THE

FIRST

HARM

THE FIRST HARM

A THRILLER

STEVEN PISKULA

WORD FIRST

Cover design by www.damonza.com

Published by Word First LLC
www.wordfirstllc.com

First Edition: September 2022

ISBN (ebook): 979-8-9858832-0-6
ISBN (paperback): 979-8-9858832-1-3
ISBN (hardcover): 979-8-9858832-2-0

steven@stevenpiskula.com
www.stevenpiskula.com

For my family

Always and forever

CHAPTER 1

Tanna Christensen lowered her fingertips onto the knurled flesh and plunged the blade deep into the muscle beneath.

"Still with us?" the instructor asked.

The first-year medical student managed to nod. But it wasn't the truth. Eight o'clock in the morning was too early for her to peel open a body.

"You have to breathe."

Tongue clicks and loud snickers rose from Tanna's so-called peers in her Human Gross Anatomy class. She didn't look up as they circled her. Scrutinized her. All eyes focused on her.

The floor shifted under Tanna's feet. She braced herself for what was coming.

"Take a breath," the instructor reminded her again.

Don't stop, Tanna thought. *Keep moving.* But her traitorous muscles hardened. Her limbs cemented themselves in place. She stood there, motionless, until the instructor reached across and pulled her hand away.

"You need to let go," he said. The scalpel stuck straight out of the cadaver, a ghastly exclamation point to her failure.

Heat stung Tanna's neck as her face flushed fever red.

If it had been just her and the cadaver, she would have been fine. Probably. But standing in front of all her fellow medical students was different. Their staring eyes and silent judgment drove a frantic pounding through her chest that left her feeling insecure. Powerless. And that infuriated her. She was twenty-four years old; she knew what she was doing. She really did.

Tanna looked around and saw her classmates reveling in her collapse, unable to hide their sadistic smiles.

"Who's next?" the instructor asked.

She squeezed her hands into tight fists, first left, then right. A trick she learned when she was nine, after she mangled the Pledge of Allegiance in front of the entire school. *Left. Right. Inhale.* She would never forget opening her mouth with confidence, only to hear her words come out wrong. All wrong. She then melted into a puddle on the cafeteria stage. Watched the room spin. Detached from herself. Unable to hide.

Left. Right. Exhale.

She ached to grab her lucky exam pen, currently tucked away in her pocket. To run her fingers over it while she mentally reviewed the photo flipbook of human organs she had created to prepare her for the real thing.

She had done the work. She just needed to trust it. No matter how many people were watching.

"I can do this," Tanna said.

She reached for the scalpel. But Nick grabbed it first.

Nick and his neon-white teeth. Nick, who wore too much cologne and was a close-talker. *There's such a thing as personal space, Nick.* Nick, the ambitious gunner whom all the students openly wished would crumble under the pressure of medical school. Except everybody knew he would finish at the top of the class and get whatever job he wanted.

"The incision needs to follow the outside edge of the trapezius muscle," Nick said as he cut into the layers of tissue.

Tanna's shoulders wilted. She might have been just a first-year student, but even she knew that medical school was not a place to expect coddling. Sink or swim, do or die. All the clichés were true.

"Here," Nick pointed out. "Infraspinatus muscle, identified."

She stepped back into the crowd of student spectators as Nick droned on, nauseating the class with his cloying honeysuckle scent. And when he'd passed the oral exposition, he flashed Tanna a condescending smirk that leveled her as if she'd been hit with a crippling gut punch.

The instructor split the students into teams of four and assigned each group a fresh cadaver for practice dissection later on. Tanna's team named their corpse George, even though they were told not to personalize their relationship with the non-person.

Tanna smiled, she joked. She pretended.

Afterward, as the others departed, the instructor approached her.

"Lots of students struggle in here," he said, filling the hard silence. "Some find out they can't cut it. Or don't want it."

"I just needed more time."

"Doctors don't get the luxury of more time. And they don't get second chances."

"I know." Tanna fought the urge to leave. She didn't need a lecture. Nothing he said could be worse than what she was already telling herself.

"And this year, you need to pass two forty-minute oral expositions. Or fail the class."

Except that.

"Do you know why I picked you to go first?"

Tanna shook her head. She didn't want to hear any more.

"I remember your admission essay. It stood out. So I thought you'd be ready. Because it's not the cadaver that stops people. Maybe you don't believe what you wrote."

"No. I mean, yes. Medicine is fascinating." The words rushed out. "Everything it can do, the endless possibilities, the people it can help. That's why I came here."

"You're tired of not making a difference in the world."

Tanna had written and rewritten her essay so many times that she still knew it by heart. But hearing someone else speak her words gave them a gravity she'd never expected.

"I am," she said.

The instructor led her out of the room, the door closing behind them, and started down the hall. "We'll be back here in a couple of days," he said over his shoulder as she heard the door's latch catch against the jamb, missing the final click. "Then, maybe, I'll let you try again. If you're sure about that."

Normally, the Los Angeles campus of Southern California Science and Medicine reminded Tanna of a resort, not a university. Precise rows of towering palm trees lined manicured lawns, and birds of paradise sprang from the soil, fanning vivid orange and blue petals high into the open air. Sun-drenched days warmed the cream exteriors of the Romanesque buildings dotting the campus. Every Tuesday and Thursday the dining hall held outside barbecues and students hung out in the sunken gardens. Add an infinity pool with a swim-up bar, and SCSM could have been the Four Seasons.

Today Tanna saw none of that. Today she saw buckled asphalt and rust-streaked windows. Today she wandered the grounds in crisscrossing arcs for more than an hour before settling at the top of the bluff near the old dormitories. There she focused on the Pacific Ocean stretching out in the distance until it fell off into nothingness.

Go check the door, her mind told her. *It didn't close all the way. You can go back in and get it right this time.*

Tanna paged through her Medical Biochemistry workbook, but the thought played over and over on repeat. The morning's humiliating events had sent her emotions ping-ponging between anger and regret. She didn't know if she could complete one oral exposition, let alone two. Who was to say the same thing wouldn't happen again? Then not only would she fail the class, she could flunk out of the university altogether.

A janitor or security guard might have closed it. But if not . . .

She remembered how excited she'd been after receiving

her SCSM acceptance letter. For six months before taking her Medical College Admission Test, she had devoured every textbook she could find while working double shifts for a shady carpet distributor. Then came formal applications, personal interviews, secondary interviews. Sleepless nights and zombie-eyed days. But when the email showed up in her inbox, and as she read the opening lines, she knew it had all been worth it. Several weeks later she had given up her studio apartment, having sold everything that wouldn't fit in her rusted blue Mazda with the mismatched wiper blades, and was driving the two thousand miles from Chicago.

All that seemed like a lifetime ago.

What are you waiting for? To blow another opportunity?

Somewhere inside her, a decision was made.

She tried to dismiss it, but her mind was already playing out the details. She envisioned herself going through her incisions, building up her muscle memory. If she practiced on her own with a real cadaver, she'd be able to pass the oral expositions. She was sure of it. And she had to be. If she choked again, that label would follow her around forever. Not only through school but on into her residency.

If she even made it that far.

To get after-hours lab admittance, students had to apply for dedicated security access and work under strict instructor supervision. But all of that took time to arrange. Time she didn't have; there were only two days before the next lab. Besides, she only needed a few minutes. Just enough to prepare her for anything the instructor threw at her. Enough to stick it to Nick for stealing her chance. Enough to prove she could do it.

Even if that meant violating the pledge she had signed at the bottom of a very official-looking piece of paper.

Go check the door.

As Tanna stood in the empty hallway outside the gross anatomy lab, the anxious thumping in her chest returned. The afternoon sun pushed thin rods of light through the building's punch-block windows while casting threatening shadows everywhere else.

The door was in fact ajar—if just barely. But it was so close to closed and locked that one wrong breath could clap it shut, and ruin any chance of redemption. Then again, walking through could also seal her medical-school fate.

Or save it for another day.

She dismissed that thought as quickly as it came. Because if not now, when? When would it ever stop?

"Here we go," she whispered, pushing the door open and slipping inside.

CHAPTER 2

The lab had no windows and, thankfully, no security cameras. The air, thick with the scent of embalming fluid, stung Tanna's nostrils, and her gaze fell onto the uneven rows of rectangular stainless-steel boxes, each of which held what used to be a human life.

Now that she'd stepped into this other world, the irony of what she was about to do struck her. The goal of a doctor was to preserve life, to encourage health and longevity. Yet she had to destroy a body in order to learn how to achieve that goal.

Tanna weaved her way through the room until she came upon George's silver sarcophagus. She slid the top open and placed her foot on the pedal that actuated the hydraulic lifting system. *You've already come this far*, she told herself as she depressed the lever. The cadaver emerged from the darkness with a metallic groan.

Poor George was face-down. They had turned him onto his stomach. That was in part to show the students what dead weight felt like, but mostly it was because working on the back and shoulders was much less personal than staring George in the eye while slicing open his chest.

After snapping on a pair of gloves and donning her goggles, Tanna unpacked her dissection kit. She lined up the five-inch scalpel and Huber probe closest to her, then slid her phone into a plastic bag to keep it clean. She knew she shouldn't take pictures, but she wanted to document her progress. And George wouldn't mind.

She grasped the scalpel and lowered it to his flesh, hesitating the instant steel touched skin.

This is where it all went wrong.

Driven forward by the fear of failure, Tanna drew the blade along the length of the trapezius muscle that ran across the shoulder. Without meaning to, she found herself saying a prayer for George. Something she hadn't done since the third grade, after God put a tumor at the base of her big sister's skull and let her die—while Tanna stood by and watched.

"George, remind me to sign up to be an organ donor."

She pushed the tip of the knife under the top epidermis layer. It was thicker than anticipated, and when she tried peeling it back, it resisted. She adjusted her grasp and pulled hard, tearing away a long triangle.

"Nooooo." Tanna stared at the ragged piece of skin in her hand, then tried to match the edges and pat it back into place. Without success.

"What are you doing to me, George?" Like every other guy in her life, he was making her work too hard for what she wanted. "Play nice now."

Tanna forced the blade back underneath, cutting as she pulled. The muscle revealed itself, and she dissected the connecting cartilage. She compared her flip cards to the real thing, noticing subtle differences that she attributed to embalming, and took pictures to evaluate further.

Behind her, the door handle rattled.

Tanna's body went rigid. Afraid to move and with no time to hide, she prepared her futile excuses at the tip of her tongue. The tightness in her chest threatened to rob her of breath.

And then she heard receding footsteps outside. Tanna took a deep breath, then exhaled slowly.

She should put George away. Get out of here before she got caught. She looked at the hydraulic pedal that would lower George back down. But then she turned her gaze to his dissected muscular system.

Just this last one, she promised herself.

She picked up the scalpel and got back to work.

"Got you. Rhomboid muscle identified," she said to the empty room.

Soon her hands were moving with surprising dexterity and her vision sparkled with lightning-strike clarity. At that moment it was only her and George, locked in a strange symbiotic relationship, student and teacher, with George giving her everything he had left.

Tanna saw the magical interplay of bone and tissue as she inspected the clean incisions, letting herself revel in the finely scraped tendons. She almost felt the electrical impulses that had once passed through them. Her own body hummed with excitement. A brief but exhilarating reminder that she could do this. That she would make a good doctor.

This is how it should have happened before.

When the muscle cramps started in her calves, she ignored them. But they clawed their way to her shoulders. Numbed her fingers. Made her scalpel slip.

She drew a sharp gasp through her teeth.

She knew she should stop before making another mistake. But she just needed to make one more incision. One more identification.

"My aunt remembered my uncle," she said aloud to reinforce the memory mnemonic. "Musculocutaneous, axillary, radial, median, ulnar. There. Brachial plexus nerve bundle, identified."

She stared at what she thought would be a series of nerve clusters. There were a lot of them. More than she'd expected, along with deep discoloration.

"Or maybe not."

She looked closer, wondering if she had it wrong, and compared the sight with her flip cards. She knew that the brachial plexus nerve bundle originated in the spinal cord, then proceeded through the neck before passing under the collarbone. It was composed of five roots and three trunks, and the smaller branches extended out into the shoulder, arm, and hand.

She accounted for all of them. And they corresponded with her flip cards, which corresponded with her textbooks. But here, now, there was a *second* set of nerve branches along with the first. These nerves were thinner, darker, and intertwined around the first set, like ivy growing around a fence post.

A hereditary defect?

Unlikely.

Then what are they? Why are they there?

Tanna stepped back and took pictures with her phone to research later.

She peered into the open cavity. She had gone further than she had planned and hoped the others in her group would understand. But after all, she had done it: apart from a couple of errant slices, she had erased her earlier failure.

With the elation of her accomplishment, Tanna's drained muscles revived themselves. Even picking up small pieces of discarded sinew and skin while cleaning her dissection site couldn't bring her down. She lowered the body back into the container, closed the lid, and checked the room. Then she snuck out through the door and left the building on a surging swell of exhilaration.

Only as she made her way across the quad did she allow herself to think about what she'd seen inside the cadaver. Whatever it was, it didn't belong there. She would need to walk into the next lab armed with answers, and she had less than forty-eight hours to figure it out.

Tanna knew of only one person both smart enough and selfless enough to help her. She typed out a quick message on her phone, attached the pictures, and sent it off.

CHAPTER 3

Thousands of miles from the SCSM campus, night infiltrated the Connecticut laboratory. Roman cut power to the overhead lights, but the equipment still twinkled with LED indicators like a concert of colored Christmas decorations. He stood over the woman sprawled out across the floor in front of him, her white lab coat changing hues under the blinking lights. Her mouth opened and closed in voiceless gasps, and he inhaled her feral scent of fear.

"Can you bring me back to life?" Roman asked again.

"I . . . I don't know what you expect me to do," the woman replied. Her quivering voice was hard to understand, and he was growing frustrated trying to listen.

He let his gaze travel across the genetics lab, taking in the workbenches stacked high with flasks and bottles, the long plastic tubes and jointed mechanical fume extraction arms that dropped from the ceiling, the hulking deep freezers and sequencing machines anchoring the back wall. Then he checked the woman's file on his phone once more.

Dr. Valerie Schaefer. Fifty-seven years old and scrappy

for her age. She was some sort of biological engineer or chemist, married to a lifetime of work and on the verge of a breakthrough. It was her drive and determination that led to her downfall. Her work could complicate things for his employer. Which meant complications for him.

Whatever her breakthrough was didn't matter to Roman. His assignment was simple: make her disappear. He had traveled all the way from San Francisco to do just that. But first he needed her to answer the question. Both of their futures hung in the balance.

"Is there enough magic in all these little tubes and potions of yours?" he asked. "Enough to bring back what was taken from me?"

Roman bent forward and watched the waves of bewilderment form in the creases under her eyes. And then came a look he recognized. That moment of pause when she underestimated him, with his slim frame and biting accent. This was the moment when her courage would stiffen—when she would harbor the belief that she could still escape.

She couldn't.

With a desperate burst of energy, she pushed herself off the floor and charged headlong into the flickering darkness. Roman sprinted after her, chasing the sound of her shoes as she darted toward the door. With a smile, he cut his way across to the exit, blocking her path.

He didn't see her swing the fume extraction arm until it slammed into his skull. The room tilted. He planted his feet wide and staggered to stay upright. He brushed his hand across the side of his head. No blood. No evidence left behind. Then he spotted Schaefer's discarded white lab coat on the floor, along with her abandoned shoes.

Scrappy *and* smart. Too bad.

He couldn't see her, but he knew she was hiding somewhere. He listened past the monotonous hum and chittering clicks of the room's equipment. Her labored breathing rose above the clatter and gave her away. She was close.

He inched even closer on gentle steps.

She charged from the darkness on his right.

Roman rammed his shoulder into the streaking figure. Her feet went airborne and her body twirled sideways. She landed hard, and the back of her head struck the floor with a sickening crack. He stood over her once more.

"Answer the question," he said, as if their talk hadn't been interrupted.

His phone vibrated, and he suppressed a sigh. He'd set it to go off only when something needed immediate attention. He glanced at the screen, then pulled it closer. He was unable to figure out what he was looking at—or more to the point, *why* he was looking at it. He stared at the pictures of the dissected human corpse, forgetting all about the trembling creature at his feet.

Clean cuts with an attention to detail. Not an accident. Not for hire.

An open cadaver. One of his?

Roman checked the raw data from the intercepted text. He recognized the receiving phone number as a contractor he'd hired. But the sender was a mystery.

Area code 310.

Los Angeles.

He would trace the number to make sure it was still in the city. This was a problem. A threat he had to contain. He needed to head back west immediately.

The sound of voices snapped Roman to attention. They were faint, somewhere outside the laboratory.

"Hear that?" Roman asked. Whoever was out there was coming this way. He looked at Schaefer for a long moment. Then he lowered his phone into his pocket.

"Now's your chance," he said. "Call to them."

He watched her turn an ear to the sound.

"There's two of them, for sure. Maybe they can take me. Get you out of here alive."

The voices grew stronger. They passed down the hallway just outside, only the wall separating them.

Roman readied himself. "You choose."

The frightened woman shivered. A part of Roman wanted her to call out to the passing voices. To save herself. To continue on and do some real good for the world. But he knew she couldn't. She was too smart for that.

"Right," he said. "Maybe they have families, children. Most likely they would die trying to help you. And you don't want that for them. Do you, Doctor?"

She filled her lungs with air and held her breath as the trailing sounds disappeared altogether.

He closed in tight. "Good choice."

Schaefer hurled herself at Roman, throwing punches in wild, uncontrolled arcs. She drove her fists into him again and again in a flurry of panicked strikes as she tried to get past him. Roman held her in place and let her pound away until her movements slowed.

She attempted one last punch, only to spin herself crashing to the floor.

He crouched down and rested his forearms on his knees. "Can you bring me back to life?"

"Yes," she said. Her eyes welled with tears. "Whatever you want. Anything."

"Too late. Too late for lies."

She released a resigned breath, her body folding inward. "No. No one can help you."

Roman took a last look at all the empty bottles and useless machines with their blinking lights of false hope. "Then you can only hurt me."

She wept.

"I'm sorry." The words did not come easy. The truth never did. He extended his open hand to her. "You won't feel a thing. I promise."

Before leaving for Los Angeles, Roman reduced the woman's lifeless form to unidentifiable ashes, then tossed them into the gutter to be carried off by a light evening rain.

CHAPTER 4

Tanna bounced out of her Clinical Skills seminar still hovering on waves of delight from her earlier achievement. She made her way to her car through a campus bathed in gray silhouettes descending from the darkening California sky.

It took several tries for the engine to turn over, and she hoped the six dollars of gas she'd put in earlier would be enough to get her through the next couple of days. She thought about using the credit card her mother had handed her before she left Chicago. The only card either of them had left that wasn't maxed out. "For emergencies," her mother had said, but Tanna decided this didn't qualify. She had enough for now, and nothing else had the power to bother her tonight.

She drove east, away from the beach and ocean surf, past the trendy shops to her apartment, a second-floor walk-up with crumbling stucco that faced out over an empty pool. The space was small but had two bedrooms, one for her and one for her roommate Krystal, a fellow med student. Between them they'd covered the walls with life-size anatomy posters and muscular system charts, a sufficient distraction from the lived-in linoleum and cracked windows. The place wasn't fancy, but it was cheap, quiet, and an ideal haven for studying.

As Tanna stepped inside, she was struck by the smell of fried garlic and curry left over from last night's attempt at dinner. Krystal loved to cook, which was unfortunate because cooking was one of the few things Krystal was terrible at. Still, they'd eaten it. On their budget, food couldn't go to waste.

Tanna plopped down on the couch, flipped open her laptop, and searched for pictures of a normal brachial plexus. She hit on several neuro-regeneration processes and even some promising work done with regenerative gene therapies, but nothing she saw online resembled what she'd found in George.

The door opened with a kick. "You're here!" Krystal squealed as she burst into the apartment.

The place may have been quiet, but Krystal was not. She was a vivacious brunette with a voice that carried for blocks. She held a Fred Segal garment bag in one hand and thrust a bottle of Beringer Reserve merlot into the air with the other. "Guess what I got? Guess, guess!"

"Not today," Tanna pleaded.

"Oh yes. *Más vino!*"

"You know I have to work tonight."

"Who cares?" Krystal went to the kitchen, came back with two glasses already poured, and pushed one into Tanna's hand. "First-year students need a life, remember? You're coming with me. Come on now. I know a party. So drink." She dashed off to her bedroom with Fred Segal in tow.

Tanna watched her disappear and smiled. She envied her

roommate. Yeah, Krystal was crazy. Loud, outgoing, energetic, morally suspect, absolutely and unquestionably brilliant, but crazy. Tanna supposed it masked some deeper, manic issues, but that didn't matter because somehow Krystal made it all look so easy. As a second-year med student, Krystal seemed to know everything worth knowing: which professors to avoid, which times were best for which classes, and how to squeeze every hidden penny from the scholarship fund. Krystal even found her a research job through the university. Tanna was indebted for every bit of help Krystal had given her.

Tanna swirled her wine and watched the red liquid legs run down the inside of the glass. The image brought her back to George's dissection. Students were never told what caused their cadaver's demise—that was part of their discovery process—but with a genetic germline mutation, all the nerves would have been around since before birth, resulting in similar size and color. The immature growth with deep pigmentation made the second set of nerves seem new somehow. An acquired mutation.

"Hey!" Tanna yelled. "Did you at least check out the pictures I sent you?"

No response from Krystal. Tanna looked back at the glass and forced herself to take a sip. The taste was smooth and seductive, a far cry from the cheap acidic boxed wine that Krystal pretended to hide in a kitchen cabinet.

Krystal fluttered back into the room. "What do you think?"

Tanna stared deep into her glass for an answer. *How could there be so many nerve endings?*

"Tanna!"

"What?" Tanna looked up. Krystal was wearing a midnight-blue slip dress cut way too low. But Tanna knew it wasn't for the party. It was for *after* the party. Krystal was seeing someone, and she always wore certain outfits for him. Tanna had never met him, didn't even know his name, and Krystal didn't talk about him, not really . . . but Tanna had put two and two together. Still, she figured every woman needed a few secrets, so she didn't pry.

"It's gorgeous," she said. "New?"

"Of course. Come on now." Krystal slammed half her wine and pulled out her phone in its pink metallic case. She twirled twice on her heels and took a video of herself with the dress in a perfect state of flow, presumably to feed her constant need to update her Instagram and TikTok accounts.

"Wait, that's mine," Tanna said. She hadn't noticed the aquamarine pendant at first. Her mother had given it to her as a present on her fourteenth birthday—the same year her father left to raise someone else's family. She kept it tucked away in the top drawer of her dresser, but now it hung around Krystal's neck.

"Oh, I borrowed it. That okay?" Krystal held out the pendant and admired it.

"Actually . . ." Tanna started.

Why are you going through my stuff? She caught the words with a bite of her lower lip before they could escape. She appreciated that they were close enough to share almost everything. It had been too long since she'd felt that bond with someone.

"It looks great on you," Tanna said and stared back into her wine. "Did you see the pictures I sent you today?"

"Hot man candy, I hope."

"Hardly. And thanks for setting me up on CollegeCrushing, by the way. I told you I don't have time to date."

"Date? YOLO, bitch. Stop trying to prove you're the good girl all the time and scratch that itch."

"Is that why my profile says I'm 'down to ride'?" Tanna forced another sip. "And I'm not so good, you know."

"Nice try."

"Would a good girl break into the gross anatomy lab to do her own dissection?"

"No, but a stupid one would."

"Oh please, you've done way worse."

"Yeah, but if I'm going to get in trouble for something, it's going to be fun. And I'm definitely not dumb enough to take pictures while I do it."

"Then you did see them!"

"I glanced." Krystal poured herself more wine. "Didn't have time to look."

"I had trouble with the brachial plexus. An extra set of nerves. Underdeveloped somehow. I can't identify it, so I figured you'd know."

"I'm sure it's nothing."

"Yeah, but I need to identify it before the next lab so I can do the oral exposition. Otherwise, I fail. It'll be easy for you. I swear."

"You know your problem, Tanna?"

"I don't drink enough," Tanna replied by rote.

"You don't drink enough," Krystal said in a singsong tone while adding more wine to Tanna's glass. "Don't worry about it. Come on now. We've got a party."

"Please, I need this. Help me out and I won't make you take off my necklace."

Krystal groaned, then breezed through the pictures. "Nothing much there. Looks like excessive nerve-growth factor." She put her phone away. "Don't even bother with it."

"But we're supposed to figure out how—"

"Forget it already," Krystal clapped back with enough force to snap Tanna upright. "Just leave it the fuck alone. It's got nothing to do with you."

Tanna was stunned by the strength of her roommate's reaction. She didn't know what to say as Krystal tilted her head back and drained her glass.

"Who breaks into a lab to look at dead bodies, anyway?" Krystal stomped around the room, gathering her purse and keys. "Trust me. Screw today and enjoy life. Come on now. Forget about the lab. Let's party."

It had become a courtesy invite and Tanna now wanted nothing to do with it. "I'll pass."

Krystal shook her head and stormed out the door. Tanna stood in the silence of the empty apartment. Had they just had a fight? Krystal had never talked to her like that before and Tanna couldn't figure out what had upset her so much. Surely it couldn't have been looking at the pictures of her cadaver. Could it?

Tanna pulled up the photos on her phone and looked for an answer in the images.

"What just happened, George?"

CHAPTER 5

"Then what's the answer?" the professor asked with the sharpened scowl of a man who had heard a lifetime of excuses.

Tanna nearly jumped from her seat, fearing she had just been called on. She had been thinking again about her cadaver and had lost her place in the lecture.

She raced to recall her mnemonics. *I dated HAL: histidine, arginine, and lysine. LEO the lion says GER: lose electrons, oxidation, gain electrons, reduction.*

"I'm waiting, Mr. Munoz."

Thank goodness.

Tanna looked down at the diagram she had been sketching in her old Hello Kitty notebook—an incomplete drawing of George's brachial plexus bundle. The gross anatomy lab was tomorrow, and she still didn't have the answer to his nerve problem. There was no way that excessive nerve-growth factor could have caused it, as Krystal had suggested last night, and all her other research had led to dead ends. Nick had bragged about knowing a neurosurgeon at Westside Hospital, but Tanna cringed at the idea of sinking low enough to ask him for a favor. She would rather take her lumps with the instructor.

The class ended, and she followed the crowd out the door. She was surprised to find two campus police officers standing outside, and then worried when their gaze zeroed in on her.

"Tanna Christensen?" one of the men asked.

Lie, she thought. *Nope, not me. You got the wrong person. Then just keep walking.*

"Yeah," she responded.

"Come with us."

She tried to force a smile while suppressing a fluttering panic in her gut. A crowd was growing around her, complete with craning necks and cell phone cameras.

"Where are we going?" she asked.

"Dean Atwell's office."

That was when she knew for sure. They had found out about the gross anatomy lab.

Tanna followed as the officers pushed through the onlookers and led her outside, then took her across the rutted lawn and into the administration building. It was one of the few original structures on campus, and the musty smell of age was embedded in the cream brick itself. Tanna thought briefly about turning and running. She figured she could beat them down the stairwell and make a break for it once she got into the open. But in the end, what would it achieve?

They arrived at the corner office of Francis Atwell, dean of the School of Medicine. The workplace was spacious, even including a sitting area with coffee tables and worn leather chairs, and everything was dark wood and brass. Massive bookshelves filled with reference anthologies of every conceivable medical specialty lined two of the walls, while a third housed a glass cabinet loaded with sports memorabilia—signed football helmets, baseballs, bats, faded player cards. An impressive collection that must have taken a small fortune to acquire. The few remaining spaces on the walls were crammed with plaques.

Dean Atwell sat behind an elongated wrap-around desk. "Sit," he commanded without looking up from the paperwork in his hands.

The two security officers departed, and Tanna sat in one of the two chairs opposite his desk. Atwell was in his late fifties, squat with a middle-age slouch. He tried to play the part of the distinguished dean, but his ill-fitting suit didn't allow him to pull it off. Piles of papers and folders were stacked everywhere across his desktop, and Tanna had to restrain the urge to straighten them up. If he needed to have piles, at least they could be neat piles.

After a long moment, Atwell finally looked up from his work. "Do you know why you're here, Miss Christensen?"

"No," she lied. "Am I under arrest or something?"

"That's up to you. We have strict guidelines at this university. Rules for your safety."

She diverted her gaze from his hard stare and looked down at his desk.

"I've been informed that you broke into the gross anatomy lab yesterday."

"I didn't." Tanna coaxed her face muscles into her best mix of innocence and confusion. "I mean, the door was open. Working outside of class is allowed, so I assumed it was okay to go in."

Atwell frowned. "Every student enrolled in Human Gross Anatomy signs a record of class management, do they not?" He shuffled through various folders on his desk, apparently looking for her form. "It states that you must apply for security access, and you must work with an instructor at all times."

"I signed something, but I don't remember what it said."

He gave up the search. "Imagine if you had cut yourself and lost enough blood to pass out. Then what?"

Tanna didn't respond.

"In addition, you know that the use of cameras, cell phones, or any type of recording device is strictly prohibited."

"But I—" Tanna stopped short. She no longer even recalled what she had been about to say. Her gaze was locked on something on top of his desk, something that had been revealed by his shuffling of papers.

Her aquamarine pendant. The one Krystal had borrowed. It was broken at the clasp.

What was it doing here?

Her hands instinctively drifted toward it.

"Unfortunately," the dean continued, "you've put me in a position where I'm forced to address the situation. First, we have to see how this impacts your scholarships."

"My scholarships?" The world came flooding back. "Just for using the lab?"

"There must be consequences for your actions. These people entrusted us with the most private parts of themselves.

Their legacy. We don't need you posting pictures of their bodies on social media somewhere."

How does he know about the pictures? How does he even know I was there?

"The door was open," she said again. "I only took pictures to help me remember the process." She pulled out her phone and scrolled through the photos she took at the lab.

"Delete those."

Tanna held up her phone. "Look. There's nothing here that could identify him. Just muscle and tissue. And it's only for my own use. That's it, I swear."

"Give me your goddamn phone!"

Atwell thrust his hand across the desk with cobra-strike quickness, but Tanna pulled her phone back just in time.

"Okay, I'm deleting them." She scrolled through, highlighted the pictures, and emailed them to herself before throwing them away. "See? All gone."

It was only then that her mind started to put the disparate pieces together. Her pendant on his desk. His knowledge of her actions, including the photos. Krystal's mysterious man . . .

The epiphany hit her like a thunderous avalanche, burying her under a reality that left her struggling to breathe.

It's him.

"This school has been quite generous to you," the dean said. "As well as your friends."

Tanna's mouth went dry. *He's the one Krystal's seeing. She must have told him about the lab. But why?*

"The extra scholarships, the coveted research position. I'd hate to see something happen to them."

"You can't. I worked so hard. I couldn't survive without them."

"Then maybe you don't deserve to be here, Miss Christensen. Frankly, you owe this institution, and myself, a great deal of gratitude. Because there are plenty of other students willing to follow my rules. Effective immediately, you're suspended from Human Gross Anatomy."

"What?" Tanna sprang to her feet. "I've paid for that class! I'll fall behind if I miss too much."

"You should hope that's all you'll be missing. This could get much more serious for you." Atwell reclined in his chair and took her in from head to toe, letting his eyes linger much longer than he should have. Long enough for Tanna to know exactly what he was looking at. "But I understand that mistakes happen. Especially with the burden of starting at a new university, a difficult curriculum, out on your own. Students feel isolated. Lonely."

Atwell stood and walked around behind Tanna, positioning himself directly between her and the door. She turned to keep him in front of her as his probing gaze plunged her into a pool of icy water.

"You see," he continued, "it's good to have people around you who can help. As long as you're willing to do what it takes."

Caged and cut off, Tanna formed a fist. *Wrist firm and lead with the knuckles*, she reminded herself while visualizing the soft spot on the side of his neck that would produce the most lateral shearing force to his vertebrae with the least amount of damage to her hand.

"We'll just have to find the right solution that benefits

all of us," Atwell said. The corners of his mouth turned up, warping his face into a plump ball. "Agreed?"

Tanna swallowed hard, not wanting to match his stare, realizing she needed to be very careful with her next move.

"Have I made myself clear?" Atwell said louder. "Whatever is needed."

She stepped around him and headed straight for the door. He didn't stop her, but he did call after her.

"By all means, take some time to consider your options. Then come by when you're ready to finalize our arrangement. Before it gets any worse for you."

Tanna picked up speed as she hurried down the hall and entered the stairwell. She was practically in a full sprint by the time she left the building. When she hit the open campus, she ran.

CHAPTER 6

Tanna stalked her way past the towering columns that encircled the exterior of the Health Sciences building. She trampled over the creeping black mold that grew along their lightless bases, fingering its way down to the concrete walkway and spreading out to infect every murky crevice.

This is how it happens, she realized.

A favor. A threat. A dark hole waiting for her to step into and disappear. Not some stalker in the night, but a trusted face. A position of authority and a proposition.

Tanna fought through the mental morass in her head for an answer. Any answer that didn't end with the fact that Krystal was involved with that man. But she couldn't find one.

She shouted when she spotted her roommate coming out of the building along with a group of students. "Krystal! I need to talk to you!"

"Saw you got arrested outside bio-chem today," Krystal said, waving her phone in the air as Tanna approached. "There's some great video of you posted all over."

"Yeah, and I just came from Dean Atwell's office. You told him. I trusted you and you told him that I broke into the lab."

"I didn't. Not like that. You wouldn't understand."

"Is it because you're seeing him?"

Krystal had started to turn away, but now she whirled back.

"Krystal, the dean had my necklace on his desk. The one you borrowed last night."

"So what?"

"Oh please. How else did it get there? He knew about the lab. He knew about the pictures. And you're the only one who could've told him, because *you're* the only one who knew. I get it, he's the guy you're seeing. But why tell him anything?"

This time Krystal bulldozed Tanna behind a rusted metal fence. "You need to stay out of this. It's none of your goddamn business."

"Fine. Do whatever you want, it's your choice. I don't care. But if there's something going on and he's forcing you to—"

"You don't know anything about him."

"Do *you*?"

"I'm a big girl. I can handle myself a hell of a lot better than you. You might want to take notes. Because believe me, you need to do whatever it takes to make this whole problem go away."

"What is that supposed to mean?"

"How do you think I got you that job and extra scholarship money, Tanna? Luck? You wouldn't have lasted a week here without me. Or him." Krystal moved closer, a clear message in her eyes. "He has ways of helping people. He can help you too."

"Excuse me?"

"Don't be naïve. You know what I'm saying. The question is, how bad do you want this?"

Krystal marched off without waiting for a response.

Tanna stood rooted to the spot, dissolving into the decay-filled cracks below her feet. Not sure what to do or where to go next. Finally, she walked to the student parking garage, where she cocooned herself behind the wheel of her car.

She couldn't understand how she'd never seen it before. The dots were there, right in front of her. All she had to do was connect them.

Tanna lifted her hand to her mouth and placed a fingernail between her front teeth. Running her tongue along the sharpest edge, she vised her jaw shut, wanting to chew the nail down to a raw, fleshy stub. A lifelong habit broken over and over again. But she was determined to be strong this time and stopped just before the nail split wide open.

How could I be so blind?

Minutes flowed into an hour as she replayed the recent events in her head. When the alert chimed on her phone for the start of her study group, she ignored it. Her study buddies would soon be huddling in a rank corner of the library, talking about amino acid properties and hemoproteins, but Tanna had no mental energy to spare for that. She needed to figure out whether she could survive without her scholarships and her job.

And then there was the situation with her roommate. Maybe Krystal really did know what she was doing. Maybe her relationship with Dean Atwell was something she wanted. Up until now, Krystal had always seemed happy. Strong and confident. The girl could handle herself.

Then again . . .

She recalled her own meeting with the dean. The aggressive moves he'd made on her. The bald-faced threats. If he had done the same with Krystal, Tanna wasn't going to stand for it.

She forced herself to start the engine and head for home.

Tanna walked into her apartment to the sound of a running shower. Krystal was already here. She knew she needed to talk more with her roommate, but also knew enough to give her time to cool off.

She took two steps into the hallway before her foot hit a wet patch of carpet and followed the growing dark stain to the bathroom door. She thought about heading straight to the sanctuary of her bedroom until the water invaded her shoe and soaked the bottom of her foot. This couldn't be ignored.

"Krystal, you're letting water out here." Tanna knocked. "Did you hear me?"

No response.

"What are you doing in there?" she yelled and put her ear against the door. "You okay?"

Silence.

"Krystal. I'm coming in."

As she eased the door open, she saw the torn shower

curtain hanging by the last few rings. Krystal's motionless body was slumped in the tub. One limp arm slung over the side. Eyes open, staring into emptiness.

"Krystal!"

Tanna rushed to her. A small stream of diluted pink blood ran from the back of Krystal's head, mixed with the spraying water, and disappeared down the drain.

"Can you hear me? Can you hear what I'm saying? Krystal!"

She reached down to read Krystal's pulse, but the surging water got in her way. "Come on, come on," she screamed and turned off the valve. She placed her fingers along Krystal's neck, searching for the carotid artery. "Please."

Tanna closed her eyes and forced the outside world away until it disappeared into a hushed distance. All her concentration focused on her roommate, hoping to feel a pulse. Praying for it.

"Give me something," she pleaded.

A feeble heartbeat pushed against her fingertips.

Tanna waited for another.

None came.

No movement. No life.

"Oh, God."

Tanna didn't remember calling 911. She barely remembered pulling Krystal's body out of the tub and laying it on the floor to perform CPR. Her mind refocused upon the nauseating crack of shattered ribs under the heels of her hands. And then the doll-like flop of Krystal's head as she tried to tilt it back on flaccid muscles. Repetitive chest compressions shot hot venom into her shoulders.

Her arms shook with paralyzing fatigue. But she wasn't going to stop. Ever.

When the paramedics arrived, Tanna shoved them back with fierce claws as they tried to take over. She needed one more pump to bring Krystal back to life. One more breath.

The paramedics yanked her from Krystal's side and rushed the body away on a stretcher.

But Tanna knew.

An assortment of police officers walked in and out of her apartment. A man in his mid-forties with dark tired eyes introduced himself as Detective Duane Lewis and rattled off a series of inane questions.

"And when was the last time you saw her again?"

"This afternoon, on campus." Tanna heard the words come out of her mouth as if someone else was speaking them. "Just a couple of hours ago."

"Did she have many friends? Different people that came to the apartment a lot?"

"A few."

"Was she seeing anyone?"

"Yes. But uh . . . I don't know his name. She never told me."

"Do you know where she got her supply of Adderall from? We found a full Ziploc bag in her room. Was she selling it?"

"I didn't know she took Adderall."

"Were you close with her?"

"Yes."

"And you don't know if she was selling pills or who she was dating?"

Tanna ignored the question. "Who calls her parents?"

"What's that?"

"Someone has to call her parents to tell them. Do I have to do that?"

"No, we have people in the department who will take care of it."

The questions continued, but Tanna stopped responding. She couldn't force herself to say another word. In other areas of her apartment, officers were standing around and talking in hushed tones. She heard phrases like "accident," "unfortunate," and "nothing else to do here." Soon they were little more than blurred figures, appearing then disappearing in front of her eyes. They were looking for answers she didn't have and didn't want to consider.

Krystal was dead. That was the period at the end of every sentence she could think to utter. Beyond that there were walls, and lives, and people living their normal routines—making dinner, checking phones, blissfully unaware of what had happened here.

The world outside continued forward. Tanna's disintegrated in water-soaked ruins on a green-tiled bathroom floor.

CHAPTER 7

Tanna pulled her knees to her chest, tears spilling out in wave after unrelenting wave. Again and again she watched herself lift Krystal's lifeless body out of the bathtub and lower it to the floor. Her hand reaching around to cradle Krystal's broken skull, held together only by a torn scalp. The endless repetition of chest compressions. Her mouth blowing warm breath past Krystal's lips, which grew ever so cold.

Her head. Why was there so much damage to her head?

Everywhere she looked, she still saw Krystal. From the tacky throw pillows Krystal insisted on buying, to the rainbow-shaped wine stain on the wall from when she tripped.

Tanna's body begged her to leave. To get away from here. As far away as possible. But her head didn't know where to go.

Trying to shake the nightmarish images loose, Tanna got to her feet. The dim overhead lights exposed the bowed ceiling and displaced furniture. She sidestepped the wet carpet in the hallway and rushed past the bathroom.

She stiffened at the doorway to Krystal's bedroom. The police had left a disaster behind. Drawers pulled open, everything scattered. They'd made a mess of Krystal's closet, too, her clothes flung across the floor. They didn't have to do that.

Krystal's parents would probably arrive the next day, and Tanna didn't want them to see the room that way. It was a pathetic consolation prize for letting their daughter die, but she didn't know what else to do, and she needed to do *something*. So she decided to clean.

Still, she stood motionless for a long time before gathering enough strength to step across the threshold.

Just keep moving, she told herself over and over.

She started with the closet, where she hung up the dresses, folded sweaters, and packed away shoes. Then the drawers. And when she'd tidied up the mess that the police had made, she kept going, afraid of what would happen if she stopped moving.

Krystal's desk came next. It was a jumble of immunology and pharmacology books, papers, open binders, empty coffee cups, a bottle of nail polish, a broken pair of forceps. Her tablet and laptop teetered on top of it all.

"Jeez, Krystal, you're such a slob."

Tanna didn't mean for it to come out the way it did, but the lighthearted words pricked a hole in the growing pressure of the hollow space.

She gathered the old coffee mugs, sorted the books and binders, then leafed through the notes and assignments in an effort to organize them.

She paused when she grabbed some folded white papers. On one side she noticed an image of lips, as if someone had kissed it. A smudged impression in Dragon Danger Red. Krystal's color.

Tanna unfolded them, and the name printed in the upper corner caught her immediate attention: Concord Funeral Inc., in San Francisco. The papers were copies of invoices that included service and processing costs for things such as intact torsos with legs, cervical spines, forearms with hands and elbows. Whole bodies. Tens of thousands of dollars in fees and shipping and tissue preparation. All laid out in cold, hard itemized lines.

But the invoices were made out to the university. So why would Krystal have them?

Curious, Tanna took out her phone to look up the company name. But that caused her to be struck by another thought: Krystal's phone wasn't here. And that didn't make sense either. Krystal's phone had been like another appendage, always at her side and never out of sight.

Tanna dialed Krystal's number, but it just rang until voice mail picked up. The sound of Krystal's voice cut deep, and Tanna closed her eyes and listened to the outgoing message one last time before hanging up.

She searched the apartment but couldn't find the phone anywhere. She faintly recalled the police asking her about it, but hadn't thought about it since. Yet now she remembered that Krystal had a tracking app on it. Tanna had helped her use it once, after Krystal had accidentally left her phone on the roof of her car. They traced it to the middle of the street three blocks away, unbroken.

It's really not important, she told herself. *The detective took it, or it got knocked down behind the couch or something. Let it go.*

Except she couldn't.

Tanna opened Krystal's tablet and logged in with her roommate's password—MasVino123—which made her smile. The home-screen picture showed Krystal and a group of friends drinking straight from a massive margarita pitcher with straws. Krystal had her arm thrown around a boy with spiky blond hair and an infectious grin. So much enthusiasm and lust for life, now frozen in a timeless memory. All of it gone.

She pulled up the tracking app and watched as a map zoomed in on a little blue dot. To her surprise, it wasn't in the apartment, nor was it at a police station. It was on campus. And it was moving.

Somebody had Krystal's phone.

Tanna zoomed in as close as possible and watched the little dot drift through the quad, past the sunken gardens, and into a corner of the administration building. The same corner as Dean Atwell's office.

Moments later, the dot vanished and a message appeared. "*Last Known Location – 1 minute ago.*"

Tanna waited, but the blue dot never returned.

CHAPTER 8

Roman didn't feel the pinch of cold air that rushed in from the coast and dropped stinging mist across the Playa del Rey neighborhood. He didn't feel the firethorn branches scraping his leg or the long piece of glass he rolled around in his fingers, its shadow casting dark prisms onto the palm of his hand. He didn't even feel it when he pressed down on the jagged shard hard enough to puncture his skin. Blood ran, but the pain never came.

Dean Francis Atwell's pretentious white BMW crunched over the bits of broken bottles Roman had strewn across the driveway. It was an old trick, the shattered remains acting as a warning signal.

Roman did nothing to hide himself. He'd watched Atwell put away four vodka tonics while gladhanding every pharmaceutical rep and medical supplier at the so-called charity reception. The man would be too impaired to notice anything.

Roman despised people like Atwell. The man was given everything he could ever need, but still took more. More greed. More corruption. More excess. There were many pies available for someone in Atwell's position, and the good dean had his fingers in all of them. And what did he add to the world? Nothing. Frankly, he deserved what he was about to get.

Atwell's feet scraped across the pockets of broken glass as he got out of the car. "What the hell?" He muttered a few choice obscenities into the night, kicking the crystalline fragments with his toe.

Roman grasped Atwell from behind, wrapping his arm around the man's neck. Atwell released a short squeal before Roman cupped a hand over his mouth.

"Shhh," Roman whispered. "Quiet."

Atwell kicked his legs in a wild attempt for freedom as Roman pulled him away. The pavement gave way to grass, then gravel. Roman yanked his prisoner up a concrete step and through the open patio door of the neighboring house, then threw him down hard.

Atwell's head bounced off the thick tile floor.

"No words," Roman said. "Not yet."

Atwell worked to steady himself, reaching out with a hand to balance, only to have it land in a pool of thickening blood. The dark liquid had spread out in long tendrils that ran into the joints between the tiles. The neighbor's limp body lay in the midst of it all.

"Jesus!" Atwell screamed, recoiling.

Roman pulled the man to a sitting position and motioned to the dead body. "Do you know who that is?"

Atwell nodded.

"She's dead for no other reason than she lived next to

you. How about that? She probably ate well, exercised, maybe devoted endless hours worrying whether she was saving enough for retirement. Then you move in next door, and none of that matters. Her days were numbered. It's sad. She'd still be alive if only you'd been at your office when I went there earlier."

Roman pulled up Krystal's picture on his cell phone and shoved it in front of Atwell's face. "You know her too. I had other plans for her. A little experiment in which she might have lived. But now she's dead. Didn't give me much choice. Boy, you've got a lot of souls to account for today."

"Oh, God," Atwell wailed. His hands shook.

"Guess you finally fucked the wrong co-ed."

"It wasn't like that."

"Fine piece of ass like that and you *weren't* fucking it? That's a shame."

"It was mostly business."

"Right. Business." Roman pulled up the picture of the deformed nerve bundle taken in the gross anatomy lab. He showed it to Atwell. "This kind of business?"

Atwell's eyes opened wide. "How did you get that?"

Roman reached into his back pocket and pulled out Krystal's cell phone in its metallic pink case. "The girl's phone. Just needed a swipe from her finger. It revealed a lot of things. Like how your little fuck-buddy sent those pictures to a man who works for us. Or I *thought* worked for us. Explain."

"I don't know what you want me—"

Roman slammed his boot onto Atwell's outstretched hand. He ground his heel, twisting and turning until he heard the sound of snapping bones. Atwell screamed in pain and his eyes rolled up in his skull.

"Don't pass out. You pass out now, you die. Hear me?" Roman eased his foot up and waited until Atwell's eyes focused once more. "Very strong girl, that Krystal. Too strong for her own good. Wouldn't say much. But she gave me your name. Now. Explain."

"All right. It was more than just sex."

"That's a start."

"She knew someone. A mortician, but bigger. Several locations. He gives us cadavers."

Roman pressed his foot back down, and Atwell released a high shriek.

"Okay, okay! The university buys them. People donate their bodies, but they need to be processed. It's not free. The university pays for it. I push business his way, he kicks money back to us."

"Why would Krystal send this mortician the pictures?"

"I don't know."

This time Roman's boot struck the side of Atwell's head. Roman stepped hard on Atwell's neck, driving his face down into the pool of thickened blood.

"Please don't kill me," Atwell whimpered.

"Answer my question."

"Sometimes their cadavers have defects. Deformed anatomy. Things that shouldn't be there. Things that are missing. It happened again. They needed to know."

Realization took hold of Roman. The threat was real. It had to be stopped.

"Who else knows?" He thrust the phone down where Atwell could see it. "What about this one?"

Atwell started to cry. Roman grabbed the back of his head, ready to drive it into the floor.

"Tanna!" Atwell screamed as he stared at the picture on Roman's phone. "Krystal's roommate. She broke into the lab and dissected the body. She took the pictures. She's the one you want, not me. Oh, God. Not me." His words were mixed with gasping sobs.

Roman expanded Tanna's image on his phone until it filled the screen. He studied her face while Dean Francis Atwell begged for his life.

CHAPTER 9

Jason Delgado clutched the top rail of the fence surrounding the motocross track and shook it loose from the ground. The air around him dripped with spent fuel and engine oil. Every racetrack he'd ever known had that same scent. It always took him back to his early days in Lancaster. He'd ridden a Yamaha then, but only because his brothers did too.

"C'mon, Sammy. Get around him!" he shouted, his Jersey accent coming out. He had moved with his family to California at age six, but the accent never left him. "What are you waiting for?"

On the course, riders careened over a series of moguls then disappeared deep into a ditch. A plume of dirt exploded skyward as two riders crashed to the ground. With the rest of the pack headed toward them, the race was about to become a yard sale.

Jason watched helplessly as his niece Samantha drove her Honda CRF110F hard to the inside of the track. Wrong choice. Samantha's foot slipped off the pedal, and her twelve-year-old arms braced against the pounding as she fought to get back into position.

"Now fucking go already!" he yelled.

Out on the track, Samantha forced her way between three riders. All four were neck-and-neck through the turn. One wobble, one false move, and they'd all go down.

Jason opened the throttle on an imaginary bike. "Come on!" he howled as the riders hit the last booter jump and the flag dropped.

Third place. Good enough to get to the final round. Jason pumped a fist. "Yes."

He hobbled off with small, staggered steps. He still felt twinges of pain if he let his stride get too long, but he'd never let that bother him. He had crutches, but half the time he didn't even bother to use them. Right now he'd left them leaning against the fence.

When he reached the track's side entrance, he paused. He wanted to see his niece, but walking through this door meant plunging headlong into his past.

Fuck it. What does it matter anyway?

Jason fished a screwdriver from his pocket, jammed it into the lock, and pushed down with a couple of strong twists. His mind pictured the metal cylinder inside, the pins fighting to hold it in place. A lifetime of experience had taught him that the right amount of leverage coupled with the right amount of force could open just about anything.

With one final twist, the mechanism gave way under the torque.

Parents and friends had gathered in the finish area to congratulate winners and console losers. Heads turned in

Jason's direction as he picked his way through the crowd, and some pointed and called out his name. Phones emerged to snap pictures. Jason was unmistakable with his long neck scar and tattoo-covered arms.

"That's how you do it," Jason said as he pounded Samantha on the shoulders. "Hard through the turns and fast down the straightaways. Every time."

A couple of kids approached. Jason took a moment to sign their papers and souvenirs and pose for pictures.

"I should have gone out around the crash," Samantha said.

"Look ahead. You have to see the track a full section at a time, not just what's in front of you."

"I'll do it," she said and smiled. "Uncle Jay, will you take a lap?"

"Yeah, take a lap!" said someone nearby, and the shout was met with cries of approval.

"I, uh, don't have my bike," Jason said.

"Use mine!" someone shouted. "Come on!"

Jason had spent pretty much his whole life, all twenty-eight years, on one bike or another. If it had wheels, he had ridden it, broken it, or fixed it at some point. To him, riding a bike was as natural as breathing—just suck in wet gasoline and exhale burnt rubber. But now, he didn't move. He couldn't. The mere thought of getting on a motorcycle welded him to the ground. He shook his head and waved off the crowd. "Not today," he said. "Sorry."

"Good job there, kiddo," a voice rang out from behind them. "Really great."

Jason turned to face the owner of the familiar voice. His

oldest brother, Matt Delgado. Matt had always had a way of imposing his will over his three younger brothers—and they all had the scars to prove it.

Matt pulled his daughter to the side and glared at Jason. "I warned you," he said through gritted teeth.

"She moved up a division, Matt. I needed to be here for that."

"Since when are you there for anyone?"

"Not now."

"You don't come here no more. Got it?" The fury in Matt's voice grew, and people took notice. "You don't come to our house, you don't come near my family. Ever."

"It's better," Jason whispered.

"I see. Walk your dumb ass out of rehab after only two days and suddenly 'it's better.' Then by all means, break on in, take what you want, screw up all our lives, and run out. Again."

"It's better," Jason said again in his calmest possible voice. "It is."

"For how long this time?"

"I came here to help, Matt. You're obviously not teaching her right."

Matt moved fast. His hand snapped up and grabbed Jason around the throat.

"You want to help, J? Stay the hell away. No one wants you around. Come near us again and I *end* you. Because it's always 'better.' Until it isn't."

Matt released Jason with a sharp push, then took Samantha's arm and led her away. Jason's niece tried to wave goodbye, but her father pulled her deeper into the crowd.

Despite the ugly show, a handful of autograph-seekers encircled Jason with limp pieces of paper clenched in their hands. Out of reflex, he scribbled his name a few times before exiting the pit and staggering over to his faded red pickup truck. He didn't take the time to retrieve his crutches. He just got in and drove.

The air washed over him as he went up one street and down another, guiding the pickup in the opposite direction of his empty apartment. There was nothing there for him, other than a mattress on the floor and a television on the wall. Gone were his trophies and championship medals. Nothing was left of the hundreds of pictures and articles that used to paper the walls. Not even a single piece of his motocross equipment remained to clutter his closet.

He curled his hands around the steering wheel and thought about calling an old friend he knew would be holding a few grams of heroin. Then he thought about calling his sponsor.

Pushing the pickup onto the freeway, he weaved around a slow-moving SUV and floored past a semi-truck.

"Move it."

The air was silent. That's what Jason remembered most. When he caught a jump, when he hit it exactly right, he felt it. Just him and his motorcycle in total harmony. One an extension of the other, and nothing else mattered. No distractions, no thoughts, no noise. Just silence. A perfect mixture of adrenaline, concentration, and tranquility. Out of all the joys from that life—the accolades, the travel, the fans, the women, the money—that was the thing he missed most. Soaring through the air in divine silence. Total control. Total freedom.

He looked down at his phone. After a moment, he shook his head and dialed.

"Talk," the voice said on the other end of the phone.

"Hey. It's me."

"JD? No shit. Where you been hiding?"

"Here and there." Jason peered out at the road. "I want to come by, but I'm a little strapped."

"What's new? Look, I got what you like, but you're still on the hook for last time."

"How about giving me a break this once?"

"Already did."

"Right. I'll figure something out."

Jason hung up and tossed the phone onto the seat. He hadn't wanted to make the call. It made him sick to do it, disgusted with himself, but also happy and excited. The need was too damn strong, and he was tired of fighting the inevitable. Maybe he had to accept that he was just another fucked-up junkie who'd thrown away everything he had and any chance of a real life for one more hit. At least now he could disappear from the world for good.

"Shit!"

Straight in front of him, a stalled car took up part of the middle and right lanes of the freeway. Jason pounded the brake pedal with both feet. Tires screeched as the pickup skidded sideways. He braced for impact. It never came.

When he came to a stop, Jason opened his eyes and looked around. Somehow, he hadn't struck the other car.

He flipped on his hazards, jumped out, ran to the other

vehicle, and yanked open the door. "Hey!" he shouted, startling the woman behind the wheel. "Get this thing off the road!"

The driver was trying to start the engine, but it wouldn't catch.

"It just died," the woman told him. "I was driving and—"

An air horn blast ripped through the night behind them, and Jason turned to see the semi coming around a curve, barreling toward them. It was too late for it to stop.

"Get out of the fucking car!" Jason screamed. He reached in, unclipped the woman's seat belt, and ripped her from her seat. "Go!"

Another horn blasted as the semi jerked into the middle lane and cut off the car next to it, almost crushing it.

Jason flung the driver to the side as the semi roared past, missing them by less than an inch. The rush of air that followed almost knocked them down. Jason pulled the woman off the road, his legs buckling.

"You okay?" he asked. "Hey. You hurt?"

"I—I don't think so."

Her words were hesitant, fragile. Standing stick straight at the edge of the road, she seemed ready to fall apart.

"What were you doing?" he said. "You could've gotten killed out there. You could've gotten *me* killed out there."

Cars flew past, honking their horns as they dodged the two stopped vehicles.

"I-I'm sorry," the woman said.

He started to snap at her again, but then stopped. Even in the deepening night, he could see a vulnerable honesty in her expression. So many of the women in Los Angeles were too made up, trying to be something they weren't, trying to be someone else. But she didn't come across that way. There was no arrogance here, no pretending to play it cool after almost being run over. She was trembling and scared . . . and not afraid to show it. As if she was still staring into the headlights of the oncoming truck, waiting to be run over.

He sighed. "Well. We're alive." He stuck out his hand. "I'm Jason, by the way."

She took his hand and shook it. "Tanna."

———————————

Though her heart was hammering against her ribcage, Tanna felt numb. Numb to the cars screaming past. Numb to the chill of the evening. Numb to the stranger who had just saved her life. *At least he didn't let anyone die tonight.* Beyond that, nothing.

"You got gas in it?" the stranger asked. Jason. He'd said his name was Jason.

"That truck almost hit us," Tanna responded.

"It did."

"No, I mean it *really* almost hit us."

"Yeah. Are you sure you're okay?"

Not in the least. Tanna's numbness was fading, but as the world seeped back in, it drowned her with the thoughts and memories from Krystal's death. She had to focus on the ground to keep her head from spinning out of control.

"Some," she said.

"What?"

"It's got some gas. Not a lot, but some."

"Okay. Probably the fuel pump then. Right now we've

just got to get your car off the road before someone T-bones it. I can push it with my truck, but you'll have to steer. Your power steering won't work, so it'll be hard. Can you do it?"

Tanna nodded. "Yes."

Jason watched the oncoming traffic and waited for two cars to pass. "Now."

They both ran. Tanna got into her car, and Jason got in his truck. Tanna turned the key, shifted into neutral, and watched as his pickup approached with surprising speed. He struck with a bang, and her car lurched forward, bucking to the right. Tanna gripped the steering wheel, but it twisted in her hands before she could get control. The car was picking up enough speed to shoot right past the emergency lane and fly down the steep embankment on the far side.

No, no, no.

She heard the tires roll over the loose gravel of the unused lane and pumped the brakes, but the car didn't even slow. "Stop!" she yelled.

With the dark ridge coming up fast, she funneled every last bit of reserve strength into slamming the brake pedal. The car slowed to a merciful stop with the front bumper pushing over a mile marker at the very edge of the overhang.

"Told you it'd be hard," Jason said as he opened the door and reached across to put the car into park.

You didn't tell me about the brakes, Tanna wanted to say, but when she turned to face him her words disappeared.

Maybe it was the soft shadows cast by the cracked dome light of her car, or the fact that this total stranger had just risked his own life to save hers without the slightest hesitation, but she couldn't help but find him winsome. A rough-and-tough teddy bear with black grease etched into the recesses of his hands and far too many tattoos, but at ease with himself . . . and definitely cute. Even under the circumstances.

"What are you going to do now?" he asked. "Call a wrecker?"

Tanna had no idea. She hadn't even thought about it.

"I can take you somewhere."

She hesitated. Being alone with a strange guy in his car at night wasn't the smartest idea. But could she even get an Uber driver to find her out here at the side of the road? Besides, she honestly couldn't afford it—especially not now that she had a tow and car repairs to consider.

She had planned to go to Dean Atwell's office, try to get in somehow, and then find out why he had Krystal's phone. If she was going to go through with it, she needed to do it now before she lost her nerve—or came to her senses.

Jason shrugged. "Unless you want to—"

"Just over to SCSM," she said before she could chicken out. "If you don't mind. And I know the most painful places on the human body to hurt someone, so don't try anything."

He chuckled. "I don't doubt it. But I'm just offering a ride is all. As long as you don't need anything else."

"Not unless you know how to pick a lock," Tanna said aloud, even though she meant to say it to herself. Somehow the words just slipped out.

A deep grin slid across Jason's face.

CHAPTER 10

Tanna bobbed up and down on the balls of her feet as she scanned the hallway. Beside her, Jason slid a screwdriver into the lock as far as it would go.

"Are you sure you want to do this?" she whispered.

"Are you?" Jason twisted the handle as he pressed. "I'm gonna have to really torque it."

"Maybe we shouldn't."

He pushed on the screwdriver and the lock broke loose with a crack that echoed up and down the corridor. They both stopped and listened for any movement. Nothing.

"Want me to wait out here? Stand guard or something?" Jason asked in a soft voice.

Tanna tilted her head to look at him, then grabbed his hand and led him inside, closing the door behind them.

The static air of Dean Atwell's office magnified even the slightest noise. Tanna saw now that the cheap plastic plaques on the wall and the shelves of books, most of which she was sure had never been opened, were just props for show.

She hurried to the desk and used the light on her phone to search.

"I thought you were here to find your phone," Jason said in a hushed tone.

"My roommate's."

"You broke in here to find your roommate's phone?"

And my necklace.

"It's complicated," she said.

Tanna combed through the piles of paper where she had last seen her necklace, but it was no longer there. Upset with herself for not grabbing it earlier, she inspected the floor in case it had fallen. Then she moved to the drawers. The first two held nothing but more papers.

The third drawer was locked.

"Hey, Jason? Do you mind?"

Jason had been searching the area around the bookshelves and memorabilia case, but now he walked over and examined the lock, taking a moment to pick at it with his rugged fingernails. "Must be important for you to go through all this trouble."

"It is. I think." Tanna sighed. "Or . . . actually I don't know."

"That clears it up. So why isn't your roommate here helping you? It's her phone."

"She's dead."

Jason stopped and looked at her.

"I found her in our shower today. She . . . slipped, I guess." Tanna had to sit on the edge of the desk to fight the weariness. "I tried to save her, but she died right there on the bathroom floor. I mean, I'm in med school. I should have been able to do something."

"Wow. Sorry."

"I pulled her out and gave her CPR, but the back of her head was a big mess."

"From falling in the shower?"

Tanna didn't really believe it either. But the alternative was not something she wanted to consider. So she ignored the question.

"When I realized her phone was missing, I tracked it online. Someone was walking with it across campus and ended up right here. Then they shut off the app. I'm still not sure why I even came, but I . . . I had to understand why her phone would be here." *And get my necklace.* "But now I have you breaking into offices and rifling through the dean's desk. I know this is crazy. I mean, it *is* crazy, right?"

"Yeah. But maybe a little crazy is what you need right now." Jason used his screwdriver to widen the gap between the desk frame and top edge just enough so that the rotating pin on the lock could no longer catch.

"I think she was sleeping with the dean," Tanna said.

"One way to get an A." Jason pulled open the drawer. But it was only stuffed with more papers, reports, and unopened mail. "No phone," he said.

He started sliding the drawer back into place, but Tanna stopped him. "Hang on."

She grabbed a worn manila folder. The name scrawled across the tab read Concord Funeral Inc.

Inside the folder were invoices and payment receipts from the university. They looked to be identical to the invoices that Krystal had in her room. But these invoices also had notes and lists with dollar amounts written on them.

"What is it?" Jason asked.

"My roommate, Krystal . . . she had some of the same invoices from this place."

"Why would she have invoices from a funeral home?"

"I don't know."

Tanna shoved everything back into the folder and tucked it under her arm. "We need to leave."

"You're taking it? Someone'll figure out it's missing." He re-engaged the lock on the drawer.

"Yeah. Any chance of getting my car started?" she asked.

"Probably been towed by now. We can call and find out where it is. Or I can drop you off at home or wherever."

Tanna shook her head. "I'm not going home. I'm going to see Krystal. She needs to answer some questions for me."

Jason looked confused. "I thought she was dead."

"She is."

CHAPTER 11

Located deep in the earth beneath the main building, level five of Modern Genetics had become an open secret among laboratory employees. Everyone knew it was there, even if they never talked about it. And that enraged Dr. Craig Emmerson. He stood there now, covered head-to-toe in his white protective lab attire, looking around at his domain. He had set up level five for ultra-deep genetic sequencing, molecular diagnostics, and reengineering, and he had made it accessible only to a few of his handpicked scientists. Yet even though he had created a facility of unrivaled magnitude, all he saw were impenetrable walls and imposing restrictions that handcuffed him at every turn.

He even abhorred the unassuming nature of the building itself. On the outside, Modern Genetics appeared to be nothing but a short, tan, corrugated metal structure on the outer edge of a deteriorating industrial park in South San Francisco. He understood why it needed to maintain a low profile, but he didn't have to accept it.

Like the exterior, the upper levels were something of

a smokescreen for the more serious work that took place down below. The first two floors held administrative offices, security, general facility labs, and a division dedicated to improving agricultural yields through gene editing. Floors three and four concentrated on medical developments: therapies for illnesses such as Alzheimer's, Hurler syndrome, and sickle-cell anemia. All noble causes. But Craig had found early in his career that although preventing diseases made headlines, it didn't make money. Tilting at windmills was never profitable.

"Show me," Craig demanded as he stared at the enormous touchscreen table display.

His head scientist, also dressed in personal protective equipment, engaged the monitor, and a lissome 3D image emerged. Two outer columns spiraled into the air, connected by multicolored bands that reached across the gap, creating a singular entity. Each humbled section reliant on the other, representing another genetic code, another piece of the puzzle, another step forward. Flawless in design and angelic in form, the twisted ladder shape of the DNA's double helix revealed itself in wondrous harmony, and as Craig's eyes swept across its curled perfection, he couldn't help but imagine the possibilities.

At its base, however, it appeared crushed, shattered, with broken splinters pushing out into nothing.

So goddamn close.

"It's not synthesizing properly," the scientist said.

"An anomaly. Maybe a problem during thermal cycling." Craig placed his hands on the image and spread them wide to enlarge it. He spun it sideways, looking deep into the center.

"It's not the thermal cycling," the scientist said. "Three months, and it's not behaving the way we projected. We have to admit that it's not a compatible polymerase."

"Are you insinuating that I'm wrong? That I led you down an erroneous path?"

The scientist tensed, looking as if she would give anything to take her words back.

"No, I . . . what I mean is that maybe we haven't found the right combination yet."

"Then when will you have it?"

"We've been working on the new formulations, as you suggested."

"So you're only doing what I explicitly laid out for you? Nothing more? I have sixty goddamn people in this building who can blindly follow my instructions. Why do I need you?"

A soft voice filtered down from overhead. "Dr. Emmerson."

"Not while I'm working," he yelled back.

"I'm sorry, but Dr. Solomon Cabral is in the lobby."

The name reverberated through the room. Craig closed his eyes and forced his jaw to unclench.

"What could he want at this hour?"

"He asked to see you, sir. What shall I tell him?"

"Tell him to get the hell out of my lab." Craig didn't have the time or patience to deal with the doddering old man.

The overhead speaker clicked off, and Craig glared at the worthless lump in front of him. "I'm running out of time. Quit making excuses and do your work. There's no new information here." He pounded his fist against the monitor, creating a break in the glass that distorted the 3D double helix. "We start again right now. I don't care how late it is. Because we're not the only ones. Every day you fail me in here, someone else gains out there."

Having made his point, he adopted a tone of compassion. "I'll make sure we get there, but we need to succeed *every day*. No matter what. Progress. Not excuses. This is too important to fail."

As the scientist sprang into motion, the overhead voice interrupted again.

"I apologize, sir, but Dr. Solomon Cabral insists on waiting. Would you like security to take care of it?"

There must be a damn good reason for Sol to stick around. Craig took one last look at the double helix before turning off the monitor and sending it back into darkness.

"No," he replied. "I'll be up."

But he was going to make the old fool wait.

He walked to the gowning room and changed out of his lab attire. At forty-three, he had chiseled himself into a robust bull, a far cry from the scrawny child who overcame a bout of Perthes disease that had put him in casts and leg braces for over two years. But age had taken its toll in other ways. As he examined himself in the mirror, he ran his fingers across the puffy skin around his eyes and made a mental note to talk to his plastic surgeon about it. There was always room for improvement.

He made his way out through the double security door access to his private elevator, which took him to the hallway outside his office. He had it installed to avoid employees who constantly came at him with their idiosyncrasies, their neuroses, their pestilence. In a perfect world, he would never have to interact with any of them, ever. The real world, however, was a different story.

A massive steel desk with matching credenza filled most of his office space, and gray leather chairs occupied the rest. Craig passed the back of his hand over a small scanner built into the top of the credenza, and a panel slid open, revealing a hidden storage space filled with an array of cell phones, custom lab tools, and amber prescription vials. He selected the appropriate plastic bottles and judiciously counted out the exact number of pills to build his nootropic stack of smart drugs, then tapped out a few more for good measure. There was piracetam for cognitive enhancement and focus. Aniracetam for concentration. Choline for neurotransmitter improvement and synaptic plasticity. The narcolepsy drug modafinil to make sure he never had to sleep, and a testosterone supplement to bring it all together, because a brilliant mind was worthless with a weak body.

When at last he made his way out to the lobby, he found his former partner resting with fingers interlaced across his lap. Dr. Cabral looked frail, with wisps of white hair ringing his balding head. Craig told himself that he would never look that feeble, even at seventy-one.

"Sol," Craig said. "I'm surprised to see you."

"I had that same feeling earlier." Sol got up and thrust out his hand.

Craig hesitated to take it. The two men had once been mentor and student, but passion and success had ultimately turned into bitterness and resentment. Still, perhaps out of some residual feeling of obligation, he acquiesced and shook

Sol's hand. To his surprise, the old man held tight, clasped his other hand on top, and pumped up and down, again and again.

"Do you still think you can scare me? After all this time?" Sol asked.

"I can't begin to imagine what you're talking about." The man's sagging skin and protruding bones against his own hand caused an overwhelming feeling of revulsion, and he yanked himself free.

"I caught your goon checking in on me. Roman. The one you send to clean up your messes."

Craig swallowed the growl rising in his throat. "You're confused again," he said, managing to project poised serenity even as hot anger shot through him.

"No. You made a mistake somewhere, and now you're covering your tracks, making sure I'm still in my place, sitting on my hands. As promised."

"Why would I have any interest in you anymore?"

"Because I know what goes on here," Sol said. "And it's not the save-mankind crap you tell the investors and the other scientists. I *developed* the Second Nature program, Craig. I built this company from the ground up. Two years away from it doesn't change that. I kept my mouth shut like you wanted, but don't expect me to stand by and watch you destroy everything I created."

Craig scoffed. "This isn't your company anymore. You couldn't keep up."

"More like you didn't want me looking over your shoulder. I brought you in and made you what you are. And then you pushed me out."

"You didn't *make* me," Craig snapped. "If anything, you held me back. How long did I carry you before I graciously cut you loose? The technology moved faster than you could handle, and you panicked. You became cautious and started thinking small. That's what killed you."

"You mean I wasn't ready to play God."

Craig laughed. "You hypocritical son of a bitch. Tell me, who is God? Show him to me. Or her. Or it. Maybe you think you see God in a tree, a newborn child, or even that perfect glass of scotch you have on Saturday night. But everything you see, feel, touch, living or not, *I* will be able to give you—only stronger, better, without disease, without degradation, without everything that goes wrong in nature. No mistakes. No malformations. None of the random errors you attribute as *divine*. I'm doing the work God should have done in the first place.

"God doesn't make us sick or let us decay," Craig continued. "Nature by its very essence breeds inaccuracies. Broken bits of DNA that get worse every time a cell reproduces. All I'm doing is taking nature out of it. Take away the unpredictability, the idiosyncrasies, the pure chance of it all, and when you finally pull away the mask of fear and demystify the things that have held us back for an eternity, you're left with the ability to *create*. With vision. With impunity. With perfection. What you have left is *me*, Sol. The true creator." Craig gave the old man a patronizing smile. "That was always your problem. You only wanted to *play* God. I set my sights quite a bit higher."

Sol paused for a long moment before speaking. "You have to stop this," he finally said. "Whatever you've done, you have to stop it right now. For your own good, Craig. For the good of everyone."

"Stop it? After I've found exactly what I need to make the biggest leap ever in our evolution?"

Sol blinked as the words registered. "Impossible."

"You've been out of the game too long. I've made advances you couldn't have imagined. Without your self-proclaimed genius."

"You don't have the mental capability for that."

"We're finished here," Craig said. "You had your chance. You failed. Now go back to your daily salad and walks in the park. Whatever you thought you'd accomplish by coming here, it's too late."

Three security guards entered the room, weapons drawn.

"Dr. Solomon Cabral," Craig said. "You were the best scientist I've ever known. The only person I looked up to in my life. The only person I ever considered even close to an equal. And I admit, there was a time when I thought we could do this together. Just imagine the worlds we could have created."

A guard leveled the muzzle of his weapon at Sol's chest.

"But that dream is over now. And mine is on the verge of everlasting glory."

CHAPTER 12

"Why are you doing this to me?" Tanna sobbed, wiping away fake tears and doing her best to make her voice shake and her lip quiver. "Why won't you let me see her?"

The nurse at the counter wasn't going to let her just walk in and see Krystal's body. Family only. Tanna had to bluff her way in, which meant crying. Most people dropped their defenses at the sight of a distraught person. Except this nurse probably had to deal with distraught people every day; a few more tears weren't going to make a damn bit of difference in her world.

"Who are you again?" the nurse asked.

Tanna reached for a tissue on the counter and dabbed her eyes. "I'm her sister. I already told you that."

"And you don't have any ID? Nothing?"

"No." Tanna went through the exercise of pretending to search for it. "When Mom called, I jumped into the car and drove down here. I wasn't thinking about my ID."

"As I told you before, without proper identification, there's no way—"

"Wait, wait, wait. Here."

Tanna pulled out her phone and scrolled through pictures until she found a bunch of herself with Krystal. They had gone out for dinner and drinks on the Hermosa Beach pier. Krystal let guys buy her shots all night long, and the evening ended with Tanna holding her hair while Krystal threw up in the bushes outside their apartment.

"See, that's us. Me and my sister Krystal. And here. And this one."

"I'm sorry," the nurse said without even looking at the phone. "Your parents are the only ones cleared to view the body."

"My sister's dead, and she's right here somewhere!" This time Tanna didn't have to fake the emotion in her voice. "I just want to see her. Can't you understand that? I have a *right* to see her. What if it was your sister? How would you feel? I just want to say goodbye!"

Her exhaustion had reached around and encircled her, squeezing out every bit of emotion she had left. She started crying again, this time for real.

The nurse picked up a phone and spoke in hushed tones. Tanna waited.

"Come with me," the nurse said at last, handing Tanna a fresh tissue.

Tanna followed the woman down a maze of corridors to a room at the end of a hallway near an elevator. The small space had a curtained window, a short couch, and an end table filled with blank forms.

"You need to fill out one of those in case the medi-cal examiner requests an autopsy. Will you be making the arrangements for removal of the body? Have you contacted a funeral director yet?"

"I don't know. Maybe."

"Find out. If nothing's been done, take care of it right away."

The nurse left the room, but Tanna didn't notice. Her mind was fixated on something the woman had said. *Contact a funeral director.* She thought about Krystal's invoices and the file from the dean's office. She wished she could look at it now and regretted leaving it with Jason.

He was waiting for her in his pickup out on the street. He'd refused to pull into the hospital parking lot—muttered something about it being too soon. Tanna told him he didn't have to stay, that he had helped her enough. She even offered what little gas money she had. But he insisted, and she felt better knowing he was around. That was probably why she leaned over and kissed him on the cheek when she got out of the pickup.

A quiet knock at the door interrupted her. An orderly pushed a gurney ahead of him, and Tanna retreated at the sight of the sheet-covered body.

"I'll be outside," was all the man said when he left.

Tanna didn't move for a long time. She stared at the shroud and wondered what she was doing here. She had been there when Krystal died. Why look at the body again?

Because you want to know if you could have saved her.

In the moment, she'd been so panicked that she didn't trust her memory. She needed to know for certain how much damage there was. And reassure herself that she'd done everything she could.

Finally, she forced herself to her feet. Her hands trembled as she pulled back the white cloth to reveal Krystal's face.

"Oh, God."

Krystal's eyes were still cracked open, as if frozen while trying to wake from a restless sleep. The dampness of the shower had made her hair frizzy. Her narrowed lips had begun to split with spiderweb-like cracks. Krystal had lived life with so much passion, but now she was expressionless and void of color. She didn't look like the same person.

And she didn't look at peace.

"I'm so sorry, Krystal. I should have been there for you."

The room grew quiet as Tanna moved her shaking hands to the back of Krystal's scalp.

"Please forgive me."

What had been so easy with her cadaver now felt like an impossible task. Tanna drew a deep breath, steadied herself, and tried again. She ran her fingers up and down the clumped and matted hair, her fingertips almost penetrating the skull.

She wished she had brought gloves.

The lacerated scalp barely held the back of Krystal's head together. The occipital bone was fragmented in several places and shifted and gave way under even light pressure.

How could a slip and fall cause so much damage?

She lifted Krystal's head and eased it over to examine the full extent of the injury. There were two separate wounds, one much larger than the other, and she reached around to—

"Step away, miss."

The administrative nurse stood in the doorway with her arms crossed. A security guard towered behind her.

"Step away," the guard repeated in a booming voice. "Right now."

CHAPTER 13

The attack pushed forward with no leader to guide them and no plan for them to follow. An unorganized shotgun blast of an assault that relied on sheer numbers for any type of advantage. Some never reached their destination, while others got washed away. Many more died of exposure. But they were resilient, born and bred for this. They had been doing it for millions and millions of years. It had always been that way: the struggle, the fight, the slaughter. That would come, and they would be ready.

As a group, they were unorganized, but individually they were complete and well-systematized. Each was nothing more than a few strands of core genetic material inside a protective protein coat, but that code told them exactly what to do and where to go—a perfect molecular parasite. And only a tiny percentage of the virus invaders needed to live for them to be successful, making them a true force to be reckoned with.

A countless number of the nearly undetectable viruses infiltrated Tanna's body. Pushed airborne by Krystal's last gasps of life and crossing the gap to their new host in tiny droplets. They didn't know who Tanna was and didn't care. They only did what they had been engineered to do: find an untapped weakness in the immune system, exploit that flaw, and shut down the immune system for good. Then this new body, Tanna's body, would become a perfect host, a living culture dish without any defenses, ready to receive the next trial.

If they didn't kill her in the process.

Ever-changing, ever-evolving, always striving for a greater existence, the virus intruders would not be denied.

The battle was underway.

CHAPTER 14

The midday sun forced Tanna to shield her eyes as she fled the hospital. She didn't remember where Jason parked, didn't know if he was still there at all, and only wanted to crawl into bed and make the world disappear. But that couldn't happen. Not anymore.

She spotted Jason's truck and hurried to it.

Through the window she saw him curled up on the bench seat, asleep. She took a moment to look at the tattoos running up and down his arm. Mixed in with the ubiquitous collection of racing images and half-naked women was a design that caught her eye: an arm with a clenched fist and the words STEEL DUKES underneath. There was a strength in its simplicity.

She knocked on the glass. He startled awake, sleep lines marking his face, and opened the door. "What time is it?"

"Almost one."

"Wow. Must have gone sideways."

"Can you take me home? I need to get out of here." Tanna heard the tremor in her voice.

"Of course."

Tanna got in and Jason brought the pickup to life, jerked it into gear, and forced his way into traffic. "Did you, you know . . . get to see her?"

"For a moment. Until hospital security came in. Ugh. I feel like such an idiot."

"Yeah, that'll turn shit upside down."

"Told them I wasn't sure why I was there. That I was too distraught over not saving her. That I was exhausted and wanted to see her one last time."

"You didn't lie."

Tanna decided not to tell him the rest. About how the nurse had gotten ahold of Krystal's parents, who informed her that Krystal didn't even have a sister. Now Krystal's parents didn't want Tanna to be anywhere near the apartment when they came to pick up Krystal's things. More than that, they didn't want Tanna at the funeral. Tanna would call them later and explain her side of the story. But not now. They were grieving a daughter.

"Oh shoot," Tanna said. "Take a right up here."

Jason turned the corner. "Now what?"

"Keep going straight for a while."

"No, I mean, *now* what? Like, have you figured anything out yet?"

The truth was, Tanna hadn't figured *anything* out. How could a simple fall in the shower result in multiple fractures to the back of Krystal's skull? It couldn't. So what *had* happened to Krystal? And did this have anything to do with Dean Atwell and all those invoices? Or with the pictures Tanna had taken of the cadaver and sent to Krystal?

"Maybe," was the only word that came out of her mouth.

Tanna tried to let her mind go blank, but too many things kept forcing their way in. The feeling of her hands against Krystal's broken skull. Her meeting with the dean. Breaking into his office. Her future with the school. The heartbreak of Krystal's parents. Everything.

"While I was waiting, I checked out that file from Concord Funeral," Jason said. "Hope you don't mind. Talked to a friend I got up there who'd heard some bad stuff about these guys. Allegedly they got in trouble for overcharging, stealing jewelry off corpses, reusing caskets, stuff like that. They got fined for it, and supposedly cleaned up their act, but word is they're still not totally legit." He paused. "You think this university guy had something to do with any of that?"

"Atwell? He's the dean of a prestigious medical school. Why would he get involved with some crooked funeral home?"

"Same reason he was screwing your roommate. Because he could."

"Hey. We don't know that for sure. Stay out of that." Tanna leaned her head against the window and closed her eyes. "But you're right. There's nothing about him I trust."

The movement of the car was rhythmic and soothing. She let some of the images in her mind drop away. But she couldn't get rid of George's double nerve clusters. The immature growth. The distinct color. The way they stretched around the others. There was something about it that kept bothering her.

She looked through the invoices again, then grabbed her phone and dialed.

"Speak to me," the voice said from the other end.

Tanna rolled her eyes. "Nick, hey. It's Tanna Christensen."

"Oh shit," Nick said. "Someone was just talking about you. Isn't Krystal Ward your roommate? I heard she, like, died or something."

"Last night. She, uh, had an accident. She slipped. Hit her head."

"Crazy. But maybe now they'll give you straight As for the semester."

"Nick, shut up and listen. I need to get into the gross anatomy lab." Tanna tapped Jason on the shoulder and pointed to the left. "I want to take a quick look at that cadaver I was working on."

"No can do. They locked that place down. No one goes in or out without an instructor now. Wouldn't do you any good anyway. They tossed your guy."

"What do you mean?"

"Your cadaver's gone. They got rid of him. Split up your group, the whole thing."

Tanna overheard him speaking to someone else. She pictured him covering the receiver with his hand, telling everyone that he was talking to her, the little weasel.

"Nick. Nick!" Tanna had to shout to get his attention.

"Yeah, like I said, we showed up for lab this morning, and he was gone, and so were you. What happened with that? Why did security come after you? Were you arrested for something?"

Go to hell, Tanna mouthed and hung up on him.

"Up another block and take a right," she said to Jason.

"Everything okay there?"

"Not hardly."

An abrasive scratch clogged her throat, and she swallowed hard to clear the sensation. With no luck, she rested her head in her hand and ignored it instead.

When they got to the corner, they saw two cop cars in front of her building, lights flashing. A handful of people had gathered around to gawk.

"What is it now?" Tanna asked.

Jason parked the pickup, and they made their way past the ogling neighbors to the courtyard with the empty pool. From there, Tanna could see police standing in her open doorway. She tried to walk inside, but an officer slid across and blocked her.

"Let her through," a voice called out.

Tanna walked inside, and Jason slid in behind her. Detective Duane Lewis stood in the middle of her living room, along with someone she guessed was his partner.

"You had a break-in," Lewis told her. "Neighbor saw someone. Called it in."

Lewis looked Jason up and down. When the two locked eyes, they held each other's stare for a long time. "Who's this?"

"My friend, Jason."

"I know you from somewhere," the detective said.

"Don't think so," said Jason.

The partner chimed in. "You're that motocross guy, aren't you? I've seen you. My kid brother used to play that video game of yours."

Jason hesitated. "Moto Madness Extreme. That's me."

"That's right. Dude, you're legit. You were like world champion, weren't you?"

"National champion," Jason said, though his voice sounded thick and reserved. "Three times."

Tanna looked to Jason. She hadn't been expecting him to be famous. Most guys she knew would have boasted about something like that as the first pickup line out of their mouths.

"Uh-huh." Detective Lewis continued to stare at Jason. "And were you with Miss Christensen at the hospital this morning?" He turned to Tanna without waiting for a reply. "I can still bring you in for that stupid stunt. Falsifying credentials. Evidence tampering."

Tanna felt small and exposed, but put on a bold front. "Go ahead. If you think that'll help bring Krystal back."

Lewis's eyes hardened, and menacing clouds rolled across the terrain of his face. Then he brushed them away with a wave of his hand. "Just look around and let us know if anything's missing."

With the detective following, Tanna went first to her bedroom at the end of the dark hall. The intruder had reduced her haven to shambles. Drawers were dumped out in tangled heaps. The bare mattress stood on end. Beyond the curtains and blue stripes of her comforter, she didn't even recognize the place.

Her laptop was nowhere to be seen. She dropped her chin against her chest. She had no money to buy a new computer, and even if she did, she'd already lost some of her work. She backed up regularly, but it had been two or three days.

She looked around to see if anything else was missing. Some of her textbooks were gone. Biology. Anatomy. An odd thing to steal, but they had been ridiculously expensive.

Next, she stepped across the hall to Krystal's bedroom. To her surprise, it was completely untouched. She couldn't understand why an intruder would ransack one bedroom and not even bother with the other one, and she wondered if she was a target somehow.

As she made her way back down the hallway, she felt the detective's eyes on her, seeming to subtly judge her.

At the door to the bathroom, Tanna stopped, trying to clear that scratch in her throat, shivering against a chill that invaded her overworked muscles. She filled her lungs with dank air from the soggy carpet beneath her feet and stepped inside.

The shower curtain was hanging only by the last few rings, but the tub showed little sign of the tragedy that had happened here. The running water had removed most of the blood. Thank goodness for that.

But then she noticed something on the back of the tub—a separation in the porcelain. And when she ran her fingers over it, a thumbnail-sized piece of it fell free, revealing the rust-colored metal underneath. Tanna picked up the chunk of hardened material, then knocked it on the edge of the tub, testing its heft and strength. She didn't know how much force it would take to break away a piece of porcelain, but she guessed that it had to be a lot.

"What is that?" Lewis said from behind her.

"A piece of the bathtub," Tanna said, turning and looking into his eyes. "Where Krystal hit her head." She held out the chunk of porcelain. "Do you really think an ordinary slip and fall could have done this?"

CHAPTER 15

The frayed lawn chair creaked as Roman settled down into it. He put in his earbuds and cracked open a can of orange Fanta. From this rooftop balcony, he could see the street in front of Tanna's apartment, and on his phone, he could watch a grainy livestream video from inside her living room.

She was old enough to be in college, but still a child in a room of adults. That was Roman's impression as he followed the gawky figure around the apartment, trailed by the detective. He understood why the roommate hadn't mentioned her. Protection. Tanna might have been good with a book, even with a scalpel, but the real world was a wild animal with real problems and real threats.

Roman didn't think she could handle it.

He listened as she told the police about the cadaver in her gross anatomy lab, the pictures she'd sent to Krystal, and the meeting she'd had with Dean Atwell. That she didn't think a slip in the bathtub could have caused so much damage to Krystal's skull or have enough force to break away a piece of the porcelain.

The police didn't give a shit. Like most cops, they put up a power trip to cover their laziness. They told her that accidents happen all the time. That it's tragic, but thieves take advantage of such situations. They reminded her that the most obvious answers were usually the right ones, and that elaborate conspiracy theories never worked out.

Still, Roman wasn't happy. The cops might have been stupid, but they were now in possession of facts that he would much rather had remained private. He cursed under his breath and crushed the empty soda can.

After making his way down to the street, he walked another block to his car, opened the trunk, and placed his can in a recycling bag with other empties.

Within the trunk, Dean Francis Atwell lifted his arms weakly. His wrists and ankles were bound, his right leg shattered. Several more bones were broken in one hand, and he had at least a couple of cracked vertebrae. Blood had crusted over his swollen left eye and dried in the creases of the dancing-vegetable tea towel used to gag his mouth.

Roman bent down, pushing his face closer, trying to recall what it felt like. Reaching into the hollow recesses of his mind for a sensation he could no longer have. He missed it so much that it owned him—and that emptiness now drove his days and plagued his nights. He had stopped feeling pain long ago, and it was like an amputated leg he still groped for sometimes.

He wished he could inhale the beautiful agony radiating off Atwell. Absorb it, experience it himself. Because with the pain, the pleasure would return.

"You're lucky for all I've given you here," he whispered,

his voice tight with envy. "Be happy when you hurt. Pain is good. Pain means life."

Atwell's one working eye searched Roman's face with hope.

Roman slammed the trunk shut.

CHAPTER 16

"They're not going to do *anything*," Tanna said as she walked out of the apartment with Jason.

"Of course not."

"I mean seriously. When I become a doctor and a patient tells me she's in pain or needs my help, I *have* to try to do something. I have to. Even if I think there's nothing wrong, that it's all in her head, I still have to try. I can't just sit back and tell her not to worry about it, or that it will all go away on its own. But these cops . . ."

Jason didn't seem the least bit surprised by the interaction. "What else did you expect?" he said.

"I expect them to do their *jobs*. That's what they're paid for."

"Tanna, if you believe what you told them—that there's more to this, and your friend died because of it—then you'll have to try and figure it out yourself."

"And how am I supposed to do that? I'm not a detective."

"I don't know. You're the one in med school. Someone's sick, what do you do?"

"Ask questions, gather information, and start ruling out all the things that it couldn't be until you're left with the best possible result. Process of elimination."

"There you go."

"Yes, and that's what the police should be doing."

Jason shook his head. "I noticed you didn't mention breaking into dean what's-his-name's office."

"I would have if I'd thought it would've done any good. But what's the point of getting myself in more trouble when they weren't going to do anything anyway?"

"Are you?"

"I couldn't save her before. What makes you think I can do something now?"

As they turned back up the street, Tanna couldn't help but think about how she had gotten here, to this present moment. It had all started with an open lab door—a door that she now wished had been shut. Then maybe none of this would have happened. Then maybe Krystal would still be alive.

"Son of a bitch," Jason growled.

She looked up to see what had upset him. Jason's truck was just up ahead. The passenger window was shattered.

Jason looked around before opening the door and searching inside his pickup. "They took the file."

"What?"

"The file you grabbed from the office. It's gone."

"Why would anyone take that?"

"We're parked on an open street in front of two police cruisers. I'm the only one broken into, and that was the only thing taken. You're the brain here, you figure it out."

"Oh my god." Tanna looked up at the surrounding apartments, feeling eyes staring down at her from behind every window. "This can't actually be happening."

"I guess this proves your theory isn't so crazy. One way to find out: talk to that dean of yours."

"No."

"He's got to know something, Tanna. You said so."

"Uh-uh. He'd just lie to me." Tanna looked Jason in the eye. "Besides, I can't be around him. He's not a good person."

Jason paused. "All right. Then go to the source."

"Concord Funeral?"

"Process of elimination, like you said. They're just up in San Francisco."

"I've got no car. No computer. Work and classes that I absolutely have to attend. I can't risk flunking out now."

"You said it yourself. The police aren't going to do shit."

Tanna shook her head. "I've already told you. I'm a first-year med student, not a detective."

"So maybe now you'll have to be both. Look, I can take you. I know my way around up there."

"And why would you do that for me? Because it'll give you another chance to steal more stuff?"

She'd seen him at the dean's office, sneaking baseball cards out of the dean's sports memorabilia case. She didn't know what the cards were, and they'd be meaningless to her if she did, but she figured they were worth a lot of money.

Jason didn't move, his eyes fixed on Tanna. Then he slid a hand into his back pocket and pulled out two baseball cards in protective plastic sleeves. He offered them to her.

She shook her head. "They're not mine."

He rubbed the cards between his fingers before returning them to his pocket. "I offered to help because I like doing it. That's all. I get it. You don't trust me. I don't blame you. But it's the truth."

"It's not even that. I trust you. I do. I just don't want to go up there and make things even worse." Tanna took a breath. "*Primum non nocere.* One of the main things they teach us when we start medical school. First, do no harm. But look at the first harm I've caused already. Krystal's dead."

"Not your fault."

"What if it is? Then what?"

"Try to make it right. Or go on with your life knowing that you could have made a better choice but didn't. And believe me, that's not so easy." Jason kicked at the broken glass on the ground. "She was your friend," he added. "You're the one who has to live with it."

The word *no* formed in the pit of Tanna's stomach and grew to a pressing lump in her throat. Just as it made its way to her mouth, ready to push forward and pass her lips, she nodded.

"Okay."

CHAPTER 17

Ablaze with a multitude of artificial lights, the San Francisco skyline pushed out against the water's edge. From thirty-seven floors up, Dr. Craig Emmerson questioned how a town that labeled itself so progressive and environmentally conscious could be so hypocritically wasteful. People talked about making sacrifices, but few followed through. A fundamental human weakness most others seemed to possess.

"Did you hear me, Craig?" Lauren Welsh asked.

"It's Dr. Emmerson," he replied.

"I didn't consider this a formal meeting."

They sat at a conference table with swirling gold inlay and touch-sensitive sensors. Surrounding them on the Brazilian rosewood walls were several Salvador Dali paintings, a Rothko, two Picassos, and, most prominently, Kandinsky's *St. George I*.

"You summoned me here in the middle of the night like some addled child," Craig said. "I hold six degrees. I'm the leading geneticist in the country, if not the world. The least you could do is address me with some common courtesy."

"Four degrees," Lauren said. "You never actually completed the other two."

"As if there was any need."

"Of course."

She worked the virtual keypad on the tabletop, and an image of three scientists in lab coats appeared on the massive video wall. A headline below it read: THE DEATH OF DNA? SYNTHETIC ENZYMES CREATED FROM ARTIFICIAL DNA.

"This comes out tomorrow," she told him. "Where do we stand?"

"Let me ask you something, Lauren. Do you know what we do at Modern Genetics? Do you have any idea what we're trying to accomplish?"

"I'm fully aware of our shared goal."

"I don't believe you are. Because if you *were* aware, you wouldn't need to ask me this."

"The people I report to are nervous. They want positive results, without complications."

"The people you report to only care about one thing, and it has nothing to do with the remarkable advances I've made. Your investors want more money and more power. That's the limit of their vision."

"You assured us you could deliver."

"I have given you everything you asked for and more. You see that? Right there?" Craig pointed to the team of scientists on the video screen. "Seven months ago, I accomplished that same thing, but you didn't want the attention. You didn't want my name splashed across the front page of any journal. I toil away in anonymity while surpassing every expectation. And this is how you treat me?"

"You promised a truly complete synthetic."

"I'm giving it to you."

"With self-replication."

Craig let his temper get the best of him. "You pathetic dolt. That next step is *revolutionary*."

"Just tell us when we can expect it."

"As soon as I have the freedom to conduct my work in the manner I require. It's *your* indecision that's costing us here."

"Justifications and delays." Lauren closed her eyes and tapped her fingers on the tabletop in a quick, uneven rhythm. The blunt professionalism disappeared from her face. "We're not going anywhere until I've concluded that you can complete the task on your own without exposing the program."

Craig shook with rage. "Who the hell do you think you're talking to? You do *not* get to sit up here and cast some sort of ethereal judgment while trying to usurp my authority!"

Lauren's voice remained calm and direct. "The investors fear your techniques have become . . . unstable."

"My techniques are none of their goddamn business. Or yours."

"Is that so?" Lauren got up and walked to the image of the three scientists. "See this woman on the right? A leading biomolecular engineer with interdisciplinary backgrounds in analytical chemistry and xenobiology. Head of the team gaining ground on you, ready to surpass your work and negate everything you've done. In short . . . she's forcing the investors to choose between her and you."

"I'm aware of who she is and her credentials."

"Then can you tell me what happened to her?"

Craig stood motionless. He didn't look at the image on the screen. Instead, he focused all his attention on Lauren, warning her with his eyes.

"She's been missing for two days now," Lauren continued. "Disappeared into thin air right out of her lab."

Craig wanted to reach his hands around Lauren's wispy neck and squeeze her into silence. It took every drop of patience to remain composed. "What's your point?"

"The point is, we've granted you the right and the resources to do what you do best, based on reassurances that you will deliver what you promised. If you want that to continue, then I trust—"

"Now you think you can threaten me?"

"I'm merely reminding you that if we cut off your resources, it would have devastating effects for you. And everyone working for you."

Craig walked over to her, getting right up in her face. "Those people up there on the screen? They haven't achieved *half* of what I've achieved. Nobody, and I mean nobody, could have accomplished what I have in the time frame you demanded, much less do so while working in that shithole you created. I don't answer to anybody. Least of all you. We leave the moment the new facility is operational."

Lauren didn't back down, didn't move even an inch. "It's been operational for three months, *Craig*. But we don't leave until I say so. Because everyone answers to someone. Including you. Realize this: you own *nothing*. Everything you have, everything you've done, belongs to my investors. Not you. You work for us."

"No," Craig snapped. "You're the one who has nothing without my work. I alone know what needs to get done, even if you're not willing to do it. Decisions will have to be made, and you don't want to be on the wrong side when *I* make them. Believe me, you do not want to get in my way."

Lauren lifted her hand and pointed at the missing scientist on the screen above them.

"You mean like how Dr. Valerie Schaefer got in your way?"

CHAPTER 18

It was supposed to be a long life, but sixty-two sure didn't seem long enough.

Sharon was a few years out of retirement as an Albuquerque high school counselor and part-time teacher. These were supposed to be the golden years. The endless days of summer filled with relaxation, shopping, and travel. The realization of any whim that came across her mind.

What a crock of shit.

The tingling had started in Sharon's fingers over a decade earlier. Without realizing it, she began pulling at them, telling herself it was no big deal, just a little onset of arthritis, and there was no way she was going to let it stop her. Had she known that her body would soon be waging an all-out war against itself, she would have killed herself right then and there, while she still had the ability to do so.

Useless doctors first diagnosed her with autoimmune peripheral neuropathy, allodynia, then syringomyelia. But numerous MRIs never located a cyst in her spinal column. They considered fibromyalgia and Guillain–Barré syndrome, and one idiot even proposed leprosy before they settled on some sort of spinocerebellar ataxia, which was just a catch-all way of saying they had no idea what the hell it was. They just needed to give it a name, and spinocerebellar ataxia was as good as any.

She endured treatment after treatment, each one more destructive than the last. But the symptoms always came back.

When Sharon began losing muscle control in her arms and legs, she knew she was in real trouble. She didn't tell anyone at first, knowing the school district would force her into early retirement. Except things spiraled from bad to worse, and she couldn't keep it secret after spasms hijacked her body. She was forced out of a job she loved, and into a life of pain. Unadulterated, horrific, crippling pain. As if someone was burning her from the inside out. Every movement, every breath, every beat of her heart sent searing agony shooting through her. But it was more than that. Chainsaw-ripped nerves allowed an overload of senses to rush in. Everything she felt, saw, experienced, came through in unrelenting waves of excruciating sensation. And it didn't stop. Ever. The fentanyl dulled it a bit, but that wasn't enough.

Death was Sharon's only hope now. She prayed for it.

Six months ago, she slipped into a coma for a week. That was bliss. And then she woke up. Things were exponentially worse after that. The doctors had done something to her while she was out. They denied it, but she knew.

She thanked God that her organs had at last begun to fail. Kidneys and liver first. Stomach and pancreas next. Everything went out of rhythm, and she lived every agonizing moment of it. She lost weight, passed blood, went on and off dialysis. There were more tests with disappointing results. Constant bed rest and antiseptic hospital rooms.

The people at Hillside Care Hospice Center were nice enough. But other than the nurses who passed through like ghosts, she had no one to help her. No family, no friends. No one brave enough to give her what she wanted most: death. It would be so easy—just unplug her feeding tube or push a pillow over her face. But she could no longer do these things for herself. She'd tried. She'd tried to give up, let go, stop breathing. But her body, her traitorous body, fought to stay alive against her every wish.

It's not even easy to die.

But when that day finally came, she cried tears of joy. Her heart misfired as it tried to pump lava-hot sludge through her narrowed veins. Her lungs sucked in raspy breaths like knife stabs. Someone sat next to her, holding her hand, but Sharon didn't look to see who it was. She didn't want the last image in her life to be some nurse she didn't know or a tattooed caregiver making fifteen dollars an hour pretending to be concerned about her. No.

She imagined herself as a young girl.

A summer dress.

A warm breeze.

A happy smile.

Then Sharon's pain vanished once and for all.

———————————

Nurse Julie let out a deep sigh and stroked the dead woman's hand. She'd been holding it for the past half hour as Sharon's body thrashed and convulsed through its last moments.

"Finally," she said to the empty room. "I mean, really."

She checked the old woman for signs of life. Satisfied that she was dead, she moved a heavy chair in front of the door and pulled out a biopsy kit.

"Okay, what do we have here?" she muttered to herself as she rummaged through the gear. "Won't need the antiseptic swabs. Not worried about infection anymore, are we?"

It had been seven months since she had gotten the call. Right after Sharon was admitted. Julie didn't know who the caller was, and she didn't care. She'd gotten this kind of call before. Usually a family member wanting her help in getting a will changed. Scheming to gobble up the scraps of their loved one's life.

But this caller didn't want much. Two grand just to provide updates. Easy money for emailing a few reports, and it wasn't a problem to rearrange her schedule.

She should have known there would be more to it. Just when it appeared the end was coming, another request was made. A tissue sample with spinal nerve root included. An odd request, but it came with a five-thousand-dollar deposit and a promise of ten more upon delivery. Julie had no idea what the caller wanted it for, but she wasn't going to pass up fifteen thousand dollars for a little piece of tissue from a dead woman no one cared about.

"Let's see here."

Julie slid her arms under Sharon's body and rolled her onto her side. She counted down the protruding vertebrae until she came to T10.

She drove the scalpel through the skin and hacked away. Neatness didn't count. She soaked up the few droplets of blood with gauze, removed a wide patch of tissue, and shoved it into a small plastic vial. Then she slapped on a bandage and rolled the body back over.

"See, that wasn't so bad."

After noting the time of death, she grabbed her phone and made the call. The courier would be there in a matter of minutes, and the ten thousand would be in her account by morning.

She smiled.

Easy money.

CHAPTER 19

Four thin wires ran along the bottom of the window before dipping down out of sight.

"Back there," Jason said, pointing.

Through the glass, Tanna spotted the alarm panel mounted on the side wall of the office. Then she rolled her neck and looked skyward at the inflamed morning clouds that had already swallowed the sun.

Jason had expertly replaced the broken window on the pickup truck with a piece of thick plastic, and they drove all night before arriving at this old office park southwest of San Francisco. The disheveled brick building of Concord Funeral was nothing much to look at, but through the dusty windows she spotted new computers, high-speed copiers, and, unfortunately, the elaborate alarm system.

"I can get us in," Jason said, "but we have to be set to run. Won't take long for cops to get here. It'll take even less time if it's private security. You ready?"

"No. Hold on. I don't even know what we're looking for." She hesitated. What was she even doing here? If someone told her a few days ago that she'd be breaking into a funeral home with some guy she'd just met, Tanna never would have believed it. "Maybe this is a mistake."

"You said you wanted to do this."

It wasn't too late. She could still turn back and go home. But that would be abandoning Krystal, wouldn't it? She just didn't want to throw her own life away, too.

Tanna wrapped herself with her arms. Her back felt stiff and her joints sore. Chills radiated from her shoulders on down into her chest and hips and seemed to drive all the heat out of her body. On top of everything else, she now wondered if she was getting sick.

"Here. Come here." Jason led her back to the truck, and they climbed inside and shut the doors. From beneath the seat he pulled out an old black hoodie with overlapping images of motorcycles stitched on the front. Under the picture, in white lettering, were the words JASON DELGADO DESIGN.

"Put this on," he said.

Tanna quickly slid into the hoodie and nestled into its warmth. It smelled sweetly of stale marijuana, but she didn't care. She was happy to enclose herself in its comfort and safety.

"You know," she said, "you could have told me you're famous."

"I'm not."

"The clothes. The motor cross."

"Motocross."

"Motocross. That officer knew who you were. They even made a video game about you. That's exciting."

"I guess." Jason failed to hide a smile. "Rode a bike before I could even walk. I had three older brothers who always tried to ditch me, and all I ever wanted to do was keep up with them. The bike was my ticket. The rest just happened. I won a few tournaments, picked up some sponsors. That opened a shitload of doors. Not all of them good. Money changes things. Changed me. I was gone a lot. Different races, different countries."

"Different countries?"

"Australia, Italy, Spain. As national champion, I had to represent."

"Why'd you stop?"

Jason let the question hang in the air for a long moment. "You don't get any younger in this world."

"Is that how you got this?" Tanna reached over and ran a finger over the scar along his neck, a sinuous white river carved into his skin. She rested her fingertips at the spot where it disappeared beneath his collar. "And why you don't like hospitals?"

"Something like that." He lowered her hand from his neck and held it. His touch warmed her fingers and relaxed her muscles.

"I've never been out of the country," Tanna said. "We barely even left the Chicago area. But it was nice there. I grew up right next to the Brookfield Zoo, and at night in the summer, you could hear all the animals howling, especially the lions. It was amazing, like . . . like their roar could carry on forever. I would lie there in bed and listen to them, pretending I was out on the Serengeti somewhere. Walking through the tall grass and looking up at the evening sky. But that's as close to Africa as I ever got."

"You should go."

"Someday. Maybe."

"Don't overthink it," Jason said. "Otherwise you'll never even try. Just decide and do it. Easy."

"For you." Tanna felt him squeeze her hand, smoothing out the wistful peaks building inside her.

As they sat in the relative warmth of the pickup, a boyish man with spiky blond hair approached the Concord Funeral building. He pulled a set of keys from his pocket, opened the door, and walked inside.

"I know that guy!" Tanna said. "I mean, I don't *know* him, but I recognize him. He's a friend of Krystal's. I saw his picture on her tablet. Brian, I think."

"Well, then let's go talk to Brian." Jason jumped out of the pickup.

Tanna scrambled out and followed him. "What are we going to say?"

"We can start with hello."

Jason pushed the door open, and they followed a threadbare carpet down a narrow hallway to what looked like the main office of Concord Funeral.

Brian was standing in front of a chirping alarm panel but spun to face them as they entered. "Can I help you?" he said. "Who are you?"

"You Brian?" Jason asked, stepping further into the room.

"I don't know you," Brian said. "What the hell do you want?"

"Hang on." Tanna moved between them. "We're friends of Krystal. I'm her roommate. Tanna."

Brian's stance relaxed a bit. "Tanna. Yeah, Krystal mentioned you. Did she . . . did she send you here?"

"I hate to tell you like this, but Krystal's dead."

"What do you mean, dead?"

"Dead is dead," Jason responded. "What do you think we mean?"

Tanna gestured for him to let her handle this. "The thing is," she said to Brian, "Krystal died the day before yesterday."

Brian looked stunned. After a moment, he turned and punched a code into the alarm panel, silencing the chirping. He stood there staring at the wall for a long moment before he turned back to face Tanna.

"How?" he asked simply.

"She slipped and fell in the shower. Hit her head. I found her, but it was already too late."

"My god."

"I'm so sorry."

Jason cut in. "Brian, what can you tell us about Concord Funeral?"

"Actually, you should talk to my dad, Wade. He'll take care of all the burial arrangements. No charge. I'll make sure of it."

"No, it's not that," Tanna told him. "Krystal had copies of invoices from here. And a person at the university had the same invoices with handwritten notes listing dollar amounts. We want to know why."

Brian stiffened. "Look, I'm sorry about Krystal, but there's nothing I can tell you."

He headed for the door, but he didn't make it more than two steps before Jason blocked him from leaving.

"We need your help," Tanna said.

"No," said Brian. "You need to leave."

Tanna mustered the strongest voice she could manage. "Krystal was my friend. She was *your* friend. And now she's dead. Like it or not, you and this company may have had something to do with it."

"What? You said she slipped in the shower."

"That's the official story," said Tanna. "But I think there's something else going on. Something you can help me figure out."

"Why would I have anything to do with Krystal's death? I'd never hurt her."

"Then why would she have the invoices? What were they for?"

Brian looked like he was about to force his way to the door, but then he paused. His shoulders slumped. "It wasn't me," he said quietly.

Tanna waited for him to continue. He didn't.

"Tell me," she said. Her tone was sharp and erupted from a place deep inside of her.

He didn't move. Just stood there staring at the floor.

Tanna looked around the office. She needed an answer. Something true. Something real she could hold on to before her world completely unraveled around her.

One wall was lined with filing cabinets. A few of the drawers had been left open, revealing their contents—file folders, some yellow and faded, others new, all with names at the top. Names of the dead.

She wondered if Krystal's name was hidden in there somewhere.

She walked over and pulled out a thick handful of files at random. "Fine," she said. "Maybe there's a record of it right here." Except she couldn't even imagine where to begin. Tanna closed her eyes, and with one sweeping motion, she threw them into the air. Papers fluttered across the room. "Hm, nothing there." She reached into another drawer and grabbed more.

"Wait!" Brian shouted. "What are you doing?"

"How about here?" Tanna hurled the files at him. "Or maybe it's one of these." She grabbed another handful and flung them across the room. "Do any of these explain what's going on? Will they tell me why she's dead?"

"Stop! Okay? Just stop." Brian let out a deep sigh. "You have to understand, it's . . . it's part of the business. No big deal. Everyone does it."

"Does what?" Tanna demanded.

Brian's eyes darted to the door. "When people bring in their loved ones for processing, sometimes we don't . . . well, we don't do what we say we'll do. Instead of burial or cremation, we sell the bodies to universities, research facilities, anyone who needs them. We might bury an empty coffin instead, or one filled with bricks, just to make it look good. I know how it sounds, but they don't know the difference. And it's big business. That's where the money is."

Tanna's mind strung the pieces together. "But Krystal wouldn't have gotten involved with any of that."

"Are you kidding? She came to us. She had a connection at the university. Someone with the authority to buy a lot at a premium price. Krystal got a cut, her guy at the university got a cut, and the medical school paid out the ass."

The words seared with white-hot truth. Tanna didn't want to believe it, but it explained a lot. Including little things, like Krystal's run of new clothes and good wine.

"It's not a big deal," Brian said again. "Every medical school and surgery lab in the country can do it. Except we get paid on the front end when Granny brings her dead husband in and again when we process him for research. Then just kick some money back to Krystal and her friend for pushing their business our way. It's an easy way to turn the cash around."

"What cash?"

"Huh?"

"You said it was an easy way to turn *the cash* around. What cash?"

Brian looked trapped. Suddenly he faked one way, then tried to charge the other way around Jason toward the door. Jason quickly stepped in front of him, and Brian responded by grabbing Jason by the neck.

That proved to be a mistake. Jason let loose with a burst of fiery punches, closed fists to Brian's head, knuckles thumping against flesh, breaking skin. Blood spilled from a split lip as Brian collapsed to the floor, his face erupting in splotchy patches of crimson.

Tanna grabbed Jason's arm. "Enough!"

Jason backed off.

She stood over Brian. "Tell us everything," she said. "Tell us now. Because I don't know if I can hold him back next time, and quite frankly, I don't want to."

Brian vaulted himself toward the exit. Jason started after him, but Tanna held him back. "No." She lunged for the alarm panel, pressing the red emergency button in the corner. The panel began to beep.

Brian slowed to a stop in the doorway.

"Are you going to let the police come?" Tanna asked. "My guess is you don't want them anywhere near this office. And Jason and I have no reason to keep quiet about what we've learned."

The beeping quickened. Brian looked caught between decisions.

"Fine," Tanna said. "I guess the police will come."

Brian continued to hesitate. The chirping sped up until it became a solid beep. Finally, he raced over to the panel and punched in the code to silence the noise.

He turned to Tanna. "All I know is that there's a guy who needs to dispose of things, okay? For whatever reason. And he hands over wads of cash for us to do it. My dad didn't want anyone else involved, but I've seen him. A slim guy with an accent. He supplies us with a lot of what goes to the university. But that's all I know. I swear."

Tanna absorbed the information. "Was this guy destroying bodies? Or was it something else?"

"At least sometimes it was bodies. I can't say if it was always that."

"Then we need to talk to your dad. He can tell us."

Brian's eyes widened. "You can't talk to him. Nobody can find out. I mean nobody."

"Brian, you still don't get it. Krystal might be dead because of this. Which means your dad might be next. This could be the only chance you have to help him, even save his life."

Brian's mouth opened, then snapped shut before any words came out. After a long pause, he spoke, his voice resigned.

"Spring Street. My dad asked me to pick up a bunch of bank records and personal files, then meet him at our mortuary on Spring Street."

CHAPTER 20

The silence of the lab put a smile on Craig's face. He preferred the solitude. Because deadlines had to be met. He paid people outrageous salaries and was still hard-pressed to find anyone willing to put in extra effort. While he labored to change the world, his employees punched a clock and cashed his paychecks.

But Craig had his prized possession. He kept it in a section of the lab that only he had access to. In fact, only three people knew of its existence; not even his head scientists realized what was behind the door. No cameras, no recording devices, no distractions. His own private sanctuary, away from the prying eyes and abhorrent uncleanliness of others.

He looked into the shallow cell-culture dish in his hand. Round and strong, it didn't have a single imperfection. Craig had made sure of that. He'd had it crafted two years ago, on his birthday, a present to himself. The only one he received. The glass was laser radiation-polished to remove all microscopic cracks and fissures. The lid fit so exquisitely that sometimes he would take it on and off again hundreds of times a night, just to feel the precision in his fingertips. It was his and his alone. The one thing he valued over everything else in his life.

He knew it was only an empty vessel, but it wouldn't always be that way. It held the power to generate low-cost drugs and vaccines. To correct malformation and cure disease. To usher in a whole new branch of medicine. Create a better world. This dish held the future, because Craig had dedicated his entire life to making it so. That was why he worked so tirelessly, constantly checking and rechecking even the minutest of details. The inglorious work that made the glorious possible.

When he walked out of his refuge, he had no idea what time it was. He could have been in there for days for all he knew, but as soon as he entered the main lab, a voice from overhead shattered his divine tranquility.

"There's a message for you, Dr. Emmerson."

"What now?"

"Sorry, sir. You instructed us to alert you when the courier arrived."

"Yeah, yeah. Leave it upstairs. I'll take care of it there."

"Yes, sir." The voice clicked off.

As he walked through the lab, Craig noticed an open drawer on one of the gel-imaging stations with a sample still in place. He took the time to catalog the results and refile it in the proper location before heading upstairs.

In his office, a small plastic vial from some dusty New Mexico hospice center sat atop his desk. Craig opened it and peered inside.

"Jeeeesus." It looked like someone had chopped it out with a dull steak knife.

He drew an aggravated breath. He had asked for a nerve

root. A simple request. He didn't know if he could even find one in this mangled piece of tissue.

He waved the back of his hand over the scanner built into the credenza, and the panel slid open. Bypassing the pill bottles and cell phones, he removed a small set of specialized dissection tools.

"Where are you?" he whispered as he carved the tissue, searching for a section of nerve root large enough to test. He cut away at the battered flesh, revealing a partial stem he hoped would be enough. It would have to do.

With expert delicacy, he made quick work of slicing the sample into micro-thin sheets. He deposited them onto slides and coated them with cell stain.

Then he waited. He'd spent half his life waiting for something or someone, and he'd grown weary of it. But it would be worth it, he reminded himself.

Craig tapped away at his keyboard until a picture of the ill-fated Sharon with the bad nerves and no family popped up on the screen. Glancing through her profile, he smiled when he came across the therapeutic strain they'd used with her. It was the first sample to come back from the NVR-31 trial, and Craig had had high hopes for it when it went out. He'd had a team working on degenerative nerve disorders for over three years, and they had made decent progress, but NVR-31 needed to break through. It had all the properties of a true regenerative therapy.

Sharon's age and volatile medical history made her a less than ideal candidate, but Craig had chosen her because her agony must have been extraordinary. NVR-31 not only had great potential to help her long-term, it could also relieve her immediate pain and give her back some semblance of life in her remaining months and days. She didn't need to suffer. Even dying was a better option than living the life she had been living. And Craig took it upon himself to save her, one way or another.

After checking the time on his Patek Philippe, he placed the first slide into the virtual microscope. The image popped up on his monitor, and he examined the dark blue and pink-stained sections. He expanded the image, then replaced it with another slide.

"Fuck."

It hadn't worked.

He reminded himself that the results were preliminary and factors such as age, health, family history, environmental influences, and biological inconsistencies needed to be considered before a final judgment could be made. But he was still disappointed. And angry.

It should have worked.

He ground his teeth in a wide clockwise motion as he looked at the mangled tissue. He should take it downstairs for more analysis with better equipment. Find out what succeeded and what didn't. Use the best parts of the results and adjust the formulation. Again.

"Why didn't it work?" he asked aloud.

Another defeat. Another setback. More time wasted.

Craig shoved his fists against his temples, trying to clear the rage clouding his thoughts. His arm swept across the desk and sent items flying. He ejected himself from his chair and glared at the mangled sample, mocking him with its insolent failure.

"Fuck you!" he screamed at it.

He knew he should take it downstairs and do it right. Something good would come. But his rage would have none of it. He crushed the sample under his pounding fists, obliterating any chance of discovering something useful. Ruining another opportunity for progress. His shouts echoed through the office as he stomped, and threw, and cursed until he exhausted himself.

Taking short, exacerbated breaths, Craig went to his credenza and pulled out an armful of pill bottles. There was no calculated measurement, no exact counting; he indiscriminately poured out handfuls of pills, filled his mouth with the drugs, and dry-swallowed.

From the rear of the credenza, he grabbed one of the hidden cell phones and made a call. After several rings, Roman answered.

"It's me," Craig said. "I have something in New Mexico that needs your attention. Without complications this time."

"I can't do it myself, but I'll make sure it's taken care of," Roman replied.

"Where are you?"

A pause. "Here. San Francisco."

"That's just perfect. You told me this Concord Funeral mess would be cleaned up."

"I'm headed there now to finish it."

"You goddamn better be," Craig snapped. "And is that why you visited my old friend, Solomon, without my authorization?"

"He doesn't know anything."

"Then why did he show up here to see me? At my lab. I

get you involved so I don't have to be. Maybe you're not the deterrent you think you are."

"It'll be done soon." Roman's voice was calm, confident.

Craig surveyed the mess before him, and his arm began to shake. "No. It needs to get done now."

CHAPTER 21

The ginkgo trees at the edge of the playground had started their annual fall ritual—a cascade of events that stripped green pigment from their leaves and left them tumbling to the ground in a spectacular display. Dr. Solomon Cabral stood beneath their branches, watching two young boys navigate their way up a slide. He observed how the smaller one grabbed the side rail, while the larger one used strength and balance to walk up the incline. Both approaches, although equally unsuccessful, had their own unique advantages and disadvantages. Both boys faced the same obstacle, and they took different paths to overcome it.

Their choices were, presumably, driven at least in part by size and motor skill. One child had more control of his muscles and better balance; the other did not and had to seek alternate means to move forward. This was adaptation at work.

Everything adapts, or tries to, Sol thought. No matter how large or small the organism, there will be adaptation, development, transformation, evolution. Or there will be death.

"Emily's over there on the swings," his daughter Caroline said at Sol's side. She pointed to a five-year-old girl digging her feet into the sand, trying to get her momentum going.

Sol followed Caroline's gaze. But the truth was, he never saw actual people anymore—at least, not the way everyone else did. Where others watched children playing, he witnessed the universe. It wasn't his fault. Decades of work as a prominent scientist in virology and molecular genetics had taught him to see behind the curtain, to discover what made his subjects tick. Behind the mouths talking and the limbs moving were cells—metabolizing, replicating, grouping themselves together in a wondrous display of unimaginable complexity to create larger systems and organs and eventually complete organisms. In his mind he would watch those bits and pieces of DNA build, copy, adhere themselves to principles and patterns of nature as minute as the movement of quarks and as grand as the cosmos, without ever knowing why they did so.

"Of course," he answered. "I saw her."

"She could use a little push."

"Couldn't we all."

Caroline released a heavy sigh.

The two boys on the slide gave up on their quest to reach the top and moved to a rope bridge suspended a foot off the ground. The law of least resistance had taken hold.

"So . . . how are you?" Caroline asked.

"Fine."

"I'm fine, too. Thanks for asking."

"I can see that. And your mother?"

"She's great, actually. In Paris now."

"I should have guessed."

"Visiting relatives and enjoying time together. Some people consider that being a family."

Sol ignored the remark. "I need to talk to you," he said. "I set up a fund for you and Emily."

Caroline shouted to Emily, who had finally gotten going on the swings. "Hold on tight!" Then she glanced over at Sol. "A fund? What for?"

"Your future. Her future."

"I make money. It's the one thing you taught me to do."

"I know, but this is something I want you to have."

"Like the restaurant you bought for me?"

Sol closed his eyes and let the sounds of playing children wash over him. He imagined their shouts and yells as a series of interwoven sound waves riding over and through each other, lessening in strength and amplitude as they stretched to reach him.

"I felt it was time for me to do something meaningful," he said.

"Better late than never I guess, but like I said, we're doing fine."

"It's important."

"Look," Caroline said, turning to face him directly. "If you really want to do something, don't give us money. Give us yourself. Be a part of our lives. At least your granddaughter's. Our door is open. It always has been."

"I know that's what you want, Caroline. And I wish that were possible. But this is everything I have to give you."

"No, it's not. Doesn't it bother you that your granddaughter doesn't even know you? Not that I do either."

"Because you don't think I was there for you?"

"Because you put your time and energy into what you wanted, what was most important to you—and that wasn't *us*. And don't tell me again how you did it to be the great provider. You would have done exactly the same if it had paid you nothing."

"You sound like your mother."

"Good."

"I know you won't believe me, but I always wanted the best for you. I just never understood what that meant. I did what I did because it was all I knew."

"Being selfish and absent were all you knew? You developed better relations with people who only briefly worked for you in the lab than you did with me over the course of a lifetime."

Sol grasped her hand. Caroline shrank back from the tender gesture.

"Yes. That's who I was," he said. "I'm trying to change that while I still can."

"With money?"

"With what I have left to give."

"The same thing you always did." Caroline pulled her hand away.

"Maybe you're right. But I need to start somewhere." His heart felt heavy and sluggish in his chest. "Just promise you'll take it. If you don't want it, then do it for Emily. And for me. That's all I'm asking. Please."

Sol waited until she agreed with a reluctant nod. It wasn't the moment of absolution he'd sought, but it would have to do.

He leaned over and kissed his daughter on the forehead. "Be good to yourself," he said and turned to leave.

As he walked away, Sol saw the two boys trying to make their way up the slide again. The larger one had switched to pulling himself up with the rail while the other one tried to climb on all fours.

Adapt or die, he thought. And smiled.

CHAPTER 22

"No cars," Jason said. "Maybe he's not here."

Tanna and Jason stood at the back of the mortuary located on Spring Street. The front of the tired old building was framed in replica white columns and plastic hedges, but that was little more than a cheap façade allowing grieving mourners to send their loved ones off with a pretense of dignity. They had immediately gone around to the rear loading dock, where they now knew the real business took place.

Jason slipped another key into the lock. Tanna hadn't seen him steal the key ring from the Concord office, but she was glad that he had. Now he was going through them one by one, so far without success. Tanna half-hoped all the keys would fail. She had come here looking for answers, but what she really wanted was an easy way to clear her conscience so she could go back to living her life.

She motioned to the chimney. "Smoke," she said. "He's here."

"Hard through the turns, fast down the straightaways," Jason muttered.

"What's that?"

"Just something we say at the track." Jason slid the second-to-last key in the lock and freed the deadbolt.

They entered a room packed with elongated cardboard boxes, each with the word HEAD printed on one end. Two doors led farther into the building.

"Which way?" Jason asked.

Tanna went right.

They pushed past a heavy velour curtain into a show-room displaying caskets of all shapes and sizes. Tanna led them through the silent assembly, looking away when she passed a silver child-sized coffin with a gold cross imprinted on the lid.

Jason stopped. "You hear that?"

Tanna closed her eyes and heard the faint sound of rustling and scraping.

They followed the noise into a dim hallway, then passed through a set of swinging doors into a wide room with a high ceiling. The crematorium.

A husky man with faded blond hair stood in front of a cremation chamber, a bulging sack of papers at his feet. Tanna couldn't be sure, but they looked like bank statements or financial reports. The man was stuffing the papers into the chamber by the armful. An adjacent chamber was shut, and Tanna heard flames roaring within.

As the man turned to grab another stack of papers, he noticed the new arrivals. Startled, he pulled out a compact pistol and pointed it at them.

"Whoa, hang on," Jason said, stepping in front of Tanna.

"You're Wade, Brian's father," Tanna said. The resemblance was clear. "He sent us to see you. We're friends of Krystal."

"Brian? He's okay? Where is he?"

"He's fine. We just left him."

"No, he's not fine. No one's fine." The gun shook in Wade's hand. "Who are you? Why are you here?"

Tanna walked out from behind Jason. "My name's Tanna. Krystal was my roommate, but she's dead now."

"No shit. We're all dead," Wade said. Then his face lit up with realization. "Wait. The roommate. You're the one who took the pictures and sent them to Krystal, aren't you? This is *your* fault! If you had just kept your goddamn nose out of our business, none of this would have happened."

"I don't understand," Tanna said. "How did those pictures lead to her death?"

"As soon as you sent the pictures to Krystal, she forwarded them to me. They saw it all. M-Gen was into everything. My email, phone records, texts. Don't you get it? You killed her. And now you've killed me."

The words tore a hole in the floor beneath Tanna. She had hoped to find a different answer here, a different truth. But there was only one truth, and it was the one she had feared all along.

I killed Krystal.

"Who's M-Gen?" Jason asked.

"Christ, you have no clue what you've gotten yourselves into," Wade said.

"Please," Tanna implored. "You have to tell us what's going on. We can help. We can go to the police. Fix this somehow."

Wade barked out a laugh. "You stupid bitch. You think they care about the fucking police? After everything they've done to all those people? No one will stop them. They're going to wipe it clean." He shook his head. "I should have just done what I was told."

Tanna suddenly understood. "You were supposed to destroy that body," she said. "My cadaver. You were supposed to cremate it for this M-Gen. But you didn't. You turned around and sold it to the university instead. Like the other bodies they expected you to get rid of."

A deep sadness rolled across Wade's face. "They're going to kill you now, too. It's just a matter of time." He set the gun down and went back to work shoving financial reports into the cremation chamber.

"There's got to be something we can do," Tanna said.

Wade had just reached into the bag to grab more documents when the air was split by several loud pops. It happened so quickly that Tanna didn't have time to react. She didn't even understand what had happened until she saw Wade's dangling right arm, muscles obliterated, shattered bone protruding from what little flesh remained. Blood pumped from the wound.

Tanna lunged to help, but Jason caught her wrist.

Three more gunshots hit Wade square in the chest, and he fell to the floor.

"Run!" Jason screamed. He pushed Tanna back through the door, out of the crematorium.

They sprinted down the service hallway but must have gotten turned around, because instead of going back to the loading dock, they came to a dead end. Tanna tried the nearest door, and when it opened, they darted through and shut it behind them.

They found themselves in the windowless embalming room. It was covered in soiled white tile, and at its center stood two stainless-steel tables. Caskets were pushed up against the wall, and a pair of rolling trays held knives, trocars, and rubber hoses.

"Oh my God oh my God," she said. "Did you see that? Did you see what happened to him?"

"Yeah." Jason looked around. "Shit. Only one door."

"Who did that?"

"I don't know. Shots came from a different doorway."

"We have to get out of here."

Jason put his finger to his lips. "Too late," he whispered.

CHAPTER 23

Roman left the crematorium through the only other exit out of the room. There were other people in the building. He hadn't seen them, but he'd heard them before he opened fire. It was a calculated gamble not to take them out right away, but he needed to eliminate his primary target first. Without error.

He followed the hallway to its end, where he stopped still. Over the years he had taught himself to be not just silent but an absolute vacuum, a dark space in the universe. The world around had no choice but to enter him. He sensed everything. And in this moment, the universe told him someone was hiding behind that door. He could almost taste the nervous energy.

He secured his grip around the assault rifle and pushed his way inside.

The room was dark, but Roman flipped on the overheads. The door closed behind him, and he smashed the doorknob with the butt of his rifle until it fell to the floor.

"No one leaves," Roman said to the room. "At least, not

alive. You might as well come out. Tell me what he told you and I'll make it quick. It's better that way."

He waited for a response, but was met with suffocating silence.

He took a step forward, looking down the barrel of his rifle as he swept the space for movement. They were hiding somewhere in here. He knew it.

"You think you can get by me? Go ahead. Try."

He moved along the perimeter, keeping a particular eye on the coffins. For the inexperienced they would seem like perfect hiding places. In reality, they were the death traps they were designed to be.

He passed the embalming tables and came to the corner of the room, where a large plastic trash bin separated itself from the wall. He yanked it forward, revealing a girl crouching behind it.

"The roommate," he said. "Tanna."

Curled into a tight ball, her eyes swirling with fear, she was clearly miles outside her comfort zone. In truth, he was shocked to find her here. He didn't think she had it in her. Yet . . . he noticed something else. Anger. Resolve. Stiffening courage. She was a cornered animal ready to leap out and attack.

He waited, unmoving, urging her to do it. He searched for the words that would make her spring into action.

"You started this," he said.

His intuition sparked. He wheeled to his left and fired three shots that blew fist-sized holes in the white tile. But his assault rifle was raised chest-high and his attacker came in low, tackling him at the knees. Roman went down, knocking a tray of embalming tools to the floor.

"The door!" the attacker hollered.

As the girl jumped to her feet and ran for the exit, the man grabbed hold of the barrel of Roman's rifle, but Roman ripped it free and swung the rifle butt around with vicious precision, tearing a gaping slash in the man's arm.

"Now what?" he said. "Huh?"

The man's eyes flicked to Tanna, who was working the broken lock, contorting her fingers to open the tumbler. "Come on," she muttered. "Open!"

Roman pointed the gun in her direction, but the man grabbed him again. Roman hammered him around the head and shoulders, bringing the rifle down over and over. The man fell to his knees, then bounced back up and plunged a knife into Roman's forearm. It must have fallen from one of the trays.

Surprised by the attack, Roman lost hold of the rifle, which clattered to the floor. At the same moment, the girl successfully opened the door. "I got it!" she shouted. "Jason!"

The man ran to follow her, and Roman scrambled for his weapon. He let loose a burst of shots that hit the door as it slammed shut behind them.

"You better fucking run!" he shouted.

He looked down at the curved blade still sticking out of his forearm and pulled it free. He went to the door, shoved the bloody tool into the broken lock, and twisted until it released. But it took too much time. They were surely gone by now.

Still, he searched the building. Nothing. Somehow, they had escaped him.

Few people earned Roman's admiration, but at this moment, the roommate and her friend did just that. Up until now, Tanna had been nothing but a nuisance—a fly buzzing around his face that he could easily swat.

He wouldn't underestimate her, or her friend, again.

He returned to the crematorium, placed the dead man's body in the cremation chamber, and propped open the door. After packing the room with cardboard boxes and wooden caskets, he overrode the door's safety sensor and pressed the ignition switch. Flames shot out of the chamber and set the room ablaze.

Roman walked out. It was unfortunate that he'd had to destroy this valued resource, but he had other locations around the country set up for the same thing. Two blocks away, he stopped to watch the beautifully destructive dance of the expanding pyre. It grew quickly, and he smiled.

By the time the fire department arrived, there would be nothing left for them to extinguish.

CHAPTER 24

Muscles expanded, chest enlarged, and lungs filled with oxygen. For Tanna, it was a breath like any other. Except that one breath brought with it multitudes of the virus invaders. That breath drew them even deeper into her respiratory system. They couldn't propel themselves on their own, so they relied on her natural movements to get them where they needed to go, and she obliged. Unknowingly and unwillingly, but efficiently.

That breath started a war.

The leading edge of the attack spearheaded its way through her body, but many of the free-floating viruses on the vanguard fell headlong into a trap. The thick and sappy mucus that lined her respiratory system latched on to the viruses' outer shells as they charged by. Unable to escape the grasp or penetrate the thick viscid layer to the vulnerable cells underneath, the viruses were left stranded, waiting for their demise.

Other invaders slipped past the gummy snare and drifted down to find open and unprotected cells, which they landed against with a soft bump. Though dwarfed in size, the viruses probed with their outer envelopes, a protein shell made up of a predetermined code, a key they had created to trick the body's defenses. The cell, with its strong outside membrane, was on constant alert against such attacks, ready to ward off any would-be enemies, but the viruses lied to the cells, told the cells they were there to help, that they were friends. How could they not be? They had the right key to prove they belonged. They fooled the cells into unlocking themselves, allowing the viruses to adhere.

And once the Trojan horse had been let through the gates, the viruses wasted no time. They ripped gaping holes into cell membranes and injected their viral material deep inside. There they unpacked multitudes of additional weapons, producing countermeasures to suppress the cells' defensive mechanisms while releasing chemicals that allowed them to take complete control of all cell functions.

After seizing full power, the viruses amped up reproduction to a frenzied state, using the cells' machinery to turn out copy after copy. The virus invaders inserted their own genetic code into the inner workings, supplanting the cells' natural building blocks to make virus clones instead.

The viruses needed to survive. And to survive, they needed to replicate. Just as viruses had done for millions of years. They knew nothing else. They were able to do nothing else. What others might see as pure destruction was merely their path to continued existence. And so the copies were turned out faster and faster until the cells swelled and bulged with thousands upon thousands of new viruses created inside their own walls.

Depleted of resources and unable to withstand the growing pressure from within, the cells burst open, releasing the mass of new viruses. Out of the gaping wounds they spewed, wave after wave, spreading out and searching for a new cell to infect, and another opportunity to start the process all over again.

CHAPTER 25

Tanna pounded on the front door of the house, then clamped her hand tighter around Jason's arm, dried blood already encasing her fingers. Jason had given her directions as she drove. Then he called a friend named Perry, who Jason promised would help them out.

Perry proved to be a man with dark snarled hair and multiple ear piercings. When he saw Jason and Tanna standing outside his door, he quickly ushered them both inside, up the stairs, and onto a worn couch in the living room.

"I need a towel," Tanna said. "Something to wrap his arm."

"Got it." Perry hurried off down the hall and reappeared a moment later holding a stained dishrag.

"Got anything cleaner?" Tanna asked.

"Sorry. That's it. Unless there's something in the kit."

"What kit?"

"There's an old first-aid kit here," Jason told her. "For things."

"Yeah, well, you have a major laceration. Possibly even

a detached tendon. A first-aid kit is more than 'things.' You need to go to the hospital."

"That's not going to happen."

"Jason, this is serious. It could get infected. You could have permanent muscle loss or nerve damage. At the very least, you need stitches. You can't just leave an open wound."

"You can take care of it," Jason told her. "You're a doctor."

"No, I'm a first-year medical student."

"Close enough."

"I'll get the kit," Perry said.

As he went off to retrieve it, Tanna wrapped the towel around Jason's wound, tied the corners tight, then looked around. This place barely qualified as livable. The house was old, with holes punched in the plaster walls here and there, and furniture that looked like it had been picked up from the side of the road.

"Interesting place," she said.

"Just a crash pad. Never know who'll show up. Perry's been here the longest. It was part of a seminary school or something, until a student hung himself out of the front window."

"That's horrible." Tanna cradled his head in her hands and looked him over. She ran her fingers over his skull, across his collarbone, and down his shoulders.

"What are you doing?"

"Checking to see if anything's broken. Are you dizzy? Do you feel nauseous? Any sensitivity to light or noise?"

"I'm fine."

"Does it hurt anywhere I'm touching you?"

"Yeah, everywhere. What do you think?"

"Okay, it doesn't seem like anything's broken. No concussion." She followed the movement of his pupils. "How did you know what to do back there? I mean, you saved our lives."

"We got lucky."

She ran her hands over his face and moved his head to examine it. When his eyes met hers, she let her touch linger on his cheeks. She meant to pull away, tell him he would be fine, but instead she found herself leaning in, closing the gap between them. But in doing so she shifted her weight, and Jason winced.

She straightened quickly. "Sorry."

Perry returned with the first-aid kit. "Are you going to do this here, or . . . ?"

"Help me get him to the bathroom," Tanna replied.

In the bathroom, she made Jason sit on the edge of the tub. Perry unpacked the first-aid kit and Tanna looked it over. A few bandages, an eyewash cup, cold compresses, empty aspirin bottles.

"This is it?" she said. "There's almost nothing here."

Perry motioned to the cabinet below the sink. "Check down there. We have needles and scissors. Some thread. I don't know what else."

"No alcohol, nothing to clean the wound with?"

Perry smiled. "Oh, we have alcohol." He ran off and returned with a liquor bottle.

"Tequila?" Tanna said. "Are you joking?"

"No, it's white. The good stuff."

"It'll be fine," Jason told her.

Tanna pulled the supplies from under the sink, then waited for Perry to leave.

"What? I want to watch."

"I need to concentrate." She pushed him out.

Perry stuck his head back through the doorway. "Hey, Jaybird. What do you want for the pain? I got some—"

"Nothing."

"Bullshit. That's not the Jason I know. At least hit the bottle a little. Don't let it all go to waste on your arm."

"Leave," Jason fired back.

"All right. I'll look into that company you wanted me to find. What was it again? M something?"

"M-Gen," said Jason.

Tanna chimed in before Perry could go. "Start by looking for medical, research, or pharmaceutical companies." Then she shut the door on him and turned to Jason. "Who's the Jason he knows?" she asked.

"Doesn't matter. Can we just do this?"

"That remains to be seen."

Tanna tried to concentrate on prepping the wound while visualizing her stitching. What her mind gave her instead were unrelenting thoughts of the trauma of the past few days. Krystal's dead body on the floor. The shooting of Brian's father. The killer standing over her, ready to pull the trigger as Jason risked his life to save them.

And through it all, the merciless words of Brian's father kept coming back to her.

This is your fault.

She raised her bloodstained hands to her face and stared at them.

"Hey. You okay?" Jason asked.

"What? I'm fine." Tanna went to the sink and washed

her hands thoroughly. "Just thinking I should keep a pair of gloves handy."

"If you're worried about germs, that tequila should kill everything anyway. Including brain cells."

"Let's hope so."

She pulled off Jason's T-shirt, revealing a series of scars circling his fit torso. Then she unscrewed the top to the tequila.

"Maybe you should take a hit of that first," Jason said.

It wasn't a bad idea. Tanna lifted the bottle and took a sip. "Ugh. This is the good stuff?"

She drizzled tequila around the outside of the wound to clean off the blood. It ran down into the tub, a small pink rivulet to the drain.

"This is going to hurt," she told him, then poured the alcohol directly over the laceration.

"It's not so bad," Jason said through gritted teeth.

"Except now I have to irrigate it."

Tanna spread the wound open with her fingers and emptied the tequila deep inside the muscle. Jason's whole body clenched as fresh blood ran.

"Holy shit!" he yelled.

Tanna immediately flushed the wound with water. "Don't be such a baby. Come on now." She grabbed the needle and thread and doused them both with the alcohol. "You realize I've never done this before."

"It's either you or me at this point."

"You really should go to the hospital. What was so traumatic that you won't step foot in there again?"

Jason shook his head. "I just trust you more."

Tanna could see that was all the answer she was going to get, so she didn't push.

She held the needle above the wound, then paused. For years she had imagined this moment: her first true medical treatment. Of course, the picture in her mind always involved a respected hospital or clinic, her actions overseen by doctors and staff. Sometimes she'd dreamed of making that rare diagnosis that everyone else had overlooked. At other times her mind had dished up nightmares of contaminating a sterile environment or inadvertently removing the wrong anatomy. But she'd never expected this. Alone in a bathroom with a bottle of tequila and a sewing kit.

She inspected the wound once more. The jagged cut ran through the Steel Dukes tattoo on his arm, and she hoped the thread would be sturdy enough to hold.

"Hey," Jason said softly. "If you really can't do it, I'll go to the ER or something. It's fine."

Tanna knew she should tell him to do just that. But her mind was already running through everything she had learned so far in medical school, picking out bits of information that might help.

"I can do it," her lips responded even if her head didn't agree.

She took a deep breath and started her first stitch. The needle stopped just as it entered the skin. On top of everything else, it was dull. She worked to get a better grip, and with a quick push, she forced the needle through and into the opposite side of the wound.

"Ow," Jason yelped.

"You need to stay still," Tanna fired back in the most

doctorly voice she could muster. She slowed down and told herself to move in careful order. "Looks like your Steel Dukes tattoo took a beating. It'll probably leave a scar through it."

"They wouldn't have it any other way."

"They?"

"My brothers. We all have the same one, in honor of our old man. Died of lung cancer. I tell you what, though—he was the toughest son of a bitch I ever knew. I mean *tough*. Four boys, raising hell all the time. We were too much for my mom. Ran her ragged. Sometimes we'd come home after getting in trouble and she'd be at the kitchen counter asking God why she didn't have girls. Then my old man would knock the hell out of us to keep us in line."

"Sounds rough."

"Nah. Typical stuff. And we had him outnumbered." Jason chuckled. "He didn't stand a chance."

Tanna watched the needle push out from underneath the skin. She brought it back over, tied it, used the scissors to cut the thread, then started another stitch. She had wanted to run it down as a continuous over-and-over stitch, but if the thread broke anywhere, the whole wound could open up again.

"Did he smoke?" she asked. Anything to keep Jason distracted.

"Oh yeah. Old-school, no filters. You know, I never even saw him take a day off before he got sick. Ever. But when he got the cancer, it took everything out of him. He was just a shell. That's when we got the tattoos."

Tanna squeezed the incision together to form a tight seal on the wound and pushed the skin up enough to get a good entry point. "Sounds like you were close to your dad."

"Not really. You know, the only advice he ever gave me was, 'Little pigs are cute, big pigs get slaughtered.'"

"Yeah, I'm not sure what to do with that."

"You and me both."

As Tanna continued her stitching, her thoughts drifted to her own father. She had to remind herself on occasion that she still loved him—as if that naive assertion would be strong enough to bridge the gaping hole he'd created the day he walked away. She understood why he did it. Losing a daughter to cancer had to have been devastating. But Tanna had lost a sister *and* a father.

He hadn't been the best father even before that. Or husband. He was always demeaning Tanna's mother—a joke here, a slight there, anything to show his superiority. Probably because Tanna's mother was smarter than him. They argued, and though it was never loud and obnoxious, Tanna sometimes wished it was. Instead, they fought in hushed tones behind locked doors, vocal razors thrust silent and deep. Subversive and painful, producing the kind of wounds that built up rope-like scars over time.

Tanna finished the row of stitches and examined her work. The stitches were crooked and close together, but at least the bleeding had stopped.

"How does it feel?" she asked.

"A little tight," Jason said, flexing his muscle. "But good. You'll be a great doctor."

She started to smile before clamping it down.

Tanna soaked some toilet paper with tequila and dabbed his arm. As she did so, she nodded at his body and touched her free hand to some old injuries. "You're a real adrenaline junkie, huh?"

"People tell me that all the time, but I don't know what it means. You want the truth? You know that little voice inside you that tells you when to stop, or be careful, or that you've gone too far? I don't have one. Never did."

"That's amazing. And scary."

"Made me a great motocross rider."

"And a great drug addict."

Jason stared back at her.

She ran her fingers along the veins in his forearm. "I have a phone," she said. "Wasn't hard to search you."

He nodded. "It's not something I'm proud of. There was nothing I didn't do at some point. And it took everything I had." He paused, thoughtful, then looked up at her. "Have you ever used? Ever been stuck in that cycle of wanting more, getting more, needing more, then wanting more again?"

Tanna shook her head.

"Well, here's the thing they don't tell you: it's dependable. You know? Always there to make you feel better. No matter what else is going on. Like laughing nonstop or finding that cool side of the pillow. Or when you're a kid and your mom wraps you in a thick warm towel after a cold swim. It's comfort, washing away all the sins of your past so they can't haunt you anymore. Because when you're high, everyday life is the low. It's unbearable. You only feel normal when you're on top."

Tanna felt suddenly like she was seeing something she shouldn't, a private space where she didn't belong. "I'm sorry," she said. "This is none of my business." She turned away and started packing the first-aid kit.

Jason spun her back, pulled her close, and kissed her, hard and fast, his rough skin rubbing against hers. Strong and confident in his movements.

Tanna allowed herself to succumb to the feeling. No hesitation, no anxiety.

And then his hand reached around and grabbed her ass while the other slid up to caress her breast.

Tanna clamped her fingers around his fresh wound and squeezed.

He jumped back as if shocked by a live electrical wire.

"Slow down, cowboy," Tanna told him. She let go of his arm, looked at him for a moment, then leaned in and reignited the kiss, this time moving with gentle deliberation. Jason followed her lead.

"I think I got something," Perry said, sticking his head into the bathroom. "Oh. Sorry."

Tanna pulled back, and she and Jason shared a smile.

CHAPTER 26

The rear bedroom was filled with an assortment of computers, beaten up and covered in motocross stickers, some monitors teetering on old beer cans. The deep hum of the equipment reminded Tanna of flapping dragonfly wings with their dry rattles and overlapping sounds.

"Not bad, doc," Perry said as he checked out the stitches.

"What is all this?" she asked.

Perry looked to Jason, but Jason responded with a slight shake of his head.

"Just work," Perry said.

"Right. You said you found something?"

"Here, look. Method General, but they're a manufacturing plant. Mobil Genesis, some sort of cell phone tech company in the valley. But you wanted medical, so I'd focus on Modern Genetics. Not too far away, down near South San Francisco."

"What did you find on them?" Tanna asked.

"Not much beyond an address. Pinged all around, but no virtual footprint of any kind. I even tried to bounce off their network, but got nothing, which is weird. I mean, I should have at least run into their firewall. But I dug up a few old articles with a basic description. M-Gen was founded by two guys." Perry pulled up an old magazine photo on one of the screens. "Dr. Solomon Cabral, that's him there, and Dr. Craig Emmerson. They were like big-deal genetic pioneers. Got together and started Modern Genetics to work on synthetic biology and gene therapy stuff. Whatever that is."

Tanna's curiosity was piqued. "It's a way to fight disease by inserting modified genes into people. Change the structure of cells instead of just treating problems with drugs or surgery. Sometimes that means DNA binding or editing, but usually what they'll do is scoop out the part of a virus that makes it deadly, replace it with a genetically altered gene, and then let the virus do what it does best: attack host cells and replicate until whatever you're trying to fix is fixed."

"Badass. Like that game, *Bio-Die*."

"Except this is real, and a lot can go wrong. Because the body will fight back to stop it. And I think that might have been the problem with my cadaver. The extra nerve bundle." Tanna took out her phone and pulled up the pictures she'd emailed to herself. She turned the screen so Perry could see.

"You get to slice people up? Damn, I should have gone to med school," Perry said.

"Think about it. If they're taking bodies to funeral parlors to cremate them, like Brian said, they're trying to cover something up. What if it's illegal research? This whole thing started after I sent those pictures to Krystal and she forwarded them to Concord Funeral. It's clear they didn't want anyone to see what I saw."

"I'm not following," Jason said. "What exactly do you think they're doing?"

Tanna's mind ran through possibilities, each connection like a flickering light that raced past faster and brighter until she dove into the blinding storm.

"Research," she said. "Like ways to regrow nerves in the brachial plexus." She nodded to her phone. "But if they're testing their methods on real people, perhaps without their consent, then it makes sense they'd want to destroy any trace of that."

"You're talking about human lab rats," Jason said. "How would that work? Wouldn't you know if someone was doing research on you?"

"Maybe not. But it's just a hypothesis. Why else cremate bodies in secret?"

Tanna turned to Perry. "What else did you find?"

"I tried to get info on the principals, but someone's made an effort to scrub them clean. You'd be surprised just how little public data there is out there for two guys who are supposedly hot-shot scientists. I couldn't find anything yet on that Dr. Emmerson guy. But I know someone who may have something on Cabral." Perry looked over at Jason.

"How much?" Jason asked.

"He won't sell a single. We'd have to buy a whole block. Five hundred."

"I don't understand," Tanna said. "Who has what and why does it cost five hundred dollars?"

Jason responded. "Perry has friends, acquaintances he works with, who collect information on people."

"Like databases," Perry said.

"Yeah, like databases. They're willing to sell this information, but only if you buy a block at a time."

Tanna looked at Perry. "You're stealing people's identities."

Perry smiled. "Sure, if you want to nutshell it."

"Will they take a credit card?" she asked.

She hated to even consider using the card. *It's for emergencies*, her mom had told her. And her mom had enough problems to worry about. But this *was* an emergency.

"You don't want to do that," Jason told her.

"Sure she does," said Perry.

"No, she doesn't."

Perry shrugged. "After two days you just need to call it in stolen."

"Why?" Tanna asked.

"Trust me. Two days and you won't be liable for any charges." Perry directed her to a crude paywall on one of the screens.

Tanna typed in the credit card information from memory and held her breath as she waited, unsure if there was enough left to cover the charge.

When the payment was accepted, Perry took over. He downloaded files and the screen lit up with names.

"Here." Perry opened the file for Solomon Cabral. "No address, just a mailbox."

"You got it that easy?" Tanna asked.

"Thank you, Equifax. But that's nothing. Texts, emails, banking . . . it's all out there for the taking if you know where to look." Perry expanded the information to another screen.

"Like these. Charges to the same place, looks like almost every night. Highland Diner in Pacifica."

"That's not far. We could be there in twenty minutes, wait around and see if he shows up. Try to find out what he knows," Jason said, looking at Tanna.

"What are you talking about? We need to go to the police with this."

"You already tried that."

Tanna turned to Perry in disbelief.

"Don't look at me," he said. "I wouldn't go to the police for anything."

"A man tried to kill us today," she said. "He murdered someone right in front of us. There's going to be evidence left behind—evidence to back our story about what's been happening. When the police see that, they'll have to follow up."

"Actually, there won't be any evidence," Perry said.

He pulled up a video on a separate monitor. A news reporter stood before a mound of smoldering ashes, reporting on the "devastating fire" that had burnt Concord Funeral to the ground.

Tanna released an uneasy sigh as she focused on the image of Dr. Cabral.

"All right," she said, turning to Jason. "Let's go."

CHAPTER 27

The Highland Diner reminded Tanna of something out of an old movie. It was cramped, with a long counter, and it looked like it hadn't been cleaned in decades. She could almost taste the years of burnt coffee and grease built up on the plaid vinyl wallpaper.

She managed to wedge herself on a stool between Jason and an overweight man reeking of rancid cigarettes and yesterday's gin. Every time he took a bite of food, his elbow bumped into her. Tanna tried to lean away, but it was no use. She clutched her fork, ready to drive it into the man's arm if it got worse.

"You think that's him?" she asked Jason in a sideways whisper. She motioned toward an older gentleman at the end of the counter working a crossword puzzle while picking at the remains of a spinach salad. He looked at least somewhat similar to the picture of Dr. Solomon Cabral that Perry had pulled up online, but this man looked thinner, more weathered, as if he could collapse at any moment.

"Can't tell," Jason responded. He shoveled down some

french fries and followed them with a swig of Coke. "Eat something. Otherwise it looks weird."

Tanna examined the egg sandwich she'd ordered. The viscous outer membrane had run out alongside the under-cooked yolk and had pooled at the center of the plate. She couldn't stand to look at it, let alone take a bite. She forced herself to drink coffee instead. It scalded her tongue. The whole place was hot. Crowded, hot, and cramped. The aching muscles in her neck twisted themselves into braided knots. She hunched her shoulders and drew a short, raspy breath that failed to satisfy her need for air.

The gentleman at the end of the counter paid his tab, folded his newspaper into a tight rectangle, and got up to leave.

"See ya, Sol," the waitress said. A chorus of goodbyes from other patrons followed, including from the overweight man sitting next to Tanna.

Jason waited a moment and then trailed him. "Come on."

Calculating the cost of the two sandwiches with drinks in her head, Tanna pulled out all the cash in her pocket. Four dollars short. She dropped everything she had on the counter and mouthed "I'm sorry" to the waitress before running out.

They followed the old man onto the street, but when they made their way around the corner, he was gone. They rushed forward, searching doorways and hidden alcoves.

Then a voice spoke from behind Tanna. "I'm calling the police."

Tanna turned to find the old man standing behind her, his phone in his hand and his thumb hovering over the send button.

"Good," she said. "Then you can tell them why you're trying to have us killed."

"I don't know what you're talking about."

Tanna was sure of it now. His face had changed, but the eyes were the same. "Sure you do," she said. "You're Dr. Solomon Cabral."

Jason snatched the phone from the old man's hand. "Who are you really calling? Another of your asshole buddies to come and gun us down?" He showed Tanna the screen— the man really had typed in 911.

"Yes, I'm Solomon Cabral," Sol said. "But why do you think I'm trying to harm you?"

"Because we found out about your company. What you're hiding there," Tanna responded.

"Ah, my company. I see. You mean the company that pushed me out and forced me into early retirement? The company that I founded with my own sweat and blood and then had ripped away from me? The company that I've had no contact with in years? That company?"

"Modern Genetics. Yes."

"I can't help you. I'm not involved anymore." Sol took his phone back from Jason. "I'm just an old man trying to enjoy a good meal."

"Someone killed my roommate. And the owner of a mortuary. Then he tried to kill us," Tanna said.

"Then you need to walk away," Sol said quietly. "That's the only thing you can do now. Forget all about this and just walk away. Don't look into it. Don't dig. Consider it . . . something that just happened."

"You don't understand," said Tanna.

"No. It's *you* who don't understand what you've gotten involved in. I can't stop them, young lady. I can't do anything anymore. No one can."

"People are dead. My friend is dead. You seriously think I can just forget that?"

"Only if you want to stay alive."

Tanna took a moment to feel the salty breeze on her skin as she gulped cool ocean air into her thickening lungs. "I can't do that," she said. "I can't act like it never happened."

Sol turned to Jason. "What about you there, sport? Are you involved too, or are you merely helping a young woman in trouble out of the goodness of your heart?"

"I got nothing to lose," Jason said.

"You have everything to lose. If you pursue this, they'll go after your family. Brothers, sisters, nieces, nephews. Anyone close to you. They won't stop. Ever."

"Then neither will we," Tanna told him.

Sol shook his head. "A couple of kids who don't know when to give up. Look at you, the good girl with the bad boy. A predictable cliché."

"You don't know shit about us," Jason fired back.

"You're right," Sol said with a laugh. "And my guess is that you don't know anything about me, or Modern Genetics. The things going on there are frankly beyond you. And trust me, you don't want to know. Because knowing makes you a target."

"We're *already* targets," said Tanna.

"You're still living, and that tells me something. It tells me you may still have a chance to take my advice."

"They're using people for live human trials," Tanna

blurted out. "Unregulated field testing. Why else would they need to destroy corpses? They could be introducing new strains of genetically modified material into unknowing hosts, and then getting rid of the evidence. That would bypass all regulations and cut development time to nothing."

Sol's gaze raised to meet hers. "Walk away."

"If we walk away now, they win."

"They'll *always* win, young lady. And you'll always lose. It's life. Enjoy it while you still have it."

"That's not good enough," Tanna said. "We're not walking away. Not anymore. It's not right."

"What do you think you're going to do? They've already thought of everything. They have money, influence, power. What do you have? You're not smart enough or strong enough to make the least bit of difference."

But Tanna couldn't let it go. She just couldn't. The growing black balloon of frustration exploded inside her head.

She pulled out her phone and brought up the pictures of the extra nerve bundle in her cadaver. "We can expose them," she said. "Tell everyone what they're hiding. What they've done."

Sol looked at her with weary eyes. "Then you've made your choice. As have I. I've fought my battles with them and lost. I've begged you not to pursue this, but I can't stop you."

And with that he turned and walked off, leaving Tanna and Jason standing at the side of the road.

CHAPTER 28

The heavy stone walls of Dean Francis Atwell's office sucked in the silence and oozed out a sour must. Even the aesthetics of the corner location couldn't relieve the listlessness of the dead space.

Detective Duane Lewis settled into his jacket as he stood in the middle of the room making mental notes to himself. Nothing seemed disturbed, but it would be difficult to tell if it had been; it appeared the dean didn't put a high priority on neatness. There were leaning stacks of papers everywhere. No trash in the wastebasket, but he figured the cleaning crew took care of that.

"We got statements from everyone on the floor," said Aaron, Duane's partner, as he entered, followed by a university police officer. "No one saw him after the charity reception."

"Make sure we get a list of his schedule for the last week. Not only meetings, but phone calls too. I want to nail down the timeline right up to that point."

"Will do," Aaron responded.

"Are there cameras?" Duane asked the university officer.

"Dean wouldn't allow them in the office. Not sure about the entrances or hallways."

"Why not in the office?"

"I, uh, I don't know. Privacy, I guess."

"I'll need copies from every camera feed in and surrounding this building for the last seventy-two hours."

It was a long shot that the video would produce any usable evidence, but Duane needed to make sure. He wasn't ready to declare the man anything more than missing, not just yet, but there were red flags. Notably that business at his house with all the broken glass, along with tracks in the driveway that could be, perhaps, dragging heel marks. No one in the neighborhood had reported anything out of the ordinary, though they were still trying to contact his closest neighbor.

"What about enemies?" Duane flipped open a folder teetering on one of the desktop stacks. The slight weight change sent the stack sideways, spilling onto the floor. "Shit."

"What's that now?"

"Do you know of any disgruntled students or faculty that might have had something against the dean?"

"Best you talk to Captain Williams about that," the officer responded.

Duane ignored the mess he'd created. "Why would I have to talk to the captain?"

"I don't know, I'm just saying."

"No you're not." Duane stepped over to the officer. "Whatever it is, we both know it's going to come out. It always does."

"Well . . . we're not supposed to mention nothing."

"Too late for that."

Cursing softly, the officer bowed his head. "Dean sometimes took meetings away from campus. Meetings that lasted, you know, like overnight. Or even a couple days. I just thought he could be on one of those is all."

"Do you know where he went for these off-campus meetings?" Duane asked.

"No, sir."

"Was it a student?"

"Some were. Some haven't been around for a while. Others are kind of regular."

"How do you know all this?"

"There were, like, complaints. From a few girls. Not on the record. Not so much anymore," the officer stammered.

"You buried them? You can't be that stupid."

"What? No—not me. I mean, I'm sure they were looked into and found to be nothing, then not reported, officially, I guess."

"Right. That's why no cameras in his office. I bet he liked to bring them back here as well."

"What the hell is it with this type of guy?" said Aaron. "A little power and everyone turns into a damn predator."

"Can of fucking worms," Duane mumbled under his breath.

He knew what was coming before anyone said another word. Months of investigation, reluctant witnesses, complicit police, and a stonewalling university trying to protect its reputation. Can of worms? No—a can of fucking vipers. In the end, everyone would do their best to sweep it right back under the rug. So could he.

"I want those names," Duane said, determined to bring it to light instead. "Descriptions. Dates. Everything you've got on the prick."

"Yeah, you'll need to talk to Captain Williams about that," the officer replied.

"Damn right I will." Duane took a slow walk around the room and sat behind the dean's desk. "I'll also need full access to the computer, emails, everything."

"Not unless the captain—"

"I'll do it myself. Now get me those names and dates. Get me whatever damn video you can find. The longer you stand there, the more times your name comes up during my discussion with the captain regarding harassment allegations against the dean that have gone unconfirmed and ignored."

It took the university officer a moment to fill in the blanks, but as soon as he did, he sprinted out of the room.

"Guy sounds like a real prize," Aaron grunted. "Think we'll find anything?"

"No idea. Especially now that half the student body and their whole damn force is involved." Duane removed a pair of black nitrile gloves and snapped them on. "I'll work here. Start at the bookshelf. Preliminary only. We may have to bring a tech in to dust for prints later."

The piles of papers on the desk revealed nothing of interest. The drawers didn't yield anything either.

"You've got to check out this collection. The guy's a real sports nut," Aaron said from across the room. "He's got Sandy Koufax, and a Mike Trout rookie card."

Duane pulled at the last drawer. Locked.

"Funny," Aaron said. "Looks like there are a couple of empty spots here. Could be something missing."

Duane took out his pad to make a note of it when he noticed the chewed-up wood around the top of the locked drawer. It looked like it had been forced open. He ran his finger over the broken grains, and sharp splinters pierced his skin through the glove. If this had happened long ago, those splinters would have been knocked off or smoothed down through normal opening and closing. No, this damage was fresh. Someone had broken in, and it was recent.

CHAPTER 29

Tanna ignored the lingering stares and sideways glances as she passed through the crowd. She was awash in a sea of black leather and piercings, slithering bodies flowing to the rhythm of the industrial trance music. A woman in a paint-streaked face mask spun her around and bobbed up and down in front of her with wide, vacant eyes.

Tanna grabbed Jason's arm. "What is this place?" Part club and part warehouse, the walls of the old building were covered in exposed brick and dried puke.

"What?" Jason shouted back over the noise.

"You told me we were meeting Perry."

"We are. This is where he wanted to meet."

Of course it is.

An enormous hand attached to an even larger arm reached out from the crowd and grabbed Jason. The bald, burly man wrapped Jason in a bear hug, lifting him off his feet.

"JD!" the man shouted. "Damn, it's good to see you."

"Big Ben, no shit." Jason hugged him back. "What the hell are you doing down here?"

"Perry sent the word out you were coming. Gonna be a damn party tonight."

At least five or six guys stood behind Big Ben, and they reached over to say hello to Jason, with hugs and fist bumps all around. Tanna could see the genuine admiration from all of them, and Jason didn't shy away from it. In fact, he seemed to soak it up, reveling in their attention, proud to show off the stitches in his arm like it was some war wound.

Drinks got passed around, and someone thrust a glass of coppery red liquid into her hand. More people joined Jason's circle, and he did his best to introduce her, but these guys were here to see him, not her, and she gradually got pushed to the side. With every handshake and pat on the back, Jason grew a bit taller. He was in his element, and she envied that. She couldn't imagine how that would feel.

Tanna took a sip of the red liquid. It was too sweet, syrupy. She was about to look for someplace to set the drink down, but then paused. Despite her share of drunken nights, she wasn't typically much of a partier. But Krystal's words about not drinking enough reverberated in her head. And standing here with Jason's close circle made her feel like she was among friends.

Except the one friend who wasn't here.

"Más vino," she said, and lifted her glass in a solitary toast only she would understand.

Más vida, her mind shot back. *More life. Always more life.*

"I love you, Krystal."

She took another sip. Then another. The world around her softened. After a while, the music stopped pounding in her ears and started flowing directly through her body. The more she drank, the more she enjoyed the taste. When Jason finally broke away from the group, there was nothing left but a thin film coating the inside of the glass.

"Have you seen Perry yet?" he asked as he led her through the swarm of people.

"No." She hadn't even been looking.

Jason pulled the glass from her hand. "Did you drink this?" he asked. "Who gave it to you?"

Tanna looked around, trying to find his friends. She could only point in the direction she thought they were.

"Don't drink anything anyone gives you here."

She felt her head nod in affirmation.

They found Perry in a corner of the bar working his phone. "The man of the hour," Perry said without looking up from the screen.

"Thanks to you."

"That's nothing. Wait till you see who else I got coming. Shit's going off tonight." Perry smacked Jason in his wounded arm and turned to Tanna. "What do you think, doc? Can't keep this guy down. No matter what. He'll keep coming back."

"Yeah," Jason said, wincing.

"You get anything out of that old man?"

"He was nice." Tanna swayed on uncertain legs. "Like my grandfather."

"He didn't give us shit," said Jason. "Just told us to walk away and don't look back."

"And are you?" Perry asked. "Or are you going to stir the pot?"

Jason grinned. "You know the answer to that."

"Okay then. How can I help?"

"I want to get all our information online. Everything we know or even think we know. Put it on websites, social media, all the feeds. They're pulling a lot of dirty shit, and so far they've been able to keep it under wraps. That ends now. I want everyone here to send it out. We'll flood the whole damn internet."

"Posting it's easy. The hard part is keeping them from bricking it up or ripping it down. But give me a few minutes and I'll hide it on the deep web. No way they can get to it there." Perry smiled. "Trust me, I got the world by the balls. Now. Tell me what you got."

"It's better if Tanna does it. I don't understand this stuff. Tanna?"

Two faces turned to her, floating in a sea of color. "What's the deep web?" she heard herself say from miles away. Except the word "deep" came out like *deeeeeeeep* and "web" never came out at all. She laughed at the absurdity of it, then fell back into herself.

"Uh, what's up with your girl there?"

"Shit," Jason said. He lifted Tanna's face to look into her eyes.

"I'm sorry," Tanna tried to say. "I didn't know." But the words dribbled out in nearly unrecognizable syllables.

"She drank the punch," Jason said.

Perry looked at Tanna. "Enjoy yourself there, honey. You're in for one hell of a ride."

Tanna watched his words jump and twirl around her head. She reached up and tried to grab the spinning letters, but they slipped right through her fingers before bouncing and floating away on musical vibrations.

"And there she goes," Perry continued.

"This isn't funny, you idiot. She hasn't done this before."

"Oh, come on. First time is the fucking best."

Jason grabbed Tanna by the shoulders. "Tanna, I need you to stay with me. Think about where you are right now. Look around. Remember what happened. Try to remember why we're here."

Perry shook his head. "It's no use, man. She's done."

"Damn it." Jason ran his fingers through his hair.

"Let it go. She'll be fine. Just tell me everything you got on M-Gen."

Tanna watched the two guys talk, their hand gestures leaving fluorescent floating trails in the air. But their conversation stopped being important to her. She didn't care and was happy not to. As a matter of fact, she was happy to be standing here at the center of the universe with the world moving around her, time and space twisting and turning, bending to her very will.

Wrapping herself in her arms, she allowed the very last bit, the very core of her essence, to succumb to the sensation. She was no more, yet she was everything.

What a great feeling it is to be God.

She closed her eyes. Or thought she did. She wasn't sure. Either way, the image of the bar in front of her remained the same. People drank and laughed, yielding to the music. She felt a communion with them, a oneness she had never before experienced. Her entire body tingled with life. She could see the waves of sound pulse and dance around her, moving across her skin with delicious throbbing vibrations.

She stepped forward into the crowd. She needed to be

with them, be a part of them. The universe commanded it. There was no forethought, no more second-guessing, no more concern over who might be watching, what they might think. No more worry about anything. Tanna's mind was freed, her muscles relaxed. She melted into the harmonious mass. This was euphoria.

The woman in the paint-streaked face mask stepped into view, and Tanna reached out to her. Their hands touched, fingertips sending jolts of electricity back and forth. They moved together in unison, music crashing, lights flashing. Tanna saw a man standing in the back, watching them both. She wasn't sure why, but she felt connected to him.

I know you.

Her mind fought to see, to remember, but the man was obscured by swirling dancers and twisting shadows. Tanna took one step toward him, then another.

I know I know you.

As she drew closer, his features sharpened. He had tight thin lips and small vermin-like teeth. He moved forward to meet her. She stared hard into his face . . . and her mind made the connection. It was him. The man who had tried to kill them at the mortuary.

Her whole body tightened. She tried to shout, scream at the top of her lungs, but nothing happened. Her muscles didn't react.

He took another step and closed the gap between them.

Her chest thumped and blood pulsed in her temples. She shut her eyes and hoped it would go away. All of it. She just wanted to be back to normal, but images and thoughts smashed into each other with no cohesion or meaning. Nothing connected.

Move, she screamed in her head, but it was no use.

The man had drawn within arm's reach when the crowd surged, knocking Tanna off balance. She fell to the floor.

Get up!

CHAPTER 30

"No," Jason said over the music. "You heard her yourself. Using real people. Like lab rats."

"Yeah, yeah, right." Perry made a note of it on his phone.

Jason had told Perry everything he could remember from his discussions with Tanna. The modified genes and live human trials, the pictures of her cadaver, Concord Funeral, destroying corpses, escaping from the killer. Most of the science stuff was over his head, but he did his best to retell it in the way he understood it.

While he and Perry spoke, Tanna was out on the dance floor, letting her body bend and flow to the music, enjoying the hell out of herself. Jason kept one eye on her, making sure she didn't get taken advantage of by some predator trying to score, steal, or destroy whatever he could get his hands on. The world was an ugly place, and even uglier when seen over the end of a pipe or through the barrel of a syringe.

Jason fought back the cravings pushing from within. Just looking at everyone indulging in their basest desires made him tingle with expectation and jealousy. He was like a six-year-old watching other people open presents on Christmas morning.

Except it went beyond cravings. It was survival.

He knew it would take only a nod or a smile, and he could get whatever he wanted. The excuses started beating a drum in his head. His arm hurt. His legs were sore. He was tired and he needed to stay awake. He needed to sleep. Because he just fucking wanted to.

Tapping his foot in a nervous tic he picked up when the hunger went unfulfilled, he turned his head to hide his eyes. One engaging look and it would be over.

When Jason looked for Tanna again, he couldn't see her. She had disappeared, devoured by the crowd. He searched the faces over and over until he found her lurching toward him, eyes wide with fear. He rushed to grab her, and she collapsed into his arms.

"Are you okay? What happened?"

"It's him."

"Who?" he asked, but he saw the answer in her face.

Jason scanned the crowd but didn't see the killer from the funeral home.

"What's going on?" Perry asked.

"The guy who tried to kill us is here. Tanna saw him."

"You sure?" Perry said. "Maybe she didn't. You know what I mean."

Jason turned back to Tanna. "Are you sure you saw him?"

She tried to point, but her arm went limp.

He grabbed her hand and held it tight as he searched the undulating bodies and the dark corners. Nothing. Then, from nowhere, the man appeared across the room. He and

Jason locked eyes in an unwavering stare, neither daring to move or even blink.

Without warning, the man vanished once more.

"He's here," Jason said. "Other side, covering the exit."

"No shit. Let's get him," Perry replied.

"Hang on." Jason surveyed the room. He spotted the man again, closer this time, like a wolf stalking its prey. Glancing down at Tanna, he saw that she wasn't going anywhere on her own. He would have to carry her out. "Too risky."

"Bullshit. We do this thing head-on. Go right at him. He won't know what hit him."

"Tanna can't even move."

"So what? We got our whole damn crew here, with more on the way."

Perry was right. "Okay," Jason said. "Yeah."

Perry typed on his phone and showed Jason the message: *JD in trouble. Need an exit. NOW!*

Jason nodded. "Send it."

People around the club began looking at their phones and showing screens to others. When Big Ben saw the message, he eased his hand around the neck of a liquor bottle and readied himself. The room was electrified with anticipation.

Then, all at once, Big Ben released a guttural howl and swung the bottle at anything that moved. He connected with one skull after another until it shattered. All hell broke loose.

Punches were thrown. People were shoved to the ground. An instant fucking donnybrook erupted, with Jason's friends at the center of it.

"There!" Jason shouted, pointing as he spotted the killer

moving toward them along the wall. But no one heard him over the cracking of fists against faces.

The killer continued his advance.

"We have to go!" Jason shouted.

He scooped Tanna up with his good arm and ran headlong into the brawl. The tightness in his legs fired with Tanna's added weight, but he charged straight into the teeth of the fighting. Perry followed, and they slipped past flying elbows and falling bodies, weaving and bobbing.

Then Perry screamed in pain.

"Don't stop!" Perry yelled as he began throwing wild punches.

Jason pushed ahead. Not looking back. Not helping Perry. Only focused on the exit just ahead. He sprinted forward but tripped over a fallen body and stumbled, slamming hard into the door. It burst open, and he pulled Tanna through.

Jason tried to run, but Tanna's dead weight slowed him down. "Come on, Tanna. Move." He lurched forward into the street.

The bar door opened behind him, and Perry stood wild-eyed inside the frame.

"Perry!" Jason shouted, but the killer rushed in and knocked Perry off his feet with a blindside elbow to the head.

Jason spun but didn't see the oncoming headlights until it was almost too late. A black Acura screeched to a halt, barely missing him and Tanna.

"Get in!" a voice bellowed from inside as the window lowered.

For a moment Jason didn't react. He was too focused on the killer charging out of the bar and heading straight for them. But then he turned to see Dr. Solomon Cabral sitting in the driver's seat.

"Get in the damn car!"

Jason ripped open the back door, shoved Tanna inside, and jumped in after her. Sol slammed on the accelerator, and the car pulled away.

"Is the girl okay?" Sol asked. "Does she need medical attention?"

Jason propped Tanna up and checked her over. "She's fine. She just drank something she shouldn't have."

"Drugs? Am I putting myself at risk here for drug addicts? If that's the case, then you can get the hell out right now."

"It was a mistake. She didn't know."

The car squealed around a corner, accelerating even faster.

"That was the guy," Jason said. "The one from the mortuary who tried to kill us."

"Yeah, I recognized him. His name is Roman. And if he's the one after you, it's too late for you to walk away. There's no escape now. He won't stop."

"We got a plan."

"Oh, you've got a plan? Congratulations. You think it all up by yourself?"

"It'll work."

"It won't. Whatever you thought of, so have they." Sol raced between two cars. "You've buried yourself. You just don't know it yet."

"Then why are you helping? And how did you know where to find us, anyway?"

"Like it was so hard. You've become giant elephants in a tiny room."

They sat in silence as the lights of downtown San Francisco appeared through the front windshield. Tanna stirred and put her arms around Jason, and he pulled her close.

Sol eased up on the accelerator and slid the car into the right lane. He turned a corner and parked in an alley next to an Omni Hotel in the heart of the city. Then he sank behind the wheel and coughed. To Jason, he looked every bit his age at that moment.

"Helping you is the last thing I should be doing," Sol said, looking back at them over his shoulder. "But they pushed me away from something I loved. Made me second-guess my abilities. It taught me a lesson. Now it's time to teach them one." He reached over the seat and handed Jason a room key. "Room twelve eleven. All paid for under the name Michaels."

Jason examined the key in his hand and looked at Sol.

"Relax," Sol told him. "If I wanted to do anything, I never would have gone to that dump and helped you in the first place. Now get her some rest."

"We'll be okay."

"No, you won't, but at least you'll be safe for a little while. I'll come by tomorrow and work on it."

"Right." Jason got out and pulled Tanna with him. He was relieved to find that she could stand on her own. "And thanks."

"Don't thank me yet. You've jumped into a world of crap, and you're not going to like what happens next."

CHAPTER 31

Darkness. Impenetrable darkness and silence. Tanna's eyes clawed at the abyss. *Do something*, she told herself. *Yell, scream, cry.*

Nothing happened.

She heard voices. Barely whispers, but people were out there, and they could help. The sounds encircled her, but she couldn't make out what they said. She waited, hoping they would talk to her, acknowledge her. No one did.

It took all her concentration, but Tanna forced her eyes open. Too bright. A white ceiling and overhead lights. More voices.

Help me.

Her abdomen bled pain as someone sliced through her from one side of her body to the other. *Stop!* The carving finally ended just below her breastbone. She wanted to cry, but the searing torture rendered her helpless as a hand peeled back her top layer of skin and reached inside her.

"Here," the voice said. "This is the descending colon. And then we have the small intestine."

Tanna strained to see her surroundings, but only the ceiling above filled her vision.

Another incision. More pain.

"And this," the voice said. "Can anyone tell me what this is?"

A shuffling of feet and shadows. Medical students in blue scrubs leaned in to gaze down at her. She recognized them from her class. Hana and Greg, and of course Nick. She pleaded with herself to close her eyes, but it was no use.

Please.

"Ilium and cecum identified," Nick said. "Looks like she still has her appendix as well."

"Very good," the voice responded. "Anyone else?"

"Here's her uterus," said a female student. "She'll never need that again."

The students crowded around even closer, pointing and poking.

"Now let's find out what makes her tick," said the voice. "Get to the bottom of what's going on here."

The students parted, and the voice had a face. The killer stood above her, scalpel in hand and a grin on his lips.

"It's time we find the truth. Open you all the way up and see what you're hiding inside. Because that's what you're afraid of. Someone uncovering what you've buried in here. We'll find it. We won't stop until we do. Isn't that right, class?"

"Yeah!" they shouted.

"We'll cut you open."

"Limb by limb!" Nick added.

The killer leaned in close, his breath on her cheek. He

pressed the tip of the scalpel into the corner of her eye. "And when we find it, you'll be on display for everyone to see."

He drove the blade deep and the world went white.

Tanna jackknifed straight up in bed. The ring of med students and overhead lights were gone. In their place was an ordinary room with long curtains, a dresser, and a small desk.

A hotel. I'm in a hotel room.

Where it was and how she'd gotten there, she had no clue. She knew only that she was safe, at least for the moment.

The pounding fog in her head suffocated her thoughts. She tried to clear her throat, but the raw tissue stung and burned, leaving her with a stabbing lump she couldn't swallow away.

"Hey," a voice said.

Tanna screamed.

"Whoa. It's just me." Jason rose from a loveseat and sat on the bed next to her. "How are you feeling?"

"I don't know. Out of it, I guess." Her head felt bloated and heavy, wobbling on her reed-like neck. "Where are we?"

"Omni Hotel. Downtown San Francisco."

"How did we get here?"

"Well, after we—"

"Did you pay for it?"

"No. We—"

"What happened last night? I don't remember anything."

"Yeah, that's what I'm trying to—"

"What about M-Gen? Did we put our information online? We have to do that."

"Finished yet?" Jason said.

Tanna paused. "Sorry."

"Okay. Let's start at the beginning. Remember last night when I told you not to drink anything anyone gave you? Well, I was a little late with that."

"Wait. I was drugged?"

Jason shrugged. "On the bright side, you had a great time."

"Are you kidding? Someone drugged me, and you think it's funny? What was it? What did I take?"

Jason recapped the events of the evening, from the drugged cocktail, to the dancing, to working with Perry to get everything posted, to the arrival of the killer and Dr. Solomon Cabral showing up to help them escape. It took effort for Tanna to soak it all in. Some elements of the evening were familiar, while others were a total blank.

Her mind fixated on the random details that she could pick out. "I danced?" she said. "Because I don't dance."

"You did last night, and pretty well."

"And Dr. Cabral, he knows this guy who's after us?"

"He recognized him, yeah. Guy's name is Roman, and he's a pro. Definitely not someone you want to tangle with."

"Then we got here, and you put me to bed"—she checked under the comforter and breathed a sigh of relief—"in my clothes. And where did you sleep?"

"On the loveseat."

"It's a king bed, you know. Plenty of room."

"Now you tell me."

"Can I see what you and Perry put online?" Her clouded head was beginning to clear, but with it came a sharp pressure building behind her eyes and a pounding in her sinuses.

Jason pulled up something on his phone and handed it

to her. "I did the best I could, though I don't understand it all. We can always add more."

Tanna scrolled through the material. It covered Modern Genetics' creation of genetically modified gene therapies and their experiments on people, possibly without their knowledge. It stated that M-Gen tried to cover up their actions by disposing of the evidence along with anyone who got in their way. And it gave all the specifics of the deal with Concord Funeral, the murders of Krystal and Wade, and the attempted murders of Jason and Tanna themselves.

"You did it," Tanna said.

"We're out there now."

"No, I mean you really did it. I can't believe you did this."

"I hope I got most of it right."

It wasn't as organized or concise as she would have liked, but it was there. All of it.

"It's perfect," she said. "You don't know what this means to me."

She hugged him tight and leaned her head on his shoulder. Jason enveloped her in his arms, and they stayed that way until she regained enough energy to pull away.

"Perry's auto-generated a click-counting system to make it trend for big outlets to pick up," Jason explained. "Once that happens, they're in the bull's-eye. So. What do you want to do next?"

Burn it to the ground, she thought. But instead she laughed, thrilled for it to be over. The tightness in her chest eased for the first time in days. "Now we let the authorities take over. We've done enough." She grabbed Jason's hand.

"Thank you. I couldn't have done this without you. I mean, you didn't even have to get involved, but you did."

Jason started to say something, then stopped and looked away. Tanna realized this was the first time since she'd met him that he'd seemed truly uncomfortable.

She put a hand on his cheek, turned his face toward hers, and kissed him. Just a quick peck of appreciation at first, but then she went back for a stronger, more passionate kiss. Jason returned it with caution, and then with abandon.

Tanna grabbed his shirt and pulled it over his head. He reached around and did the same for her. She gripped the front of his pants, unhooked the top button, and thrust her hands inside. He grabbed her pants at the waist and ripped them down over her hips.

Clothes flew in all directions. Bodies entangled on the bed. Tanna held him tight and swung her body on top of his. She released a stilted gasp as she relaxed her hips and allowed him inside of her.

As sweat rose on excited skin, they ignored their vibrating cell phones and let their soft cries of pleasure fill the room.

CHAPTER 32

Dr. Craig Emmerson stepped out of the isolated pleasure of his private elevator and looked across the hall into his office. Roman sat in one of his guest chairs, his polluted fingers tapping away at the desk. Craig could almost see the microscopic trails of expired skin cells and oily secretions left in their wake.

"What are you doing *here*?" Craig snapped. He grabbed a sanitizing wipe and cleaned the desk.

"You don't know?"

"No games, Roman. Not now."

Roman pulled out his phone and held it up.

Craig started to reach for the device before stopping himself at the last moment. Phones were the world's petri dishes. The screen showed an article, with the words *Modern Genetics* and *Unregulated Testing* in the headline. Craig motioned for Roman to scroll down and skimmed something about cremating corpses. A photo of a dissected body was included.

"When?" he asked.

"Last night some time."

"Who was it?"

Roman only had to nod his head and Craig knew.

"God damn it! I *told* you. I told you to take care of this. If you had finished it at the mortuary, none of this would have happened. How hard could it be? They're *kids*."

"They're more than that. And they had help."

"Who?"

"Solomon."

Craig took a step back. "Impossible."

"It's true."

As the treasonous revelation sank in, Craig fell back into his chair. "Why? What does he have to gain?"

"Revenge. Respect," Roman said as if thinking aloud. "Or maybe he's just an old man with nothing to lose."

"Bullshit. Everyone has something to lose. Even Sol." Craig's dismay gave way to rage. He was tempted to let it overtake him and blot out the rest of the world. "How could he do this to me?"

Roman leaned forward. "Are you finally willing to do what it takes? Or are you still too scared to deal with him once and for all?"

Craig tried to let the question pass. Petty words from a petty man. He needed to think ahead. Think smart.

"I always thought Sol would be happy to fade into the background," he said. "Give up the endless hours of mind-numbing tedium for a quiet life. I was wrong. He came to warn me about that, but I didn't listen."

"We need to do something. Now." Roman pointed

to his phone. "This has traction. Once it's viral, it's out of our hands."

Craig struggled to find clarity. There was an opportunity here somewhere, he knew it. He contemplated the options until the answer came to him. What on the surface appeared to be a monumental setback might instead be the answer to all his problems.

He looked at Roman and smiled. "That's right. It will go viral."

CHAPTER 33

Always patrolling and forever on alert, the white blood cells roamed through Tanna's body looking for anything out of the ordinary, searching every conceivable corner to hunt down trespassers. From the circulatory to the lymphatic to the respiratory, bodily systems were scrutinized, and it wasn't long before they came across the virus invaders in mid-attack.

White blood cell macrophages, resembling lumbering jelly-like blobs, were at first unaware if the viruses were friend or foe. But they had access to a vast database of known helpers and foreign enemies that Tanna's body had encountered over time. Tipped off by chemicals released by the infected cells, the macrophages soon realized that the viruses were something they had never seen before.

A definite foe.

The macrophages began to engulf the viruses, surrounding them and drawing them in, trapping them in a pocket where they released caustic enzymes that broke down the viruses' outer coating, allowing it to seep deep into their inner workings. The viruses were unable to escape the death hold, and the enzymes dissolved the virus cores until there was nothing left but shattered debris.

But the macrophages couldn't win the battle on their own. They sent out signals to others, telling them that the enemy had been identified. They had to annihilate it, eradicate it, down to every last one, and they had to do it fast, before the virus had a chance to mutate and they would have to start all over again.

They fought relentlessly, but all around them, infected cells of Tanna's body were erupting, bursting forth with hundreds of thousands more of the replicated viruses. It was as though all the stars had poured out of the night sky, each point of light a newly duplicated virus looking for another cell to infect, another opportunity to replicate, another chance to continue its existence.

The macrophages were outnumbered and overrun. Everywhere they turned, the enemy spewed forth to spread its infection. The defenders' only hope was that backup would arrive before it was too late.

CHAPTER 34

Steaming hot water ran down Tanna's body. She couldn't remember another shower ever relaxing her quite so much. The rhythmic rushing calmed her mind and soothed the congested cough rumbling in her chest.

She thought about what had just happened with Jason. In the madness that her world had become, he was the one constant she could rely on. The only positive thing to come out of this senseless disaster. Having sex with him had been impulsive, but impulsive felt good for a change. Great, actually. She felt at ease with him. As she climaxed with nail-scratching release and melted down into the mass of tangled sheets, she was able to forget about everything but the slowing beat of his heart and the cooling sweat of her skin. She even let herself consider the possibility of something lasting coming out of this.

After stepping out of the shower, Tanna curled her toes on the thick bathmat. She dried off, drenched herself in a white hotel robe, and walked back into the bedroom. When she saw that room service had been delivered, she grinned and popped a strawberry in her mouth.

"Fresh fruit, I love it. And mimosas? You thought of everything."

Jason didn't respond. He was staring at his phone and didn't even acknowledge her.

"Jason?"

When he looked up, his face was pale, the color of smoldering ash.

"They, uh . . ." He handed his phone to her.

Tanna scrolled through page after page of websites and media feeds devoted to Modern Genetics. Many contained the information they had posted. A few mentioned the great strides they'd made in medicine and all the accolades they'd received. Then there were others with wild claims that M-Gen had tried to clone humans, and that they had created a super-disease to kill off the world's population except those who could afford to pay for the cure. One article from a former employee claimed to have an autopsy video of a human-alien hybrid. There was even a site dedicated to M-Gen's zombie apocalypse.

"Zombies? Are you kidding me? Where did all this come from?" Tanna asked. "None of this was out there before. Perry said he could hardly find anything, but some of this stuff is dated from years ago."

"It's not really from years ago. It wasn't even there this morning. There was nothing, then all of this."

"I don't get it."

"Camouflage."

It took a moment to sink in, but the heavy realization

came as a stabbing knife, tearing through muscle and hitting bone.

"What we posted last night is now just another crazy conspiracy theory," Jason explained. "Not as crazy as the zombie apocalypse, but not as good as the Gregory Miller Humanitarian Award they supposedly received. It'll get lost in the shuffle. How do you find one true tree in the whole forest of lies?"

Tanna had to sit down. All their work. Everything they had risked. It came to nothing.

"That's not the worst part."

Jason took his phone back, pulled up the CNN home page, and handed it back to her. It featured a picture of Jason straddling a motorcycle, surrounded by race fans. Right next to it was a picture of her, taken the first day of orientation during her White Coat Ceremony, where she was given her short white student's coat and took the Hippocratic Oath.

"That's us!" Tanna shrieked. "Why are we on CNN?"

Her hands shook as she read. The article detailed how police had found Dean Atwell's body that morning in San Francisco, almost four hundred miles from his home in Los Angeles, where they also found his closest neighbor murdered. The dean had been beaten badly, but the coroner suspects the cause of death was several puncture wounds to his heart and lungs made with a precise instrument, possibly a scalpel. The body was severely dehydrated, with ligature marks on the wrists and ankles, indicating the dean had been held against his will.

The primary suspects were Tanna and Jason.

Tanna's life was falling apart as the entire world watched.

She felt the weight of it pulling her down. Unable to find a pinpoint of light in the enveloping darkness, she sank to the floor.

The phone vibrated with new announcements.

"San Francisco Police have started a manhunt for the two suspects," she read aloud. "A manhunt for us? We didn't have anything to do with it."

"They have video of us outside the building entrance before we broke into his office. And that was the same day you were arrested by the university cops. We've also been spotted in San Francisco. It's circumstantial bullshit, but just imagine what else they can come up with. Your fingerprints on the murder weapon. Not too hard to get ahold of one of your old scalpels, I bet."

"My mom," Tanna said. "I have to call her. I have to let her know it wasn't us."

Jason took the phone from her hand. "No. You can't do that. You can't let anyone know where you are."

"She needs to know the truth. I can't let her think I killed someone."

"Oh fuck." Jason was staring at his phone.

"What now?"

Jason showed her the screen.

As Tanna read, her mouth fell open in shock. "A killing spree? We're on a *killing spree*?"

"The guy at the mortuary. His son Brian told them that I beat the hell out of him to find out where his dad was. They found bone fragments in the cremation chamber and are waiting to identify them, but as he's gone missing, they suspect it's him."

"The two suspects are believed to be in the San Francisco area, and police have doubled their efforts to find them," Tanna quoted from the story. She rocked back and forth. "How could I be so stupid to think I could change anything? I should have never tried."

"This isn't your fault."

"Of course it is." She brought her hand to her mouth and mashed a fingernail between her teeth. "We have to tell someone what's happening. Anyone who'll believe us."

"We'd be lucky if they don't shoot us on sight."

A muffled scrape sounded in the hallway, and Tanna whipped her head around. "That's our door," she whispered. Her heart hammered against her chest. She jumped up to examine the windows for a way to escape, but they didn't open.

Jason grabbed a heavy wrought-iron lamp, ripped off the shade, and held it like a club. He tiptoed toward the door but stopped before he reached it.

They both heard the sound. Someone was working the lock from the other side.

CHAPTER 35

The lock sprang open with an electronic beep.

Tanna reached for the first weapon she could find—a butter knife from the breakfast tray. Jason cocked his arm, set to swing with full force.

"It's Sol," a voice whispered through the cracked door.

"Sonofabitch." Jason took a step back.

Sol entered. His gaze traveled from the lamp in Jason's hand to the knife in Tanna's, then he shook his head. "What did you think you would do with those? You're a couple of damn children who don't have a clue what you've gotten yourselves into."

"We didn't murder those people," Tanna declared. She couldn't help herself. She needed to tell someone who would believe her.

"What difference does that make now?" Sol ran a hand across his sweating forehead. The skin on his face appeared ashen and loose. "You had your chance to walk away, and you didn't listen to me. Now you've brought a damn butter knife to a gunfight, for Christ's sake." He took a labored breath and put his hands on his hips. "But I can't say I've been any smarter. I told myself not to get involved with you two, that this wasn't my fight, and I didn't even listen to myself."

"They're making it all up," Tanna said. "The stuff in the news. It's all lies."

"So what?" Sol said. "Lies or truth, it doesn't matter once it's out there, unless you have evidence to exonerate you, which I expect you don't. Why should I even believe you?"

"Because somebody has to." Tanna quickly tried to explain everything that had happened, starting with the cadaver and working all the way up to the present moment.

Sol sighed. "If you're lying to me, I'm harboring two wanted murderers." He collapsed into the loveseat.

"We're sorry," Tanna said.

"It's too late for sorry."

Jason's cell phone vibrated with another alert.

"You still have your phones?" Sol said. "You really are children. Destroy them now. If they haven't tracked your location yet, they will soon."

Tanna looked to Jason, and they both looked at Sol. Destroying their phones meant cutting their lifeline to the outside world.

"Now!" the old man shouted. "If you want my help, you'll do what I tell you. No questions. I've put my life's work and reputation on the line for you."

Tanna and Jason took turns smashing their phones on the corner of the dresser. Jason then fished out the SIM cards and dropped them in the trash.

"Does anyone know you're here?" Sol asked. "Did you call or see anyone since you arrived?"

They shook their heads.

"Wrong. You ordered room service," Sol said. "*Everyone* is a potential witness. Everything you do must be calculated. Quit looking at the world right in front of you and see what's behind it, making it move. One mistake and it's over." He shook his head in frustration. "I'm tempted to walk away and leave you both to your fate. It'll be over quick—look how fast your little plan last night blew up in your face."

"Excuse us for not being expert fugitives," Tanna shot back. "Just tell us what's going on. Why are they doing all of this? What else are they trying so hard to protect?"

Sol rose and looked out the window, then turned back to face them. "No time. They know you're here."

Tanna ran over and looked through the glass. Two squad cars were parked on the street, and police officers were clearing pedestrians from the sidewalk.

"I can get you somewhere safe," Sol said, "but you must be willing to go all the way with this. If you want to prove your innocence, there's no choice but to take down the whole complex. No matter what. I won't get involved otherwise. It's your life. Your decision."

Tanna's body radiated with heat. Twelve stories down, the physical world disappeared beneath her. She stared into the chasm, unable to look away, and felt the room turn on an unstable axis. She wanted to grab it and make it stop spinning, just for a minute, but there was nothing left for her to hold on to. Even looking at Jason, with his unyielding expression and concentrated stare, offered no relief.

"Okay," she said. "Tell us what to do."

"Move!" Sol barked.

Tanna took only enough time to run into the bathroom and throw on her old clothes before they were out the door and into the hallway.

"Stairs," Sol said, pointing.

They raced down the stairwell to an underground parking garage. Wheezing, Sol led them to his car and opened the trunk, which was packed with boxes and papers. "Shit, no room," he muttered. "Back seat then. On the floor."

In moments Tanna and Jason were both wedged in the rear footwell, Jason wincing in pain from contorting his legs.

"Stay there," Sol told them as he drove through the parking garage. "Whatever you hear, whatever you see, don't move or say anything."

The sun streamed through the windows when the car exited the structure. They slowed to a roll, and Tanna heard Sol's window lower.

"Officer," Sol shouted with an air of authority. "Dr. Solomon Cabral. On my way to UCSF Medical. I've got a cardiac patient with three blockages prepped and waiting. I need to get through the intersection."

"Where are you coming from?" the officer shouted back.

Tanna heard the officer's boots approaching. She forced herself into a tighter ball.

"Five-fifty building," Sol said as the car continued to roll forward.

"Hold up," the officer yelled. "Wait."

"Thanks for the assistance."

The engine revved as the car lurched over a curb and fell back down with a jolt. It picked up speed and made a series of abrupt turns before straightening out.

"You can get up now," Sol said, breaking the long silence.

Tanna and Jason unwound themselves from the floor and sat on the rear seat.

"You asked me why they're doing this," Sol said. "It's because you were right. Not about everything, but enough to scare them. In some ways, it's my fault. Decades of work, projects I started and perfected, are now coming to fruition. And they'll stop at nothing to see it finished."

He wiped away the sweat forming across his face and checked his mirrors. "They've been testing genetic therapies in vivo, in living people, without their knowledge, then covering it up. You guessed that part right. Then again, that's been going on in one form or another since Peter Plett and Edward Jenner started inoculating young children against smallpox to see if it would work. But at M-Gen, that's just the beginning. You're a med student?"

"First year," Tanna replied.

"Familiar with XNA?"

"You mean like DNA?"

"Artificial DNA. Xeno nucleic acid. Synthetic. Man-made. Engineered to be anything, do anything, create anything you could imagine. I helped invent it." Sol's pride was evident. "It's stronger, more reliable, and has a much longer life span. Most important, it doesn't break down like organic DNA."

"You created DNA? Artificially?"

"XNA. Yes."

"How?"

"Well, that's the trick, isn't it?"

"Alien life forms," Jason said. "Like that article. You're creating alien life forms."

"The scientific community uses the term *synthetic*. We called ours the Second Nature program."

A police siren split the air behind them.

"Get down."

Tanna and Jason ducked. The car bolted forward and Tanna felt it weave between other vehicles on the road. The movement made her nauseated.

"How far back is it?" Jason asked.

"Let me drive."

The siren grew louder, and Sol carved a hard right that forced Tanna to grab on. Then they jerked even harder to the left, the tires squealing to hold position.

Tanna heard the siren continue straight, heading off into the distance.

"I'm getting too old for this," Sol said under his breath.

Tanna and Jason straightened themselves. As her heart rate slowed, Tanna contemplated what Sol had said about XNA. It was like a wall in her head, one she never knew existed, came tumbling down. The implications, the possibilities, were overwhelming. "They're going to change the nature of medicine," she said.

"You have to get out of sight. I can take you somewhere while I get what we need."

"Aren't they?"

"No. They're going to change the *world*." Sol took a labored breath as if he didn't want to continue. "New drugs. New therapies. Eradication of disease. The answer to how life began. Everything. Altering cell structures to something that can't be broken down or even seen by our own bodies because our bodies have never been told to search for it.

"Look what the SARS-Cov-2 virus did. How fast it spread. Think about HIV and Ebola. These are the great white sharks of the virus world. A perfect delivery system. Now think what we can do if we replace their normal payload with engineered XNA strands that can target whatever disease you want. Once inside the cell, it'll do whatever we programmed it to do. No more cancer, Parkinson's, AIDS, Alzheimer's. You name it, it's gone. And that's just the beginning. Whoever perfects it, well . . ."

"They'll be beyond rich," Tanna finished.

"They'll be beyond *powerful*," Sol corrected her. "They'll have the ability to wipe disease off the face of the earth . . . or not, if they choose. The power to create life. Or *un*create it."

"To play God," Tanna said.

"To *be* God."

"Until it spins out of control." Tanna took a deep breath. "Because it always does."

A police car sped around the corner and shot past them in the opposite lane. Tanna turned her head and hid her face in her hands.

"What makes it different now," Sol said, "is replication. Evolution." He checked his mirrors. "That's been the problem for everyone. For this to work, self-replication must happen. If Emmerson solved that, well, I couldn't even begin to imagine what he could do next."

"They can't just go around creating synthetic life forms, can they?" Tanna said. "Aren't there laws?"

"Not if your lab sits on top of a retrofitted oil platform in the middle of the Pacific. That's where Craig is moving level five of Modern Genetics. He's been planning it for years. Out in international waters, there are no rules, no regulations, no laws. Craig can create what he wants, how he wants, with no interference from anyone."

Tanna slid her hand over Jason's, hoping to calm her nerves. "I can't believe this is happening."

"It's happening. And the science will move ahead, with or without Craig Emmerson," Sol told her. "It's human nature—to strive and create. And it's the right thing to do. He's just the wrong person to do it."

Jason had listened patiently to the scientific discussion, but now he cut in. "This is all fucking great, but how does any of it help us? Everyone thinks we're on a killing spree."

"I need to make sure you know what you're getting into. Who you're up against."

"Sounds like we're up against God or something. What we really need to know is how to fight back."

"Follow the money," Sol said simply. "Before Craig moves the lab and it's too late. Money always leaves a trail. Start by exposing those funding it, and why they're doing it, and the rest will fall like dominoes. Because that's one thing people understand: money. Let them get outraged about the rich and greedy profiting from these heinous crimes in order to get wealthier and more powerful. Then they'll get outraged about the science going on there. I promise you. It's the only way to save yourselves now."

"How are we supposed to do that?" Tanna asked.

"I'm working on it," Sol said, gripping the steering wheel until the leather creaked.

Tanna slumped back in the seat. Her head throbbed, sending echoes through her skull, and a heaviness swelled behind her eyes, pushing her down, trapping her at the bottom of a deep pool, struggling to escape.

She tried to look at Jason, to apologize for getting him involved, to tell him how horrible she felt about it, but she didn't have the strength. She wished she could take it all back.

But it was too late now. She couldn't think of a thing to say that would make any difference.

CHAPTER 36

Looking past the sun-faded fabric of a dated maroon dress, Roman used the reflection of the shop's glass window to track his target. The bulge on the man's hip, probably a Glock 19 pistol, and the extra-thick ankle wrap, for sure a Kahr CM9, announced his presence with amateur arrogance. It didn't help that he was constantly adjusting the body armor hidden under his civilian flannel shirt. The man may as well have just worn a sign that read MERCENARY FOR HIRE written in kid-printed crayon.

Two blocks away, Roman had seen another squad member camped out on the corner. Standard surveillance procedure for setting a perimeter. There would be more as they tightened the noose around La Bella restaurant.

Even Craig wasn't stupid enough to draw so much attention to himself. No, these were Lauren's people. She had made the decision. A desperate one. And her direct involvement meant even more problems.

The squad member turned and took easy strides, trying

his best to blend in, but ruined the effect by talking into a miniature microphone clipped under his collar.

"Idiot," Roman muttered.

Broad daylight. Busy street. But if Roman waited too long, they would reach the shuttered restaurant before him. He didn't have a choice.

He ducked into a narrow alley between two buildings, closed his eyes, and touched the tips of his fingers to the wall in a vertical runner's stance. The smell of damp brick and sour urine filled his nostrils. He listened past the barking dog and arguing couple to a deeper sound. The measured clack of industrial leather shoes moving toward him. Determined steps with a quickening pace. He waited.

Clack, step.

Waited.

Clack, step.

Roman snatched the soldier from the street and jerked him into the alley. The man emitted a rough gasp and pulled his Glock free, but Roman gripped his wrist, twisted his arm up behind his shoulder blades, and snapped bone. In one quick move, he ripped the microphone from the man's collar, pulling the earpiece with it.

"Fuck you, motherfucker," the soldier grunted. He swung with his good hand, but was unable to connect.

Roman was on top of him in a flash. He pulled his double-fixed blade knife from the sheath at the small of his back and pushed it against the man's neck.

"It's you," the soldier said, recognition on his face. "What the fuck do you think you're doing?"

"How many are there?" Roman asked.

"You broke my arm, you asshole."

"How many?" He dug the tip of the knife deeper.

"What difference does it make? Two kids, and you couldn't get it done. Now we have to clean up your shit."

With blazing speed, Roman swung his elbow down into the man's temple. "You don't think I can handle this? You think I failed?" Roman twisted the broken arm. "They're *mine*. Understand? Stay out of my way and stop fucking this up."

"You had your chance. Now we'll get them."

"Then you'd better have sent a whole goddamn army."

The man laughed. "We did."

Roman looked up and saw another mercenary diving at him, already airborne. The man crashed into Roman from the side, sending him hard to the ground. Off-balance, Roman used the momentum of the fall to hurl the man against the brick wall. The mercenary pulled his pistol to fire, but Roman reached across and slit the man's throat.

He spun back to face the first soldier and found the man using his good arm to try to release the CM9 from his ankle holster.

"Don't," Roman warned.

"We're not stopping."

They watched one another through a thickening cloud of distrust, each waiting for the other to move.

The soldier freed his pistol first, but Roman got off the first shot as he drew his Sig from his hip belt and pulled the trigger.

Head shot.

"Neither am I."

Roman noticed blood on his shirt from a shallow injury to his stomach. It would have to wait. He looked at the two dead bodies and reminded himself that it would all be worth it. Success required sacrifice. But those thoughts were getting harder to justify.

He straightened up, pressed his arm against his injury to conceal it, then strolled out of the alley onto the sidewalk.

He had work to do.

CHAPTER 37

In chipped paint and broken neon, the sign above the restaurant door might have read LA BELLA, but it had clearly stopped operating years ago. The windows were covered with black plastic, and layers of fine gray dust had settled on tables still set for a dinner service that never happened.

Tanna sat under a canopy of fake grapevines and ran her finger along the edge of a wineglass, remembering how her father taught her to wet the rim and make it sing. She thought it was magic until she learned it was simple physics. The stick-and-slide motion of the finger created vibrations that caused the crystal glass to resonate. It didn't sing at all. That was the day she realized there was no real magic in the world.

"What time is it?" she asked.

"I don't know," Jason replied into the stagnant air.

The plastic on the outside of the windows fluttered in the ocean breeze, and the shadows lengthened through the small rips and tears. Sol was late.

"He should be here already," she said. "We're running out of time."

The inflammation in her throat made it difficult to talk. She felt heat clawing its way through her body as if it was blistering her from the inside. She tried to convince herself that she was fine, it was just exhaustion, and she'd feel better after she rested. But she was beginning to suspect it was more than that.

Her weary and watery eyes focused on Jason. He'd found a corner booth large enough to stretch out in and rest, but his foot tapped away, an unconscious tic that kept him half in and half out of the waking world. Tanna sensed that his impatience mirrored her own.

"He'll come," Jason said.

"If he doesn't, we'll need our own plan. Or we just die with the world thinking we're murderers."

From the back door came the sound of metal scraping metal, and both Tanna and Jason jumped to their feet. A hunched figure appeared in the main dining room.

It wasn't Sol.

The man appeared to be in his late thirties and had a bushy red beard. He was out of breath, and an oversized black messenger bag was slung over his shoulder.

"Who are you?" Tanna demanded.

"My name's Eric. Sol told me to come."

"Where's Sol? And how do we know you're with him?"

"You know I'm with him by the fact I came here to help two people wanted for murder and put my life on the line to do it."

"Then when's Sol coming? We need to know what's going on here."

Eric took a deep breath. "Sol's in the hospital. Heart attack, stroke, not sure. He called me this morning and told me what he needed. Then he called later from Saint Francis Memorial. I tried to see him, but he was unconscious by then. So I came right over to find you."

Tanna buried her face in her hands. She couldn't believe it.

"And who exactly are you?" Jason asked.

"I'm Eric."

"Yeah, no shit. What do you do for Sol, and what do we do now that he's in the hospital?"

"He didn't tell you about this?"

"No," Tanna said. "He didn't tell us anything."

"Right, probably for the best." Eric pulled up a chair at an empty table, and Tanna and Jason joined him. "Sol told me you need access to M-Gen's database so you can find evidence of who's funding them and show the world all the bad shit they're really doing with that money. Well, I worked in their IT department. Until they let me go, along with the rest of the IT staff. A few years back we started a project to take their entire computer network offline. Completely offline. And once the new system had proven itself, they unplugged from the outside world, and then they replaced everyone involved.

"You see, they moved everything in-house. Now they have no connections beyond their building. All their information, all their financial records, all their scientific data is kept on-site. They're the only ones who can access it."

"Hackers," Jason said with a nod. "If you're connected, you'll be attacked. It's just a matter of time. But without a connection, no one can get to you."

"Not just hackers—governments, too. You think you can stop the NSA from getting into your system? What about China? North Korea? The only way to keep yourself safe is to break the physical connection. Isolate yourself. So that's what they've done. And now the only way to get to it is—"

"Break in and take it," Jason finished.

"Yep. Everything about them is there, in one spot. Research, lab work, security, finances. All the proof you need. Their greatest strength is their greatest weakness.

"Now, I can show you the important drives to take—the ones that will hurt them the most. But you can't just pull the hard drives out of the servers. That'll trigger the system to start wiping them, and you'll have nothing but mush. You won't be able to pull them out fast enough. I designed it that way, and the backup system is buried deep under the building, in a bomb-proof enclosure you can't access. But you can overcome that with a temporary override program I'll give you."

"Stop." Tanna held up a hand. "Why are you telling us all of this?"

"You're kidding, right?" Eric asked.

"If you know what we need and where to get it, why don't you just grab it?"

"One whiff of me and they'll drop me on sight," Eric said. "I can't get within six hundred yards of that place. They have more security than the damn White House."

"Then how are we supposed to pull it off?"

"Not my problem. You want to expose the people paying them to do this stuff? Try to prove what's really going on there? Then you need the hard drives."

"This is crazy," Tanna said.

Eric pushed his chair back from the table. "Yeah. It is. But Sol asked me to tell you everything I know, and that's what I'm doing. I can tell you where to go and what to do, but you're going to have to do it. And if you fail, make no mistake, Craig Emmerson will stop at nothing to find out who helped you. When he figures out it was us . . . then we're dead too."

CHAPTER 38

"It's too much," Tanna said, pacing across the floor in a figure-eight pattern. "I don't know how we're supposed to do this."

Jason knew exactly how he would've handled a situation like this in the past: he'd just sit back and let it take care of itself. Pack the pipe, fill the syringe, crush a monster hit of anything he had on hand, and let it be. No worries. Unless he wasn't holding, but he could always get what he needed by lying, stealing, whatever it took. But things were different now that he was sober. A sober reality was a lot harder—and way more fucked up.

"We need to go straight at them," he said to Tanna. "Strong and fast. Hope for the best." It was the only thing that made sense to him anymore. Track down Craig Emmerson, beat him to a pulp, kill the piece of shit if necessary. Jason figured he was already wanted for multiple murders— what was one more? And at least this one would actually be his doing.

"We can't rush into it. There's too much on the line."

Tanna stopped to look at him. "Maybe we should wait to see how Sol is. He could still help us."

"No, Tanna. We're on our own. The longer we wait, the more chance we get caught before we even make a move. It's a miracle no one's found us yet."

"What about him?" Tanna looked toward the back bathroom, where Eric had gone. "Do you trust him?"

"Hell no. But what choice do we have?"

"That's what I don't like. I mean, there's got to be something we're overlooking. I just need to think." Tanna resumed her pacing.

Jason watched her walk back and forth across the floor. She had become indecisive when she needed to act. A set of spinning wheels stuck in her own head. For someone so smart, Jason didn't understand how she couldn't see something so obvious.

"Hard through the turns, fast down the straightaways," he said. "That's how you win. Thinking about it won't get it done. Sol was right. They won't stop. They'll keep coming after us until they destroy us. The only chance we have is to get to them first."

"We only get one shot at saving our lives here, so excuse me if I want to take a few moments to make sure it's right," Tanna fired back. "This isn't a stupid motorcycle race. There are no second chances here."

"Everything okay?" Eric asked, returning.

Jason looked to Tanna, but she stared at the floor. "Fine," he said.

"All right then, you two have a plan?"

"Not yet," Tanna replied. "Working on it."

Jason shook his head. His impatience was red-lining and his body crying out for relief. Anything he could sniff, snort, or inject would do. Anything to take him away. He needed to get under control fast, so he excused himself and went to the bathroom, where an unbalanced overhead fan made a clanking sound as one blade repeatedly hit the dirty plastic housing.

He checked his zombie-pale reflection in the mirror, then closed his eyes. Sleep would be good. A big fat speedball would be better.

Maybe Tanna was right. What did he know anyway? It wasn't his fight, and he kept getting in her way. Maybe she'd be better off on her own. The urge to walk off and leave infested his thoughts, suffocating everything else. He wouldn't even have to explain it. She'd understand.

He splashed cool water onto his face and tried to take a deep breath, but his muscles cinched a rope around his chest. When he reached for a paper towel, the metal dispenser came up empty. He slid his hand up into its gaping mouth and felt around. Nothing. It hung there on the wall, silently mocking him.

"You think this is funny?" he shouted at it. "Huh?"

Jason threw a quick right that dented the front of the dispenser. A second punch rocked it loose from its anchors. He grabbed it with both hands and ripped it free from its mounting, sending chunks of plaster to the floor, then hurled it across the room. It struck the wall and crashed to the floor with a clang. He picked it up again and threw it back down. Again and again. He didn't stop until he was covered in sweat.

"Yeah, fuck you, too," he said and kicked the distorted hunk of metal to the corner.

Wiping his forehead, he returned to the dining room. But Tanna and Eric weren't there.

"Tanna?" he called out, but his world went black.

CHAPTER 39

"Keep moving!" Eric said.

"We can't leave him there. We have to go back."

Eric grabbed Tanna by the wrist, pulling her off her feet as he dragged her along the sidewalk.

She wrenched her hand free. "They're going to get him."

Eric ducked around the corner of a building and grasped her shoulders. "Either he escaped or they already have him."

Tanna knocked his arms off of her. "Then we need to wait."

"He won't find us. We have to keep going. It's our only chance." Eric continued to lead her away from the restaurant, traveling parallel to the water's edge.

It had all happened so fast. Eric had been lecturing her about the importance of some type of data when she saw movement through a tear in the plastic window covering. When they went to look, they saw people standing suspiciously in front of the restaurant. That was when Eric panicked and shoved her right out the back door. She called out for Jason, but when Eric screamed at her to run, she did.

Tanna made up her mind and stopped dead in her tracks. "I'm not leaving him. He'd never do that to me."

"I'm not so sure of that, the way you guys were going at it."

"What the hell does that mean?"

Eric sighed. "Nothing. Listen, if you go back there, they'll catch you, and it'll be over, for both of you. Is that what you want?"

Tanna glanced down a side street and saw a silver Camry approaching. She had seen it before as they ran from the restaurant—or so she thought. Now she followed it with her eyes.

"What is it?" Eric asked.

"That car. It's the second time I've seen it."

"Run!"

Eric shot forward at the same instant that the car hit the gas and roared up fast behind them. Tanna caught up to him and raced stride for stride as they took a hard corner. They found themselves at the entrance to a park with the water on one side and a thick forest on the other. In between was an open, grassy field, filled with picnic tables, people, and no place to hide.

"The woods," Tanna said.

"We won't make it."

"Then move your ass!"

She forced her legs into a higher gear and ran through the park, straight toward the tree line.

The Camry jumped the curb and followed, tearing through the soft grass, launching sprays of mud through the air. Tanna weaved around picnic blankets and families enjoying a day at the park, but the pursuing car had no interest in weaving: it shot straight through two picnic tables, sending parents scrambling for their kids.

"Hurry up!" Tanna shouted. Eric had fallen behind and was clearly winded.

Directly in front of Tanna was a small playground, with children swinging on swings and hanging from climbing bars. The woods were just behind it—a straight shot through and they would make it. But Tanna took one look at the kids before cutting away, back out toward the open field. She couldn't risk the car hitting them.

"Where are you going?" Eric shouted. He kept on racing straight into the playground.

Tanna was both relieved and terrified when the car followed her instead of Eric. She was out in the open now, without any cover, and she willed her legs to go faster, pushing herself to her limits. Still, she knew she couldn't outrun it. She had to get to the trees.

Planting her foot into the ground, she cut hard, making a sharp turn back toward the woods. The car's engine revved, but its tires spun on the soft grass and it had to settle for swinging wide.

Tanna saw Eric just inside the tree line, waiting for her with his hands on his knees, trying to catch his breath. *Keep running, you idiot.* She tried to wave him ahead, but he didn't move.

"Keep going!" she yelled, and Eric moved deeper into the woods.

Behind her, the car bounced up and down as it crossed deep ruts in the ground. She heard a thump and looked back to see that its front tires had gotten stuck in a wide ditch. For the moment at least, it had stopped dead.

Tanna practically dove into the trees. From over her shoulder came the sounds of car doors and men shouting as they continued the pursuit on foot.

"Eric? Where are you?" Tanna called, weaving her way between soaring oaks. "Eric?"

"Here," a voice floated in from her left.

Tanna found him bent over as if he was about to throw up. She put her finger to her lips, then pointed ahead where the ground sloped upward and rugged boulders were littered among the trees. They treaded softly up the hill, using the rocks as cover. Tanna could no longer hear their pursuers, but she knew they were still there, searching.

"They saw me. I know it," Eric said. "I'm a dead man." He removed his messenger bag and handed it to her. "Here. Take the whole thing." He opened the flap. "This sheet here is the map of the servers and the hard drives you need to pull out."

Tanna held up a hand. "Hang on."

"But you have to get down to level four where the server room is. There are retina scanners and biometrics in place, but you can't change your face if a system gets compromised, so I backdoored most everything with passcodes and some two-factor. I put them here." Eric pointed to a series of handwritten letters and numbers.

"Eric, wait."

He pulled out a USB flash drive and held it up. "Most important, you have to plug this into one of the servers before you do anything, or you're screwed. It'll work automatically, so just stick it in and wait for it to quit blinking before you start."

"Stop!" Tanna demanded, too loud.

"Tanna, they've seen me, and they know who I am and where I live. I need to hide. And if you don't get this done, I'll have to find a way to disappear for good."

Several cracks pierced the air from below. Tanna peeked around the boulder but saw no one.

"Here's the bad news," Eric said.

"That was good news?"

"The interior door to the server room needs to be unlocked with a rotating code that I don't have. But Sol and Craig both have master keys—microchips, actually—that give them access to every inch of that place. They can't be duplicated. Sol's was shut down when he got pushed out, but he was able to set it up so it will still work as a one-time override. That's it—one time only. Try it again and the system will go into complete lockdown."

"Where is it?"

"Implanted in the back of Sol's hand. Smaller than a grain of rice. When he left, I reported it as having been removed, but it wasn't."

"His hand? Are you serious? But Sol's in the hospital."

Eric shrugged. "That's all I can do for you. I have to go. Don't follow me. Don't contact me. Nothing. I'm done." He sprinted away and disappeared into the forest.

"Unbelievable," Tanna said under her breath. She slid the messenger bag over her shoulder and peered around the stone, back down the hill. One of the men was down below, moving silently upslope. She had to move.

Tanna continued upward, using the boulders as cover. But the slope grew steeper, and soon she was facing a sheer cliff.

Turning around wasn't an option.

She dug her fingertips into cracks in the rock and pulled herself forward in a desperate climb up the side of the rocky wall. Her feet found footholds to support her, but her hands were slick with sweat. When she pushed ahead, she lost her hold, lunged out, then dropped six feet. Her body bounced sideways as her knee slammed into an outcropping that stopped her momentum. She scrambled to regain her balance and felt a trickle of blood run down her shin.

Take your time. Go slow.

She looked down and spotted the man as he emerged from the trees, heading toward her. The sight gave her a shot of adrenaline, overriding her fatigue and congested lungs. She moved her arms and legs in frantic unison, scaling the rock, her hands guiding her forward, driving hard until she reached the top of the ridge and pulled her body over.

Tanna collapsed onto her back and took a moment to force air into her constricted chest. Then she crawled to the edge and peered over.

The man was almost halfway up and moving fast.

Why can't you just leave me alone?

She looked around for a rock, and found one almost the size of her head. She raised the stone high. It was a straight shot; all she had to do was drop it. She imagined the man's cracked skull and disoriented fall, a flailing marionette with the strings cut.

An eye for an eye, she thought.

Her arms trembled with the weight of the stone. He deserved it. For everything they were doing. He deserved to die.

Just drop it!

She pulled back from the edge and let the stone fall harmlessly to the ground.

She just couldn't do it.

Turning, she ran. The other side of the ridge was a gradual slope, and she threw herself down the descent with reckless abandon. When the trees got heavy again, she zigzagged her way through. Low branches and dense underbrush tore at her body, but she didn't slow. She had to keep moving.

At the edge of the park the woods thinned and gave way to a residential neighborhood. She had no idea what she was going to do next, but for the moment at least, she was safe.

But Jason wasn't. He was either captured or dead already. Like Krystal. Maybe Sol too. They had trusted her, and she had let them down.

Another failure on a long list.

CHAPTER 40

Jason tried to concentrate, but the beating of his heart pounded in his skull with such force that it made it difficult to focus. He opened his eyes into darkness and movement. A car. He was in a car. The gentle rocking turned his stomach, and the pain threatened to make him pass out again. He fought back with deep breaths and clenched teeth. He tried to straighten himself, but his arms were bound behind his back, his feet tied at the ankles.

They had put him in the damn trunk, the motherfuckers.

Voices and muted laughter drifted in. He strained to make out the words, but nothing in his world was clear.

He rolled over through the enclosure and determined that he was alone. Tanna wasn't here. That was for the best. Maybe she had gotten away.

Maybe.

Right now he needed to focus on his own escape.

He felt around the trunk with his fingers, but found nothing. No loose piece of metal, no sharp edges, no scrap of carpet to grab. He thought back to the last time he had been handcuffed like this, stuck in a makeshift holding cell in Madrid after getting drunk and running naked through the Plaza Mayor following a crossover motorcycle event at the Las Ventas bullring. In the end, they called him *el estúpido Americano* and let him go.

Now he pulled his knees up to his chest—his thigh muscles screaming in agony—and stretched his arms down as far as he could to see if he could pass his feet through the opening above his bound wrists. He couldn't quite reach, so he pulled his legs up tighter.

The trunk went red from brake lights as the car came to a sudden stop. It idled for a moment, then someone hit the gas and it took off again.

Knowing it would hurt like hell, he yanked his knees up hard and quickly passed his feet through the opening above his wrists as if he was stepping through. Pain exploded across his body, and he had to bite back a scream—but he did it.

He was still bound, but now he had his hands in front of him. He ran his fingers over the restraint around his ankles—a thick plastic cable tie—and smiled. This was simple mechanics. The locking mechanism relied on small plastic teeth meshing against the ridges in the cable, creating the distinctive clicking sound these ties made when pulled tight. He bent back the loose end of the strap and dug around with his fingernail until it caught the locking teeth, then pulled those away just enough to disengage them from the cable so he could loosen the restraint.

The car picked up speed and began to weave. Jason heard an aggravated shout from inside the car.

The restraint around his wrists was the same cable tie

design, but there was no way his fingers could extend far enough to open it.

The car accelerated further and took a sharp turn, sending Jason tumbling into the side wall.

Stop and think, his mind shouted. *What would Tanna do?*

He had an idea.

He unlaced his shoe and tied one end of the shoelace to the top eyelet. With effort, he managed to feed the other end between his wrists and the plastic tie. Then he clamped down on the loose end of the shoelace with his teeth so that it ran taut from his mouth all the way to his shoe.

Finally, he slid his wrists back and forth in a sawing motion.

"Go, go," he heard someone shout from inside the car.

The heat burned his skin, but he continued sliding the cable tie across the makeshift friction saw.

The car took a hard left. Jason rolled around inside, and the shoelace snapped. "Shit!"

The brakes shot on for a second, and in the brief red light Jason saw a heavy groove cut into the plastic. It had been working. He just needed to finish the job.

He reached down, untied his other shoelace, and repeated the process. Back and forth he sawed.

Hurry up. Back and forth. *Keep going.* Back and forth.

The second shoelace broke. "No!"

By now the plastic must be nearly cut through. Jason flexed his wrists and twisted his forearms so hard that he cut off circulation in his hands. Still, he continued to twist until the strap broke with a crack.

He was free.

He quickly searched the inside of the truck for the emergency latch release, but they must have removed the handle. And just as he was contemplating his next move, shouts erupted from within the car, and Jason felt the entire vehicle go airborne. He too floated into the air, then crashed down hard as the car impacted the ground again. The trunk was flooded with red as the vehicle skidded to a halt.

Jason scrambled to find the trunk cable at the point it entered the latch. His fingertips found the thin wire, and he pulled.

Nothing happened.

"Come on!"

He grasped it tighter and ripped it hard.

The latch unlocked, and the trunk opened.

Jason launched himself out from inside. Before he was even clear of the rear bumper, he saw another car driving straight at them, headed for the passenger side of the vehicle. He heard shouting and the whine of the other engine as it increased its speed.

He leaped out of the way just as the other car plowed headfirst into the vehicle he'd just exited, so close to him that he could almost feel the twisting metal and splintering glass. Landing on aching legs, he rolled away.

As the two cars careened across the pavement, horns blared and tires screeched. Jason forced himself to his feet and ran.

When he heard pursuing footsteps, he glanced back. One man was now chasing him. And to his surprise, another man got out of the second car that had caused the accident.

It was the killer from before. Roman. He immediately started chasing them both.

Jason dodged traffic, pushed around a corner, and found himself in a suburban subdivision. But the footsteps grew louder, and a man tackled him from behind. As Jason struggled to get up, the man rose to his feet and stood over him.

"You're lucky they want you two alive," he said, panting for breath. "This time I'm going to strap you to the—"

The man screeched in pain and dropped to the ground, holding his thigh. Blood poured between his fingers. Jason saw Roman running down the street at them, his pistol out in front.

The man turned to fire, but Roman sank another bullet into the assailant, this time in the shoulder.

As more shots were fired, Jason pushed himself upright and took off. He angled between two houses, through an open gate, and into a backyard surrounded by wood fencing. He swung himself over the fence and fell into a bougainvillea on the other side, its long thorns piercing him.

Gunshots exploded through the fence above Jason's head, and he crawled deep under the plant's overhang of flowers. He now heard sirens approaching, and voices were shouting for an ambulance.

"You keep running!" Roman yelled from the other side of the fence. "The moment you stop, I get you. You hear me? No one else. I'll be the last thing you see on this earth. So keep running."

Jason lay motionless and waited for the sound of Roman's retreat to fade. He looked up at the plant above him—the colorful flowers, the intertwined vines, and the razor-sharp thorns hidden within. The beauty of this world could be so cruel.

CHAPTER 41

Flanked by two security guards from his lab, Dr. Craig Emmerson marched through the lobby and headed straight for the conference room.

"Don't do it," Lauren said, emerging from a hallway to one side. "You're making a gigantic mistake walking in there."

"Wrong. You made the mistake when you unleashed that so-called hit squad of yours without my knowledge."

"Something had to be done, and decisions needed to be made. Isn't that what you told me?"

"Well, you sure did something. By the looks of it, you created a monumental shitstorm that put the entire operation at risk. Years of research, billions of dollars invested, and you may have destroyed the venture in one catastrophic decision. You've done more damage in the last twelve hours than I ever could have. Be grateful I'm still willing to pick up the pieces."

"You lost control."

"I lost nothing."

"Jesus, you can't see it, can you? Your arrogance and egotism are why we're in this mess. I warned you about performing your own trials. You lied about compliance, and it finally came back to bite you. And that's just what we know about."

Craig took a moment before responding. "I only did what was necessary. Nothing more."

He started once more for the conference room. With a quick nod, Lauren sent two of her men to block his path. Craig's own security guards pulled their weapons, and the four faced off.

"Walk through that door and they'll shut you down for good," Lauren said. "I'm the only reason you're still allowed to operate. You need me."

Craig stared at the polished marble floor, recalling the events of the past several years. The acquiescing. The kowtowing. The endless setbacks. He had shown them a unique way of thinking. An original vision they never could have imagined. They would not take it from him. They didn't deserve the gift he had given them.

His hand shook with anger as he pushed past Lauren's men and grasped the door handle. "Shoot me then," he said. "If you have the audacity. Either way, it's the last decision you make here."

The men looked to Lauren, who appeared uncertain.

"That will always be the difference between us," Craig said. "I wouldn't have hesitated."

He opened the door.

"I'm going to sit in the front row and watch them take your life away," she told him as he entered. "It'll be more painful than any bullet."

Inside, investors milled around, talking among themselves. They represented vast wealth, both personal and industrial. They were well-known capitalists and board members. CEOs and so-called pillars of the nation. The one percent of the one percent, wielding enormous financial, political, and ideological influence. Brought together by the prospect of innovation and, especially, money. Simple greed.

"I see we've been busy today," Craig said as he walked to the front of the room. "Hopefully you haven't destroyed every chance we have of making this work. Although I have my doubts about that at the moment."

The investors gave each other questioning looks, unaccustomed to the aggressiveness of his demeanor.

"I'm just curious: were any of you actually *thinking* earlier when you called out your mercenaries? Or were you overreacting to questionable information you were given? Either way, it was irresponsible and destructive."

"Watch your tone, Dr. Emmerson," one investor grumbled.

"My tone? Oh, I see. My *tone*. You've compromised years of research, put my work in jeopardy, and possibly exposed your involvement, but you're concerned about my tone. Maybe that's why we're in the position we're in now."

"Do you understand the risks we've taken to be here?" someone asked. "To have us all together in one room like this?"

"Oh, indeed. Conspiracy and collusion, that's what they'll say. Your names will be jokes to a disillusioned public just waiting for such a misstep. And that's a best-case scenario."

"You've become reckless, and now you've dragged us into

it," said another investor. "We've given you everything you asked for, but you lied and omitted information, even after you promised to stop."

"Plausible deniability. For your own good." Craig glanced out the window at the Omni Hotel. He had laughed out loud when he heard the news reports that police had locked it down for hours while they did a room-to-room search for Tanna and Jason, based on an anonymous tip, only to have it turn up empty.

"You created deadlines, I met them," Craig said. "You demanded results, I produced them. On my own, putting myself at risk, to shield all of you. And now this? I am giving the world the greatest gift it could ever receive while you sit around bickering about compliance."

"The situation threatened to expose everything. It needed to be dealt with."

"You have no clue as to the damage you've done nor the liability you've opened yourselves up to. I am in command of the situation. At least that was the case before you and your little mouthpiece there"—Craig pointed to Lauren—"got involved. I will continue to take care of it, and your interference will not be tolerated. Not anymore."

"Don't forget who you're talking to here," another commented.

"Oh, I know who I'm talking to. A bunch of short-sighted figureheads who made their money by lying, cheating, and stealing, but couldn't come up with a single visionary thought if given a lifetime to do so."

Craig glared at the spineless statues in front of him.

"You think you can shut me down or lock me out? That

will never happen. That's why I've already begun closing level five. We're moving to the new location immediately. No more waiting."

The room erupted in protests, but Craig shouted them down before they got rolling.

"The world deserves this. How we get there is irrelevant. Be thankful that I'm allowing you to be a part of it."

"You think too much of yourself, Dr. Emmerson," an investor yelled from the back.

"There you are mistaken," Craig said with a cold smile. "*I* control access to the data. I'm the only one who knows how it works. I'm the only one who can continue with the research. If you try to stop me, I expose you. From now on, you don't make another decision without me. You don't get that choice anymore."

CHAPTER 42

As Jason scrambled up the stairs to Perry's apartment, his legs almost gave out on him. Without his phone, he hadn't been able to order a car, so he'd found a cab instead. He'd had the driver drop him off a few blocks away, and when it came time to pay, he took off.

"Perry, you here?" Jason shouted.

He heard pounding and crashing from inside and pushed through the open front door. Following the noise, he moved down the hall on quiet steps. When Jason poked his head around the corner, he saw a mound of broken computers piled up in the back bedroom.

"Fuck," Perry grunted as he yanked out a hard drive.

Jason let out a sigh of relief.

Perry spun and yelled in surprise. "Damn it! Don't do that."

"What the hell's going on?"

"You tell me. They tracked me down. Blew a hole right through my security, and my system gave it up quicker than a freshman on prom night. Speaking of, where's your girl?"

"Thought she might've come here. We got split up. Could be bad."

"Bad all around."

Jason looked at the purple bruises creeping up on Perry's face—the result of his fight with Roman. Then he looked down at the broken electronics. "What'd they take?"

"Everything. Who knows? By the time I realized it, they had me locked out of my own system. Only thing I could do was shut it down and rip out drives."

Jason snapped his fingers. "Tanna's credit card. They could have followed it here."

"Except I got my shit closed tight. I'm under attack all the time, and no one gets in, ever. They even took down the M-Gen site we posted. No forwarding, no registry, nothing. Like it never existed."

"You put that on the deep web. They can't get to that. No one can."

"They did." Perry went into his closet, rummaged around, and returned with a cordless drill and ball-peen hammer. Standing over the hard drives, he revved the drill's motor, then paused.

"I hate to ask, Jason, but I have to. I mean, there's a lot being said about you out there."

Jason saw the sliver of distrust in his friend's eyes. "We didn't kill anyone."

"Figured. But I know you always bring the crazy. Trust me, I enjoy it more than anyone, I just needed to make sure it wasn't getting out of control again."

Perry became a whirlwind, drilling holes through the hard drives with one hand and hammering them to death with the other. Bits of metal, plastic, and silicone flew as Perry destroyed his life's work.

"I'm sorry for bringing you into this," Jason said. "If I'd known, I never would have done it."

"Like I said, you always bring the crazy, and I love you for it."

"But I was trying to help this time. I really was."

"Maybe you cut her loose and save yourself for a change."

Jason pushed his hands through his hair and walked around the bedroom. "You have to leave."

"What?"

"Get out now. If they tracked your system, they've got your address."

Perry gestured to the mess. "They already got everything they wanted. There's nothing left."

"Doesn't matter. You're a part of it, and they know that now. They're not going to leave any loose ends."

"I'm not scared of them."

Jason shook his head. He saw Perry's phone on the top of the desk and grabbed it. Then he dialed 911. When the operator picked up, Jason tried to sound winded, and spoke in a shallow voice to disguise himself. "Yeah, this is Perry Young. I'm at 1821 Holson Way. He's here. Jason Delgado. The one you're looking for. He broke in, stole some of my stuff, beat the hell out of me. You have to come now. Hurry."

Jason hung up and tossed the phone to Perry.

"What the fuck did you just do?" Perry screamed. "You're bringing the police here? *Here?*"

"I'm sorry, but you can't just sit around and let them

find you. The police can protect you. It's the only way to keep you safe."

"Safe? Are you nuts?" Perry circled his room in a state of panic. He ripped out a dresser drawer and flipped it over to reveal a giant black bag taped to the bottom. He opened it and showed Jason the hundreds of colorful pills inside. "What am I supposed to do with this?"

Jason instinctively reached in. Red, yellow, and blue pills stuck to the sweat on his fingers as he pulled his hand out. He stared at them as if he was looking deep into a heavenly constellation of evening stars, and it took everything he had not to impulsively shove them in his mouth.

"Flush them," he said. "Who cares?"

"Flush them? Are you kidding? That's like four grand of Molly."

"These people will destroy you. Your computers are just the beginning. Look what they're doing to me."

"But this is good stuff."

"Get over it. Now, I need a burner." Perry didn't move. "Perry!"

"Yeah, yeah." Perry reached under his pillow, pulled out another cell phone, and handed it to Jason. "What am I supposed to tell the cops when they come? They'll know we're friends."

"Tell them the truth. It has to come out one way or another now. But one more thing. Your keys."

Perry crossed his arms. "No. No way in hell."

"They'll be here any second. I have to go."

Perry dug into his pocket and handed over his keys. "Will I ever see her again?"

"I promise."

"What a relief."

"Thanks for everything. I mean it."

"Just go already."

Jason bolted into the hall, down the stairs, and out the front door, grabbing Perry's helmet as he went. Parked at the edge of the curb was Perry's Kawasaki ZX-10R motorcycle. A flat black supersport built to go fast. Really fucking fast. The sight of it pushed the pain from Jason's thighs into the pit of his stomach. Not that long ago he had sworn to himself that he'd never get on a motorcycle again. After what happened last time, he wasn't sure he could ever trust himself on one.

Now the motorcycle taunted him, daring him to get on. For a moment he was unable to move, gripping the keys until they cut into his skin.

It was a squeal of tires that got him moving. A charcoal-gray SUV with tinted windows screamed around the corner and charged down the street toward him. A wall of police sirens sounded not far behind.

Jason slid his leg over the seat and brought the machine to life. The engine shuddered and snarled beneath him. He made sure the SUV had seen him, then slipped on the helmet and revved the motor until his entire body shook. He popped the clutch and fishtailed away from the curb, heading straight at the oncoming SUV.

Jason adjusted the damper and traction control to loosen the steering. The motorcycle hitched a bit when it switched gears, but damn could it fly. He hugged his body in, settled down on the frame, and opened the throttle.

He corrected his path to put himself right between the

SUV's headlights. The two vehicles aligned themselves on a collision course. As the world whipped past, Jason continued to accelerate.

Jason knew they each needed to make a decision. It wasn't a matter of who would flinch first; neither would do that. No, Jason had to get by this guy, and to do that he had to guess which side to pass on. The driver of the SUV had the same choice to make.

The wrong choice, and it was all over.

The distance between them closed fast. Jason shut his eyes. He needed to feel the cycle as much as see what was happening. He sensed the pistons ramming back and forth in the engine block, the movement of the chain as it transferred power to the rear wheel, the rubber of the tires as they gripped the road, the stiffness of the suspension, the variance in the steering, the feel of the throttle under his fingers.

Now!

Jason leaned left, then twisted the handlebars right. The speed and momentum kicked him sideways, and he used all his weight to stay upright. When the SUV barreled down on his left, its front bumper almost clipped his back tire as he shot down the driver's side of the vehicle. On instinct, he raised his arm to shield himself just as the side mirror was about to strike him. It broke off and smashed into the driver's window, sending a spray of shattered glass everywhere.

The SUV skidded to a stop and turned around, heading away from Perry's apartment, as Jason had intended. He smiled to himself, rounded the corner onto a busier street, and pushed forward—straight toward a line of five squad cars coming at him stacked single-file.

Jason eased off the accelerator just enough for the SUV to catch up.

As the police convoy came closer, cars pulled to the side, leaving Jason with an open road. He gunned the engine, and the force lifted his front wheel off the ground. He took off down the street with the SUV trailing and flipped the cops his middle finger as he flew by. The last two squad cars peeled off and turned to chase them while the other three continued on.

Jason made a hard turn and led the group into an area of town where there would be little regard for police sirens. He raced through four red lights before the SUV turned off, unable to keep up. One of the squad cars followed it, while the other continued to pursue Jason.

Cutting a series of quick corners, Jason zigzagged through a dilapidated neighborhood. When he spotted an empty graffiti-covered garage, he pulled in, killed the engine, and waited in the dark.

The police cruiser shot past.

Jason's muscles vibrated with leftover adrenaline, and his inner thighs stiffened. He got off the cycle and walked around before they cramped up.

The sound of sirens filled the air. More squad cars were apparently joining the search. Jason knew it would be a while before he could safely go anywhere, so he eased down onto the broken concrete and leaned against the wall.

He pulled out the cell phone he'd taken from Perry and thought about who he could call. Names from his past rolled through his head. Some of the people he had known well, while others were distant blurs, remnants of drug-altered memories. Either way, most of them wouldn't trust him—not anymore. He had screwed up a lot of friendships in his life, and they were probably happy as hell to see him getting what he had coming.

And they were right. They were better off without him.

So was Tanna. She was strong, smart, building something for her future. What could he offer her besides disappointment and despair? She didn't need any part of his life. Best to let her down now and get it over with.

Jason put the phone away. There was no one left for him to call.

He reached into his back pocket to pull out the few pills he'd taken from Perry's stash, and the two signed baseball cards he'd stolen came with them. He sat on the cold concrete floor and stared at them in his hand, while outside, police patrolled the streets in an unrelenting hunt to track him down.

CHAPTER 43

Just another moth to the flame, Tanna told herself. Without a plan, without knowing what had happened to Jason, without any idea of where she was, she followed the outline of the city. That was all she could think to do. She gave up on figuring out new possibilities and stopped herself from imagining different scenarios of how she could have done things better. What was the point? She needed to survive. One foot in front of the other, head on a swivel, keep moving forward.

She pulled the edges of the hoodie closer to hide her face, retreating inward. Her muscles begged for rest, and the piercing pressure in her sinus cavities forced her to breathe through her mouth. Even then, she could barely draw a simple breath. She placed her fingers against her neck and felt her lymph nodes, swollen and tender. Her body was turning against her, and she had to eat, drink, recover . . . or she'd never make it.

The image of downtown San Francisco was the flame that drew her in. On tired, burning legs, she continued to head for the heart of it.

When a red pickup pulled up alongside her at the curb,

she didn't even turn her head. She crouched down, pretending to tie her shoe. The driver hopped out, and Tanna noticed the tattoos up and down his arm.

"Jason!" she yelled, springing to her feet.

"Who?" the man said.

This wasn't Jason. He was shorter and chunkier and had a goatee. His tattoo sleeve was intertwined images of knives with skulls. She wondered how she could have been so mistaken.

"Nothing," Tanna muttered as she pressed forward.

"You looking for something there, honey?" the man called out. "Maybe you need a date?"

Tanna continued ahead, his footsteps following behind her.

"I'll show you a good time. A real good time."

"Go to hell," she said with enough force to carry down the block.

"Oh, I like a girl with some fire." He quickened his pace.

Keep walking. It's not worth it.

But she didn't. She planted her feet and spun around. "Is that so?"

"Bet you bring the fire down below too."

"You think you can say whatever you want to me? Huh?" Tanna marched right up to him. "Because I'm the good girl, I need to be afraid of you? Is that it? You can just do anything? Maybe you want to roll me over right here in the street."

The man clearly hadn't been expecting this. He stared at her, speechless.

"Or are you too scared now?" Her voice bounced off nearby houses and echoed back to her. "Started something you can't finish. Petrified of making the wrong decision."

The man regained his nerve. "I ain't scared of some bitch."

"Then what are you waiting for?" Tanna practically spat the words in his face. "Come on. Take your shot."

Something in her voice made him take a step back.

"Do it!" she screamed at the top of her lungs.

All around, doors opened and curtains were parted. She felt eyes on her. But Tanna couldn't stop. She couldn't halt the flood rushing through the cracks, breaking the dam.

"You're gutless and weak," she growled.

"Stupid cunt," the man barked at her before turning and walking away.

"And now you screwed this up, too. Can't do anything right!" she hollered as he disappeared down the block. "Yeah, go run and hide. That's what you're best at, isn't it?"

It took Tanna a moment to remember where she was—standing in the middle of the street, hands balled into fists, people watching her from porches and behind windows.

Breathe, she told herself. *Just breathe.*

She pulled her hood around her face and moved on, navigating past abandoned cars while trying to keep the view of downtown in front of her. The rush she'd felt a moment ago faded, leaving her empty and exhausted, her mind collapsing in on itself and her body about to follow.

Too far. You went too far.

She kept walking. She didn't know for how long. When she passed a worn-out convenience store, she ducked inside, grabbed a bottle of water, and then studied the snacks near the front. As she reached for a blueberry granola bar, she caught sight of herself on a small television propped up behind the counter. It was a newscast, and it showed her running through the park with the silver Camry following.

The news then switched over to a video of Tanna's mother trying to get into her house through a throng of reporters who were sticking microphones into her face. Her motorized wheelchair could barely move through the pack, even with Tanna's aunt doing her best to clear a path. Tanna could only imagine what they were saying to her. Talking about how her daughter had kidnapped and tortured the dean. How she'd killed the mortician and burned his body to cover her tracks. They were probably asking her what it felt like to raise a monster.

Then Tanna was struck by another realization. *If reporters can get to her, anyone can get to her.*

"Leave her alone," she said aloud.

"Excuse me?" the cashier asked.

Tanna turned and looked straight at him. The moment she saw his expression, she knew. He'd recognized her.

"Never mind," she said.

Tanna dug through her empty pockets, then frantically searched the black messenger bag Eric had given her. Not a cent.

"I, uh . . ."

Take it and run.

Tanna retreated a few steps and looked to the exit. Trapped between panic and rage, she glanced once at the cashier before rushing out onto the deserted street.

CHAPTER 44

Detective Duane Lewis sat along the wall and watched the frantic calmness with amazement. Officers rotated in and out with purpose and quiet efficiency while computer keyboards clacked and phones rang.

This was not the way of things back at his own precinct. His bullpen was a constant barrage of shouting, dick jokes, and pointed obscenities. On a day like today, it would have been pure bedlam. They were expected to get results—that was the measuring stick—and no one cared if they had to roll a couple desks or beat the water cooler with a baseball bat to relieve the tension in the room. Common courtesy and professionalism were the first things to be sacrificed.

Not so at the San Francisco Police Department Headquarters. Perhaps that was because the building housed the police chief himself, and so everyone was put on a short leash. When the chief was involved, image and outward appearance were critical—especially now, with the city and nation watching.

"Deputy Chief Marcos has a moment for you now," a gentle voice said over his shoulder.

An assistant guided him to a modest office with walls covered in pictures of handshakes and forced smiles. Deputy Chief of the Field Operations Bureau was a thankless job, a bureaucratic nightmare. As the person in charge of overseeing the Patrol Division and Investigations Bureau, he needed to liaise between the chief and staff, and he was responsible for maintaining all ongoing investigations and patrols. Anything positive would get credited to those higher up, but when the shit hit the fan, it would fall straight into his lap.

"Sir," said the assistant, "the LA detective is here."

"Detective Duane Lewis," Duane put in as the assistant walked out.

Deputy Chief Marcos was an imposing, rigid figure. He looked as if he might once have played linebacker, and probably still had a wall of muscle underneath the subsequent weight gain. He paused a long moment before looking up from his monitor.

"Detective Lewis. Welcome to San Francisco. Now what's so important that you felt the need to come all the way up here to talk to me in person? Because right now, I've got a long line out there—including the mayor, the chief, and about a hundred reporters camped outside. Lucky for you, I was a detective in my previous life. I know what it's like to deal with administrative assholes like me."

"Sir, I was hoping to talk to some of your people, see if there's anything I can do to help with the investigation."

"Do you know where those two are right now?"

"No."

"Then there's nothing to talk about. They have your report."

"Yeah, but my experience with the case and the suspects might let me add personal details not in the official report. Maybe I could help anticipate their next move or give you an idea of—"

"You could have arrested them a couple of days ago and saved us a world of misery. We've got open gun wars in the middle of the street, for Christ's sake."

"You're right. I should have done something."

The assistant walked in, slid a thick folder onto the desk, and departed once more.

"Fine," said the deputy chief, "then bottom-line it for me. One detective to another."

"I can't buy this whole Bonnie and Clyde crap," Duane told him.

Marcos shrugged. "Us too. But the evidence is strong. Nothing's out of place. Our only job now is to catch them and nail them to the wall."

"That's the part I don't buy. Everything's all wrapped up. Very convenient. And these two?"

"Jason Delgado has a history of drug use and incarceration. You arrested him a couple of times yourself."

"Credit-card fraud. Petty theft. Once for possession with intent. Kicked it down to simple possession when he volunteered for rehab."

"Maybe this time he was dealing for someone and things got out of control. Couldn't reel it in."

"He's a user and likes to have fun. That's all. Now we're

talking three dead—the dean, his neighbor, and the mortician. Four if you include the roommate."

"Possibly two more found in an alley close to where
the girl was spotted last. And these guys were dressed for
combat."

"So now they're supposedly capable of killing soldiers?
The guy's a recovering addict. The girl is just a med student."

"A med student who got mixed up with the wrong guy
and now can't get off the merry-go-round." Marcos leaned
back in his chair and started counting off on his fingers. "Her
roommate, whom she 'found' in the shower. Dead. We have
video of her at the dean's office. He's dead. We know they
went looking for the mortician. Dead again. The evidence
speaks for itself."

"That video is another thing that bothers me. The university office hasn't sent it to me yet. I don't even know what
else is on it. But somehow that clip already got leaked."

"Detective Lewis, I appreciate your interest in this case,
but we've got a dozen detectives on this, over one hundred
patrol officers, and every idiot out there with a cell phone
trying to track them down. There's nothing you can add."

"Just let me tell your people what I know," Duane said.
"I won't get in the way. But maybe I can shed some light on
their next move. How could it hurt?"

Marcos shook his head. "I'm sorry, but the answer is—"

"Please," Duane said, leaning across the desk. "From
one detective to another. I didn't listen to her. I didn't care
enough and I let it get away from me. Now I've got to be
part of fixing it."

The assistant thrust his head through the open door. "They lost him."

"Damn it," Marcos yelled. "Can't we catch one break here?"

"Well, the kid is on his way to us." The assistant opened a file. "Perry Young. Seems he and Jason Delgado are friends. It turns out that Jason Delgado made the 911 call himself. Wanted the cops there for protection."

"Protection from what?"

"Maybe whoever was driving the gray SUV that got away. You might want to hear what this Perry has to say. It's messed up."

The assistant handed Marcos the file, and he scanned it quickly. "Great. A cyberhack tweeker with a record of exposing himself in public. Just what we need to crack this thing." He showed the open file to Duane. "You recognize him?"

Duane looked at the newest picture and the older mugshots. He didn't recognize this guy at all, but he knew that answer would put him on the outside looking in. So he lied.

"I've seen them together, yeah."

Marcos looked at Duane, hesitated, then frowned. "Okay, you can listen in. Tell my people what you know. And if anything rings your bell, I don't care how small, speak up this time."

CHAPTER 45

With the battle tilted against Tanna's body, her immune system leaped into overdrive. Helper cells swarmed the combat zone, coordinating the fight and reporting back. They called up specialized attack cells and ordered virus debris cleared and identified. Next, they diverted vast amounts of energy and resources to increase the production of all virus-fighting cells in the hopes of stemming the tide of the assault. The overwhelming choreography of activity required every aspect to work perfectly.

Reinforcements charged to the front lines. The fearless and battle-hardened killer T-cells attacked with reckless abandon. They, too, had been born and bred for this. Warriors adapted over time with the simple purpose of destroying infected cells that had been tricked into becoming virus-creating machines. If this war was going to be won, they needed to stop the cells from replicating. Without that, there would be no chance.

Marked with indicators after the virus assault, the infected cells became homing beacons, alerting T-cells that they had been compromised. Hurrying to attach themselves to any infested cells, the killer Ts bored holes in the cell walls and poured in their toxic payload, liquefying the host cells' inner workings and stopping the viruses' only means of reproduction. The body had to destroy itself in order to save itself.

Unfortunately, as strong as the T-cells were, the virus assault had a significant head start. It had already spread deep into Tanna's lungs, and from there had pushed through the rest of her body. Before long the viruses would find more cells to infect, destroy more tissue, wreak more havoc. The cycle would endlessly repeat itself, unless Tanna's immune system either found a way to stop them . . . or succumbed to defeat.

CHAPTER 46

Roman examined the gunshot wound that curved across his abdomen. The heat had cauterized most of the injury, which meant he wouldn't lose much blood, but burns took a long time to heal, and just when that healing was nearly complete, it would inevitably split open, spill out pus, and start all over again.

His two-room apartment bordered the Hunters Point district, an area where no one cared who came and went. His only furnishings were a folding table with chairs and a twin bed, while his kitchenette held nothing but a single set of dishes and a well-used moqueca pot. Utilitarian and efficient—that was all he needed here in the States. He directed his money and passion toward his five-bedroom, six-bath villa in Costa Rica. There, he'd just renovated the primary suite to add a wrap-around deck, giving him a glorious view of the impenetrable jungle, full of feral mantled howlers that screeched through the night.

He wished he was there now. He wasn't born there, but it was the closest thing to a home he'd ever had. He could be there in hours. Just walk away, leave all this damage and degradation behind for someone else to deal with.

"Looks like you need to be more careful," Dr. Craig Emmerson said from the rear of the room.

Roman didn't bother to turn around. On his way to the apartment, he'd spotted Craig sitting in a car two blocks away.

Craig circled around to assess Roman's wound. "Not too bad."

"It's fine." On the table next to Tanna's stolen laptop, Roman bypassed her biology workbook open to a chapter on nerve impulses and grabbed his canvas travel bag that doubled as his medical kit. He pulled out tape, bandages, and a penknife. "It'll be over soon."

"That's hard to believe."

"Lauren's people got in the way."

"I saw. The whole city saw. Hell, the whole world has seen it by now. But that doesn't matter. Let them run around town and make a complete mess of things. It's better for us. By the time anyone figures out what's going on, we'll be long gone. All you have to do is take care of our loose ends."

"Those two are stronger than you think," Roman said. "They're not out for fame or glory like you. Just survival. That makes them dangerous. Unpredictable. They're fighting for their lives. But I'll take care of them."

Craig stepped closer. "You'd better. I don't accept failure."

"Neither do I."

"Then if you can't get them, get to their families, their friends. Go after the girl's mother. Go all the way. Just put an end to it."

Roman shook his head. "No need. They're separated,

on the run, and on their own. There's only one place left for them—and I'll be there."

"Have you given any thought to what happens if you're not?" Craig asked. "You need to cover every angle here. And you'll do it. You'll do it because you want what I can give you, more than anything. So you need to be willing to do whatever's necessary."

"Are you?" Roman asked.

Craig smiled. A smile that made it seem there wasn't a problem in his world. It was the smile of the blissfully reckless and pathologically corrupt. "You're right," he said. "They have proven themselves more formidable than they look. But so are you. We have to look inside ourselves for the strength now, Roman. Then your loyalty will be rewarded."

Roman had heard all the bullshit before. An endless stream of lies spewed from the crooked mouth of the little man. He eyed the penknife on the table. He was split between the world he knew and the world he wanted.

"I'm trusting you to finish what we started," Craig said.

Punching down his desire for vengeance, Roman nodded. His mind was made up. "I'll do whatever it takes."

CHAPTER 47

The door to Dr. Solomon Cabral's hospital room opened in silence, and Tanna slipped inside, wearing a long white doctor's coat and carrying a stack of papers, both of which she'd picked up while slipping in through the service entrance. She snuck through the hospital by keeping her head down while pretending to examine the vital documents in her hands. In reality, they were just stolen janitorial forms, and it appeared the hospital needed floor polish and bleach.

The monotonous chirp of the patient monitor station resonated in the quiet air. It recorded Sol's pulse, respiration, oxygen level, and temperature, keeping perfect track of his deteriorating health and his inability to wake up.

Sol lay motionless, tucked neatly beneath the thin blanket. His hair looked finer than before and his face gaunter.

"We really do make a pair," Tanna said as she stepped up to the side of his bed. "You unconscious and me with no idea what I'm even doing here." Her gaze swept over the bag feeding Sol intravenous liquids. "Any chance you want to snap out of it and tell me what to do?"

Notes scribbled in black marker filled a whiteboard on the wall above Sol's head. Most of them were already crossed off in red. It appeared the doctors didn't know what was wrong with him, which meant there was no reason to believe he was going to come out of it any time soon, if at all.

Tanna stretched her sore muscles. She had walked to Saint Francis Memorial Hospital on blistering feet that resented every step.

"Like the disguise?" she said, gesturing to her outfit. "It suits me, don't you think? The truth is . . . I would have made a good doctor. One of the best. I've never had the guts to say that before. To anyone. Not even myself."

The familiar sound of the monitor station stirred up memories of her sister. The repeated hospital trips. The endless waiting. The constant disappointment. She wanted to ignore them but couldn't.

"You know, after my sister died, people treated me differently. They never saw me for who *I* was. Only that I wasn't her. Everyone expected me to be strong. To be good. To be silent. To keep my emotions to myself so I wouldn't create more problems for my parents. But in the end, look where that got me."

She took a deep breath and removed the white overcoat. "Too bad this will never happen now."

A bouquet of tulips stood on the side table, and she ran her fingers over the blooms. Tucked between the stems was a child's picture of green grass and a lemon-yellow sun. The words I LOVE YOU GRANDPA were scrawled across the bottom.

"What a mess I got everyone into. That's what I get for trying to do the right thing. Don't worry, I won't make that mistake again. Lie, cheat, steal. Seems like the one sure way to get what you want. I should have done more of that. Lesson learned. Looks like Dr. Emmerson got it right after all."

And perhaps he really had. Tanna had wanted to become a doctor to help people, but doctors hadn't been able to save her sister. They wouldn't be able to save her mother. They hadn't saved the millions who had died during the pandemic. Whereas Dr. Emmerson had a different approach, a new way of thinking. Stop picking up the pieces of shattered lives and instead fix everything *before* the problem starts. He was taking shortcuts, yes, but they were leading him to what might be the ultimate cure.

And the sooner he figured it out, the better.

Tanna eased into the chair next to Sol's bed and wrapped his hand in hers. He was peaceful and composed; he even had a slight smile on his face. And why not? He had nothing more to worry about now.

Tanna thought maybe he had the right idea, too. Just let it all go. Forget your hopes and dreams. The world didn't need another doctor anyway.

A wave of exhaustion made her rest her head on the side of the bed. She wasn't doing well. Her heart was beating so hard she could feel it in her skull. And with her throat ripped raw, each new breath felt like it tore away a chunk of her fluid-filled lungs. Her shivering muscles buckled, and her body told her it was time to quit.

She closed her eyes, and her head was all too happy to follow. In an instant, she was asleep.

CHAPTER 48

With the streets closed off, Detective Duane Lewis had to park three blocks away from the convenience store and walk from there. That seemed excessive when all they had was a store clerk who'd briefly spotted one of the suspects, but then nothing in the case made much sense to him.

Like the interview with Perry Young.

San Francisco PD had been trying to nail Perry for a long time on identity theft, drug dealing, and credit-card fraud, but they had never been able to make anything stick. Now that they were almost sure to turn up something in that pile of hardware he'd left in his bedroom, Duane figured the kid would say whatever he could to cover his own ass. But what he told them instead was an almost incoherent conspiracy theory involving a lab called Modern Genetics and a prominent scientist conducting secret human trials.

Chief Deputy Marcos dismissed it as a bullshit smoke-screen, but Duane wasn't so sure. On the surface it made no sense . . . yet it fit with what Tanna had tried to tell him back in Los Angeles. Yes, it was far-fetched and improbable. But it also felt like adding more pieces to a larger puzzle.

Unfortunately, until they turned up some hard evidence on the kid, they had nothing to hold Perry on, and so after questioning him he'd been released.

An officer stepped in Duane's path. "Hold up right there."

Duane pulled his badge and showed it.

"LA?" the officer said. "That badge won't get you in here."

"I'm assisting on the case. Deputy Chief Marcos asked me to help."

"Good for you. Wait over there."

"I have to talk to the detectives."

"Over there," the officer said.

"If you think I—"

"We got enough assholes inside already. Don't need one more."

"It's okay," a detective yelled from the store's entrance. "He's with us."

The officer looked Duane up and down suspiciously before turning his shoulders to let him pass.

Duane walked up to the detective. "Thanks for that."

"No problem. Marcos told us to give you access." The detective smiled. "And to keep an eye on you."

"Sounds about right. So what have you got?"

The detective gestured to the cashier, who was giving his statement to a handful of officers. "Idiot tweeted to the world that she was in the store before he called us. There were twenty people here before we even showed up. Any evidence will be shit."

Duane looked around. "Cameras?"

"Yeah, thank goodness. Two weren't working, but the one behind the cashier was up. Got my guys transferring it now."

The detective led Duane into a cluttered back room where a pair of officers were finishing up the video transfer from an antiquated security system to a tablet. They replayed the footage for Duane.

"What's she got in her hands?" Duane asked, looking at Tanna standing in front of the cashier.

"Looks like a bottle of water. She didn't pay."

"From where she was at the park to here, seems like she's headed back into the city," Duane said.

"That's how we see it."

Duane couldn't figure it out. Why would she willingly go somewhere she knew the police would be searching for her?

They both watched as Tanna stood transfixed, staring at something before finally digging through her pockets for money. "Do you know what she was staring at?" Duane asked.

"No clue."

Duane walked back into the store, trailed by the detective, and stood in the approximate location where Tanna had stood on the video. He spotted it immediately—a small television propped up behind the cashier.

"I'd like to find out what she was watching on that television while she stood here," Duane said.

He also planned on having a talk with someone at Modern Genetics, but he sure as hell wasn't going to mention that to anyone else.

CHAPTER 49

The water of the North Pacific Ocean was a fathomless black well. The swelling waves and deepening troughs rolled across the horizon on their way to the closest landfall, over eight hundred nautical miles away.

Above the undulating surface, a pristine new building complex climbed four stories off the deck of the retrofitted oil platform. The hulking main spar stood defiant and steadfast against the constant pounding of the ocean and supported the sprawling compound with ease. A massive crane stuck off the back like an inky broken finger, ferrying materials to waiting workers who rushed to join metal supports that sent showers of sparks into the water.

"No!" the foreman yelled at one of his welders. "Bring it all the way across to here. Over here!"

He made his way below deck, where immense generators were chugging to life. All around the structure, floodlights came on, illuminating the sheer scale of the station hovering above the ocean. He had seen it almost every day for two years, but the sight still amazed him.

The lights clicked off with a heavy thud and sent the foreman into darkness.

"Damn it!" he shouted and flipped on his earpiece. "It's still tripping. There's a short somewhere."

A crackling voice responded in his ear. "I requested a new tracer from the mainland, but it'll have to come with the first round of staff."

"I told you we're not waiting that long. We open on time."

"Salt water keeps eating through the connections. It could be anywhere. I don't know how the hell I'm supposed to find it."

The foreman ran through the options in his head. "Do it by hand. Turn every unit on individually until it trips again. The most critical first. At least we can isolate it."

"Do you have any idea how long that'll take?"

"Not as long as making you run all new lines."

"Copy that."

Section by section, the station awoke from its hibernation. The foreman led a group of workers through empty corridors, their flashlight beams slashing through the dark. They passed a storage unit bulging with canned goods stacked from floor to ceiling, and a kitchen that clanged as refrigeration compressors kicked on for the first time. Computer systems came online, and monitors blinked and flashed. The foreman measured output velocity as air-conditioning units pushed a chilled breeze into the server room.

Inside the main research lab, he helped remove thin plastic dust covers to expose the pristine new equipment beneath. The lab was a beautiful combination of design and function, easily surpassing what he'd seen at Modern Genetics' mainland location. His workers examined the machines for any signs of damage, then calibrated the devices with as much precision as time allowed. It should have taken two weeks to adjust to protocol standards. He had days.

Sleeping berths were made up with clean linens, and he ordered folding chairs delivered to the one open courtyard on the upper corner of the rig. Back up on the main deck, the foreman shouted at workers to reinforce a wobbly part of the guardrail. The last thing he needed was someone slipping and falling into the Pacific.

Finally, he took a moment to look around. The truth was, he enjoyed the sudden chaos. After sitting idle for months, he was chomping at the bit to pull a few all-nighters.

The command to initiate location startup had come as a surprise. The foreman didn't know who had changed their mind or why, and he didn't care. For all their supposed intelligence, none of those scientists could make a practical decision to save their lives. *Not my circus, not my monkeys*, he reminded himself.

The first supply ship and more crew were expected in thirty-six hours, followed by a series of staff deliveries that would start with engineering and laboratory personnel. It wouldn't be long before the station was functioning at maximum capacity, and that was a moment he had been anticipating for a long time. He'd spent two years cradling this baby from concept to reality. Soon it would be time to show off what it could do.

It would be ready. He'd make sure of it.

CHAPTER 50

Images flickered madly through Tanna's head. She couldn't connect the people she knew in them with the places she'd been. Everything moved too fast. Image on top of image. A swirling collection of morphing likenesses. *Slow down.*

"Wake up."

The outer edges turned black as her world spun faster. She rushed forward. *Please stop.*

"Tanna, wake up."

The spinning mass grew, drawing her in, and she was tumbling, falling, disappearing into the darkness.

"Tanna!"

She woke with a jolt, disconnected from her surroundings, unable to place herself.

"Are you okay?"

Reality rushed back. The hospital room. Sol. The chirping monitor next to the bed. And Jason—standing in front of her.

Tanna launched herself up and threw her arms around him.

"It's really you."

He squeezed her tight. "It's me," he said.

She let her body melt into his. "I didn't know what happened to you. It was all so fast."

"I'm just glad I found you here. It was the only place I could think of to look."

"I shouldn't have left you. I'm so sorry."

"No. You had to save yourself. What happened to me is my fault. I tell young racers to look a full section down the track, not just at what's in front of them; I didn't do that, and I wasn't there for you. *I'm* sorry."

Tanna went silent, letting herself relax in this moment of warmth and tranquility. She didn't want to move, didn't want to think, but she noticed Jason's eyes roaming across the room and realized he had been speaking to her.

"What happened to Eric?" he asked again.

She stepped away from him, and felt the exhaustion again. Her muscles were spent, and the weight of her head almost pulled her forward. She was tired, sick, and afraid of what was happening to her.

"He ran away. But first he gave me that messenger bag." She opened it and pulled out a handful of loose papers with notes and diagrams scribbled on them.

"What is all that?" Jason asked.

"Codes. Locations. Instructions for what drives to take and how to take them. He didn't explain it all that well." She pulled out the miniature USB flash drive. "He also gave me this. I have to insert it into one of the servers or everything will get wiped."

Jason sighed. "This keeps getting better."

As he reached out to pull her close again, Tanna pushed back. "Don't. I think there's something wrong with me."

"I don't care." Jason slipped past her defenses and held her. She didn't want to let him, but she didn't have the energy to stop him. "We'll figure it all out," he said.

"How? I'm sick. And I don't know what I'm doing."

"Yes you do. But first we have to get out of here. Besides the police, there's an army of people out there looking for us. And honestly, I can't believe that I even came here in the first place."

Tanna waited for more. In part, she just wanted to hear him talk. To get lost in his voice, to be taken away somewhere before reality inevitably came around to smack her in the face.

He relented. "I got into a bad accident a while back. Don't even remember what happened, but I woke up in a hospital room much like this one and the doctors told me I had a combination of alcohol, cocaine, and hydrocodone in my system. Apparently I was cruising the freeway, missed my exit, and turned straight into a concrete divider at forty miles an hour. I forked up over the handlebars, but not before the bike split me in half down the middle. Blew my pelvis apart. Had two surgeries just so my legs wouldn't flop sideways."

"You had your helmet on?"

"Part of the routine." He shrugged. "I had no idea where I was going, or even if I had someone with me. Every minute in that hospital bed, I watched the door and waited for the police to walk through and tell me I had killed someone. That I had another person on the back of my bike who died. It was the worst feeling in the world.

"But that's the thing, getting fucked up was my life. That was all I knew, and it didn't matter who I hurt or what I had to do to get fucked up all over again. But then I ended up someplace like here." Jason looked around the room. "That's when I told myself I wouldn't get high again. That I'd never step foot in a hospital again. And I would never get on a motorcycle again either.

"For the last few months, I kept that promise. But it was hard. I wasn't used to living sober, and . . . it didn't seem worth it. I felt . . . hopeless."

"I'm sorry. You don't need to tell me all this."

"No, it's okay. Because being around . . . being around you has made me want to do better in ways I didn't even realize I could." Jason reached out and grabbed her hands. "But I never want to hurt you like that."

"You won't."

"How do you know that? I don't. Why do you think I stole those baseball cards? I was going to sell them and get fucked up again. Because I don't think I can live a sober life."

"You can. I believe it."

"What if I don't want to?"

The question pierced Tanna's heart. It was the most honest thing he could have said, and she wasn't sure she was ready to hear it. Maybe she never would be. But it was the truth. His truth.

Tanna realized her world would never fit into a perfect box, and she was beginning to accept that. "I'm sorry to have put you through this," she said, then wrapped him in her arms and squeezed him as tight as she could.

"Don't be. As screwed up as all this is, at least it has

meaning. Fighting for my life gives me something to focus on."

She stepped back and looked him in the eye. "I don't want you fighting for your life. I don't want *me* fighting for *my* life either. I know that M-Gen needs to be stopped, but by us? You and me? Really?"

"You're a hell of a lot stronger than you think, Tanna. I've seen it. But no one would blame you for stopping now. Especially me. Maybe we take our chances with the police. Or just go hide. I'm with you, whatever you decide."

She looked down at the wound on his arm, the one that ran through his Steel Dukes tattoo. Images from the last few days rotated in and out of her head, punishing her. There was too much pain. Too much death.

But it was Krystal's death that still haunted her the most. Her limp body stretched out on their bathroom floor. Her wet hair and lifeless eyes. Another sister ripped from Tanna's life too early.

"What do you want to do?" Jason asked.

Tanna lowered her fingertips onto the back of Sol's hand and felt along his skin until she came across a hard nodule about the size of a grain of rice.

"What we have to," she said.

CHAPTER 51

With the lab starting to pack up, Craig was working largely out of his home office. But it was worth it—instead of months or weeks, it would now be mere days and hours before he was at the new location, looking out over the endless ocean, with the freedom to expand. To imagine and create. Nothing holding him back. It gave him a boost of energy, and he was deeply involved with his work on synthetic enzyme compounds when the call came.

A detective was at his door.

As he passed through his condo, he couldn't stop himself from pausing to inspect it. It was immaculate as always, with never so much as a throw pillow out of place. Although he spent almost all his hours at the lab, he insisted the staff come every day to clean the bedding and sanitize the bathroom, no matter what. The thought of crawling between sheets that had already been slept in, even if only by him, repulsed him. Several months ago, he caught a maid rubbing his bedding with a dryer sheet to make everything smell newly washed.

He fired her on the spot. That was when he installed the hidden cameras.

Craig opened his front door to find the detective standing outside.

"Dr. Emmerson? Detective Duane Lewis. Sorry to bother you so late." Lewis extended his hand.

Refusing to return the handshake, Craig moved to block him from entering. "The doorman rang and said it was important. What do you want, Detective?"

Lewis peered into the apartment. "Maybe we can talk inside."

"You expect this to take long?"

"Too long to stand in the hallway."

Craig looked the man over, judging his careless choice of clothing and overall slovenly appearance, then allowed him in with a sweep of his hand.

"Thank you." Lewis gazed around the space, then stepped across to the massive windows that overlooked the glittering city below. "That's a hell of a view."

"I don't get to enjoy it much. As a matter of fact, you're lucky you caught me here tonight."

"Yeah, you're not an easy man to find. Figure you must be a bit of a workaholic. Me too, I guess."

"I doubt that. So, Detective, you came here, to my home, late at night, to talk about something?"

"Right. That is one magnificent view," Lewis commented again, and helped himself to a seat on the white leather couch. He pulled out his notepad but didn't open it, crossing his hands over his knees instead. "I'm assisting the

San Francisco Police Department with their investigation into Tanna Christensen and Jason Delgado."

"Who's that now?"

"Tanna Christensen and Jason Delgado. The two all over the news who are wanted for murder. The ones everyone is looking for, but no one can seem to find."

"I haven't had time to follow the story."

"I understand. You're a busy man. Still, no one has reached out to you? No one from the local police department?"

"I received a call, but they didn't feel the need to show up at my home and disrupt my work. You're just assisting, you said?"

"On loan from Los Angeles," Lewis said, shuffling in his seat. "I'll try to make this brief."

"I wish you would." Staring at the detective sitting on his couch, infesting his private home with filth and sickness, Craig found himself grinding his teeth in slow, circular motions.

"These two, Tanna and Jason. You don't know them? They haven't tried to contact you?"

"Absolutely not. For what purpose?"

"I was hoping you would know." Lewis opened his notepad and started writing. "Maybe I should back up. Tell me about your relationship with your partner, Dr. Solomon Cabral."

"Solomon is not my partner. We merely worked together until his retirement."

"You're not conducting any projects with him right now?"

"No." Craig scoffed. "He can't offer me anything anymore."

"So he's not involved at Modern Genetics in any way?"

"Detective, I understand that you don't have the mental capacity to comprehend the concepts I grapple with on a daily basis, but I assure you that this is not the kind of work one just leaves and returns to at one's convenience. Solomon had an exceptional mind in his time, but science moves fast. Once you walk away, even for a moment, you can't come back."

"Sure. And the last time you saw him?"

"Eight or ten months ago at a cancer benefit. He's taken up traveling. I couldn't even imagine where he is now."

"Saint Francis Memorial Hospital. Here in San Francisco."

"I know where it is."

"But you didn't know he was admitted there earlier today? Doctors think he won't make it."

For a moment Craig felt as if he had laughed out loud, but he wasn't sure. He had certainly wanted to. To fill the room with a raucous roar that shook the walls. But it was probably only in his head. And in his heart.

"I don't have time to keep tabs on everyone I've ever worked with," he finally said.

"I just thought with someone so close, it would've been different."

"Apparently not."

"You're telling me you didn't know?"

"Asked and answered." Craig began walking to the door. "Thank you for the personal update, but we're done here. I wish you the best of luck with whatever it is you're trying to do."

"Of course. There's just one thing I need you to clarify."

"Actually, there isn't. I've been cooperative and forthcoming, but I'm busy, and quite frankly, you're out of your jurisdiction and in over your head."

Lewis didn't make a move to get off the couch. "The thing is, with all this media attention on Delgado and Christensen, there have been a lot of tips flooding in. People have either seen the couple, or they think they've seen them. But there was one call from a waitress at the Highland Diner in Pacifica. She says she remembers them for sure. They stiffed her on the bill. But here's an interesting detail. She said when they ran off, they seemed to be following one of her regulars who had just left. Dr. Solomon Cabral."

Lewis paused as if waiting for a reaction. Craig refused to give him one.

The detective continued. "It's interesting, don't you think? I mean, with everything going on, with the police on their tail, why would these two go out of their way to track down your ex-partner at some diner he frequents? Why not just run?"

As Lewis waited once more for an answer, Craig tried desperately to keep his teeth from grinding, but it was no use. The repugnant noise spread through the room.

CHAPTER 52

Jason led Tanna through the hospital parking garage to Perry's motorcycle.

"Where's your truck?" she asked.

"Towed, impounded. Who knows? This is Perry's bike. It's all we've got."

"I'm not getting on that."

"What do you mean?"

"I mean I've never been on a motorcycle before, and I'm not starting now. Can't we find your truck? Or get something else? Maybe we can steal a car."

Jason couldn't believe this. "Hey, I know not everyone's comfortable with motorcycles, but it's what we have. There's no choice here."

"I don't care. You know the first two things they tell you in medical school? One, always listen to your patients. Two, never get on a motorcycle."

"Tanna. Do you trust me?"

"That's not the point."

"It is the point. I've put myself on the line here. Now I'm

asking for a little trust in return." Jason grabbed the helmet hanging from the handlebars. "All you have to do is sit down and hang on. I'll do the rest."

Tanna drew a steadying breath between her teeth before yanking the helmet from his hands. Jason found himself trying to hide a grin—and failed. This woman, who had come so far and been so fearless, never stopped surprising him. The thought of running and hiding, escaping into a world clouded by drugs and masked by chemicals, continued to tempt him. But the need to be with her was stronger. Tanna allowed him to be himself without judgment. Something no one else did. Not anymore.

"What are we waiting for?" Tanna asked as she slipped the helmet over her head.

Jason helped her with the strap. The helmet was too big for her, but he made it as tight as he could. "How does that feel?"

"Like I stuck my head in a coffin."

"I'll go slow." He mounted the bike and held out his hand to guide her on.

"Where's yours?" she asked.

"You're wearing it."

"Do I need to remind you of the statistics regarding motorcycle accidents, especially for those not wearing helmets?"

"Except we only have one. Now you need to get on."

Tanna swung her leg over the seat and hoisted herself onto the back. Jason guided her feet to the foot pegs on either side, then grabbed her hands and tucked them in front of his body.

"There's no backrest, so you have to really hold on," he said. "Tighter. And keep looking over my shoulders. That'll tell you which way to move."

The motorcycle roared to life, and he glided out onto the street as smoothly as possible.

"Hang on," he shouted, and he opened the throttle.

When Jason took the first turn, he leaned into it. Tanna didn't. In fact, she countered his movements by leaning the opposite way, even loosening her grip. Jason clutched her hands and pulled her tight.

"Stop fighting it," he said.

He took another corner, and again she instinctively went the other way. This time he yanked her arm hard in the direction she needed to lean.

"When I move, you move with me," he said.

At the next curve, Tanna leaned along with him. "Good. Very good." He reached down and squeezed her hand.

Ahead, two motorcyclists were dismounting from their cycles in front of a bar. Seeing an opportunity, Jason timed it so that he passed them just as one of the riders had removed his helmet. Jason snatched it right from the unsuspecting rider's hand, then yelled his apologies while speeding away.

"Happy?" he shouted to Tanna as he put the helmet over his head.

She squeezed his hand, and Jason suspected she had a reluctant smile hidden behind her visor.

CHAPTER 53

Roman stood beside the hospital bed and watched Sol's chest rise and lower with each labored breath. He was happy for the old man. After years of struggling, it would finally be over.

"I guess it's time," Roman said over the sound of the chirping medical monitor.

He moved his gaze from a bouquet of flowers to the wastebasket. Inside were a few bloody tissues, an empty gauze wrapper, some colorful pills, two worn baseball cards.

Someone had been here.

Roman yanked back the hospital blanket and spotted it right away—a fresh bandage on the back of Sol's right hand. He peeled off the dressing and examined the shallow incision.

It was them. Tanna and Jason. It had to be.

Roman couldn't help but shake his head and chuckle. Even with everyone on their tail, they had somehow stayed one step ahead. But now he had to hurry.

He pulled out a small black case with two preloaded

syringes inside. One had a red cap and the other green. He removed the green cap and inserted the needle into the injection port on the IV line. Then he rammed the plunger home. The fluid began its short journey through the plastic tube and into Sol's waiting vein. From there, his blood would carry it to his heart.

Roman stepped over to the monitoring station and ran his fingers across the small louvers at the back that brought in fresh air and expelled excess heat. He hefted the power cord in his hand and tugged on it to test the connection to the wall outlet.

When it made its first set of erratic beeps, Roman waited. After a moment, Sol's heartbeat returned to normal.

"Come on, old man. What are you waiting for?"

Two quick beeps, then silence.

Four rapid beeps followed by a long pause.

"About damn time," Roman said. He pulled the red cap off the other syringe.

The monitor erupted in flashing lights and piercing sounds. Roman slid the needle all the way through one of the thin louvered openings, then unloaded the contents into the inner workings of the machine. It popped and sparked, sending out wisps of white smoke that smelled of charged electricity. The monitor died and the room fell silent.

Sol's eyes fluttered.

"What the hell is going on in here?" a female voice shouted.

Roman looked up to see a nurse standing just inside the door. Before she could react, he shot over to her and grabbed her arm.

"Get your hands off me."

"What's your name?"

"I'm calling security."

Sol's breathing became choppy and labored.

"No, you're not." Roman clenched his fingers tighter, digging them deep into her muscles. "You must not be paid very well."

"Stop it. Please."

"And such a hard job. Very unrewarding."

"Let go. You're hurting me."

"I'm *helping* you." Roman squeezed even tighter. "What's your name?"

"Amy. It's Amy."

"Okay, Amy. Did you see who was here earlier?"

"What?"

"In the room. Who was here?"

"I don't know. I just came on shift. I didn't see anyone, I swear."

He twisted her arm, inflicting even more pain. "You sure?"

"Yes." She was tearing up, and her voice cracked. "No one. Please."

Roman looked back at Sol. The old man's eyes opened and shut rapidly.

"Well then, Amy, today's your lucky day," Roman said. "Because you get to do me a favor."

CHAPTER 54

"You did great. See how easy that was?" Jason said.

Tanna glared at him. "You said that already."

"But it's true. You did great."

They were walking side by side across an empty parking lot toward the rear of a squat tan corrugated metal building. They turned the corner and headed to the front.

"We got everything?" Jason asked.

She patted the black messenger bag slung over her shoulder. "I hope so."

Tanna's swollen joints and stabbing headache were now constant reminders that something was wrong with her. She suspected it had something to do with this place, with the work that went on here, but she wouldn't allow herself to think about that. Not yet.

They walked up the sidewalk and stopped in front of the glass double doors. On a flimsy plastic plaque were the words Modern Genetics Inc.

That name, etched in her mind, made her pause. A name that created so many problems and caused so much death. A simple name on an ordinary building with unimaginable consequences.

Tanna put out her hand.

"Hard through the turns," Jason said. He handed her one of the two bricks he had picked up from the deserted lot where they'd parked the motorcycle.

Tanna ran her fingers over the chipped edges. She calmed her nerves. Gathered her strength.

"Fuck you," she roared and launched the brick with every ounce of energy she could muster.

It hit the door dead center. The glass cracked and spiderwebbed out from the point of impact, almost reaching the far corners. But it didn't break.

Floodlights came on. An alarm buzzed somewhere deep in the building.

Jason hurled his brick at the exact same spot. The force knocked the pane free from the frame, leaving a gaping hole into the lobby.

"Don't even think of moving," said a voice behind them.

Before Tanna could spin around, a security officer appeared in the lobby ahead of them. He paused to inspect the damage to the door, his feet crunching over the fallen glass as he stepped through the opening.

He nodded at Jason and Tanna as if they were expected, then pointed to cameras mounted on the building. "Night vision. With thermal scanners. Did you think you could surprise us?"

Tanna watched as he wrapped his hand around the pistol in his holster. "We, uh, we just want to talk," she sputtered.

"Really? Then talk."

"We need to talk to Dr. Emmerson."

"I don't know who that is."

"Dr. Craig Emmerson. He runs this place and—"

"Don't know him. Now, here's what I'd like to talk about. You two are trespassing on private property. And you were apprehended in the act of breaking and entering." He pulled his pistol free and pointed it directly at her. "In fact, you attacked us. And then I shot you in self-defense."

Though she expected fear, blistering anger rushed through her instead. She let it invade every inch of her body.

Tanna balled her fists.

Left. Right. Inhale.

She stared into the barrel of the man's weapon. Round and smooth. Her eyes couldn't penetrate the darkness to the deadly bullet buried within, but it was there, waiting for her.

She leaned forward, closing the gap, making sure it pointed to the middle of her forehead.

Left. Right. Exhale.

"You're an idiot," she said. "We know all about your illegal work with gene therapy and synthetic XNA. We know about your experimental tests on people without their knowledge, and about your plan to move your operation to international waters so you can continue your work without oversight. Now you have to wonder, what else do we know? And who have we told? Kill us, and you'll never find out. More important, your bosses will never find out. And how's that going to make you look? Think it through. You have one chance to make the right decision here. Just one. We're here to make a deal. Don't screw it up."

She remained still, watching the man's finger on the trigger.

"Oh, Christ, don't buy that shit," a guard said from behind them. "Just drop them so we can be done with this."

But the man in front of her, apparently the one in charge, paused. "What's your deal?"

"Not with you. Get Emmerson."

For a long moment no one moved. Then the security officer lowered his weapon.

"Make the call," he said.

"Are you crazy?" said the guard behind them.

"Just do it!" the man shouted. He turned to Tanna and Jason. "Come with me."

"No." Tanna stood firm. "We're not going anywhere. Bring him here."

The officer laughed. "Young lady, you may think you've got some leverage, but trust me, you're hanging on by a thin fucking thread. Right now you're on my property and in my world, so when I tell you you're coming with me, you're coming with me."

"And if we don't?" Tanna asked.

"Then you've given me all the reason I need. The boss will understand."

Tanna glanced at Jason. They both looked over their shoulders. Not one but now two guards had moved up right behind them.

"This way," the lead guard said with a smirk.

He led them through the broken door and into the lobby. He walked up to a door on the other side—this one far more secure than the cheap glass doors leading outside—entered a passcode, and guided them into a long hallway.

As soon as the door slammed shut behind them, the

guards attacked with lightning quickness. Tanna felt her legs swept from under her and saw Jason getting tackled at the same moment. In the blink of an eye they both had guards on top of them, pulling their arms behind them and driving their heads into the floor.

"What are you doing?" Tanna cried, struggling.

"Tanna, don't. Just let them—"

A knee came down hard in the middle of Jason's back and was followed by a right fist to his jaw. The guards then pulled out plastic cable ties and bound Tanna's and Jason's hands behind their backs.

"Check it," said the lead officer.

One of the guards rummaged through Tanna's messenger bag. "It's empty."

The man looked down at Tanna and Jason. "Did you really think you could *negotiate* your way out of this? You can't even imagine what they're going to do to you. In a couple of hours, you'll be wishing we shot you."

The guards hefted them roughly to their feet, then walked them through a confusing maze of intersecting hallways. At last they opened the door to an office, shoved their two prisoners inside, and slammed the door behind them.

From the hallway came the voice of the lead guard. "Stay here. If they try anything, do whatever you want." His footsteps faded.

Tanna looked around in silence. Their new prison was an ordinary office, equipped with a desk, phone, and two chairs. No windows. No way to escape.

She started to say something when Jason cut her off with a shake of his head. He came close and whispered in her ear. "Camera in the ceiling. Top right. Maybe a microphone too." He led her behind the desk where they knelt down. "Hopefully this will block their view."

"Your jaw is swelling."

"Yeah, he got me good. Move this way."

They turned back to back, and Jason went to work on her cable tie. He dug at her clasp, and after several attempts, it released. "Leave it on so they see it on. Just keep it loose so you can get out when you need to."

"How did you know how to do that?" she asked.

"Long story. Here, help me with mine. Grab the loose end and bend it back while you pull on it slightly."

Tanna did that.

"Now dig your fingernail in right where the teeth catch."

She tried but only managed to tighten it more. When she attempted it again, she was able to grab the locking teeth with her fingernail and release the cable tie.

When they spun around to face each other, she planted a kiss on his swelling jaw.

"Ow."

"Sorry."

"It's okay." He kissed her back.

"So we're in."

"We're in," he repeated. "Now we just need Perry to come through. Because if he doesn't . . ."

Tanna nodded. She knew exactly what that meant, and it wasn't good. Relying on Perry to help them was a risk she didn't want to take. But she didn't have a choice. They had run out of time. And options.

Appearing as if they were still bound, they moved out into the middle of the office in direct view of the camera.

She leaned her body up against his. "Fast down the straightaways."

CHAPTER 55

Craig looked down from his home to the city below. From up here, he couldn't see the dirt and disease that ran rampant through the streets, flooding the gutters until the ooze backed up and rolled over the sidewalks in never-ending waves. From where he stood, the world looked clean, untainted. And that was fine with him.

He turned back to face the detective. "I wouldn't have any idea," he replied.

Detective Duane Lewis eased back into the corner of the sofa, pushing his pestilence into the creases of the leather. "For the record, then: you don't have any clue, none at all, why these two fugitives would try to contact your ex-partner, Dr. Solomon Cabral."

Craig's cell phone rang from the other room.

"If you need to get that . . ." Lewis said.

"I do, but you're leaving."

"It's okay. I'll wait."

The phone rang again.

"Show yourself out, Detective, or I'll have security come

help you out." Craig walked back into his office. "What?" he shouted into the phone as he answered.

"We have them," Lauren said from the other end of the line. "The two we've been looking for. In the lab. Showed up at the front door and rang the bell."

The realization sank in. "Then it's over."

"No. They have information from an old friend of yours."

"Bullshit!" Craig yelled, too loudly. He looked back into the living room and saw Lewis still milling around.

"Did you know they were in contact with him?"

"Seems to be the question of the hour."

"Is that what the detective there wants to know?"

Craig stopped short. "You're having me watched?"

"Waiting for you to step on your dick."

"Too bad. This ends now."

"No. They already know about the relocation. What else do they know? Nobody touches them until I find out everything. Maybe it's time I send my squad down there to take care of it."

"Your squad screwed everything up from the moment they got involved. My people will handle this."

"Your security officers at the lab called *me*, Craig. Not you. What does that tell you about your people?"

Lauren hung up without giving Craig a chance to respond.

Seething with anger, Craig stormed into the empty living room to demand the detective leave, only to find the front door already shutting behind the man. Robbed of his opportunity to vent his rage, Craig flung his phone at the wall. It fell to the ground in shattered pieces.

When he'd gathered himself, he grabbed his keys. He would go to the lab himself and fix the problem for good—before someone else could screw it up again.

CHAPTER 56

Eric white-knuckled the steering wheel. With the van's headlights turned off, he couldn't see where he was headed and feared running the damn thing off the road at any moment. Sure enough, the right front tire ground against the curb with a wretched jolt. Eric overcorrected, sending the van across the street.

"Damn it," he said as he plowed into the opposite side. "Slow down."

Ever since leaving the girl behind, he'd half-expected for someone to gun him down at any moment. But he'd made it back to the van. It didn't really have what he needed—everything had happened so fast after Sol's call—but it would have to do.

He eased the vehicle through the unlit roads of the South San Francisco industrial park, a bulky brown shark slipping through the night. As he came over the top of a slight ridge, he stopped and parked. And there it was, down below. Modern Genetics. He had told himself that he would never go back, never lay his eyes on that goddamn building again. But here he was.

He pulled out his digital camera and aimed it at the building, still several hundred yards away. Zooming in, he waited as it focused on the front door. That was when he saw the shattered glass.

"Holy shit." Something had already happened.

And it was still happening. As he watched, a figure entered the frame. It was Dr. Emmerson, approaching the building, pausing at the entrance to look at the destruction, and then marching inside.

Eric rushed into the van's cargo area. On one side, multiple server racks were pushed up against the wall. The first set of high-capacity drives were labeled with bright red stickers, the second with yellow, and the third with green. On the other side of the van, an array of battery backup units bottomed out the truck's suspension.

He flipped the switch on the batteries. The indicator read twenty percent.

Not enough. Not nearly enough.

He hadn't had a chance to charge them after getting them out of storage, and the van didn't have a working outlet connection.

"Come on, be here." Eric dumped over a large plastic crate. Rummaging through coiled cords and broken electrical motors, he found what he was looking for. Pulling the grime-encased power inverter from the pile, along with a set of jumper cables, he hurried to the front of the van and opened the hood. He connected the red and black clips to the van's battery terminal and then ran the wire through the driver's side window and into the back. The inverter would convert the DC power of the battery to regular household AC current so he could plug in the charging stations. Once he'd checked his connections, he started the engine, plugged in the battery units, and flipped the switch.

A tiny popping noise went off like a bomb inside the enclosed van.

"Fuuuuuuck!"

A fuse had blown, and he didn't have a replacement.

Think.

Eric stripped a piece of wire and used it to override the safety feature in place of the fuse. He unplugged all the battery units except one to lighten the load, hoping it would be enough. If not, it'd be over in an instant, punctuated by arcing electricity and showering sparks.

But this time the unit started in silence.

He would need to charge one at a time and keep rotating them as they drained. It was slow, but safer. And it had to work. Because if it didn't, he'd be dead.

Making a quick sign of the cross, he turned on the servers. The hard drives lit up and started spinning, and he breathed a sigh of relief.

Finally, he plugged in his laptop and adjusted the settings for his location. Then he stood back and tapped his foot in anticipation.

He was ready.

CHAPTER 57

Tanna's immune system threw everything it had at the virus, and the war raging inside her body left devastation in its wake. Abraded nerves, hammering chills, and unrelenting lethargy.

And still nothing was finished. Viruses hunted everywhere for weak spots to exploit, continually probing for a fatal flaw they could take advantage of, and Tanna's immune system responded by calling for B-cells to join the fray. Arriving to find a wasteland of ruptured cells and inflamed tissue, the B-cells scoured the battlefield, picking up and ingesting the broken and discarded pieces of virus carcasses. In so doing, they memorized the virus's genetic code and created antibody receptors that attracted the invaders like a magnet. These receptors would latch on to the viruses, clumping them together in large groups, making it easier for the macrophages to come along and eat them en masse.

Once they were armed with the exact knowledge of what they were looking for, the B-cells replicated themselves at an impressive rate, releasing thousands upon thousands of antibody receptors that flooded Tanna's body. The counterattack was devastating to the virus invaders. Their time was running out.

But all they needed was one more cell to infect. One more chance to start the process over. One more opportunity to destroy Tanna's body in the process.

And they had a plan to do just that.

CHAPTER 58

Tanna didn't react when Dr. Emmerson entered the room. She didn't want to give him the satisfaction. The man looked her up and down, then did the same with Jason.

"That's it? You're the ones who have been making my life a goddamn mess? All this effort for you two?"

Emmerson was shorter than she would have thought, and generally . . . unremarkable. Not the fang-filing sociopath or mad scientist she had somehow envisioned and hoped he would be. Just a man. Flesh and bone.

"You could have stopped at any time," she said.

"And let you destroy something I've worked my entire life to create?"

"What about all the lives *you've* destroyed?"

"Sacrifices are part of the process." Emmerson stood tall. "I'm giving the world the greatest gift it's ever known."

"While you take the glory."

"This coming from a postpubescent med student and a used-up junkie. You couldn't comprehend the tiniest bit of what goes on here."

"We have a good idea."

"Oh, that's right, you've been talking to my old friend Solomon. And he filled your head with wild fantasies of virus modification, disease eradication, and the ability to turn back time. Maybe he even told you that I'm creating genetically pure strands of XNA to build novel life forms from thin air. Or that I plan to pick up this entire lab and move it into the middle of the ocean somewhere."

Emmerson shook his head. "What I'm sure he didn't tell you is that he suffers from vascular dementia. That's his dirty little secret. His mind is failing, and everything he told you is just a twisted figment of his imagination. I'm sure you thought you could accomplish something by coming here, but I'm sorry to tell you, you won't. There's no deal to be made."

At that moment the door flew open, and Roman stormed in. He grabbed Jason by the neck and shoved him against the wall. "Told you I'd see you again, you fuck."

Jason smirked. "A real accomplishment, seeing as I had to come to you."

Roman tightened his grip around Jason's throat. "Your mistake. You came all this way to die here in my hands."

"Enough," Emmerson snapped. "Whatever this is can wait until the issue with Solomon is finished."

"It's already done," Roman said. "I was just at the hospital."

A shuddering gasp left Tanna's body.

Sol is dead.

She forced herself to blink away the building tears.

But Emmerson gave a smile of relief. And pleasure.

"Good riddance," he said.

He turned his gaze on Tanna. "Your last hope, Miss Christensen. Gone forever. How does it feel to have lost everything?"

Tanna let the room grow quiet. She listened past the throbbing in her ears, ignored her raspy wheezing, and searched for the answer. But the silence was deafening. She scrambled for the words that would keep him talking. Anything to delay him. Before it became too late.

"You're lying," she said. "He wasn't delusional, and he wasn't sick. You are. You're creating God knows what for your own vile purposes."

Emmerson chuckled, then addressed Roman. "Find out what the old man told them, and who else they've shared it with. Start with the girl. See what she says with a few hundred milligrams of amobarbital and sodium thiopental in her system. But don't overdo it. I want her to feel what's happening to her."

"Looking forward to it," Roman replied.

Emmerson reached over to Tanna as if he was about to place the tips of his fingers on her cheek, but he stopped just short. "Tell me, Miss Christensen, what did you want to be when you grew up? A doctor, yes? You wanted to cure disease? Help people? Make a difference in their lives?"

Tanna could sense the groping tentacles of his near-touch.

"We're the same, you and I," he intoned.

"I'm nothing like you," Tanna growled. She slid her right hand out of the plastic restraint and eyed the spots along his neck and jaw where she would strike. It would all be over the moment she hit him, but she was willing for it to end right then and there.

"You gave up everything you knew and trusted in the world to go to medical school," said Emmerson, "then threw it all away. Because you needed to do something special. I can see it in your tenacity. You have the strength to do whatever it takes. Very few of us have that."

"You're a monster," Tanna said.

"What would you have done to save your sister? Or your mother? How far would you have gone?"

That was when she heard it. Past the walls. Beyond the silence. In the distance, muffled shouts and yelling filtered through.

"But you couldn't save your sister, and your mother's time is coming ever closer. So you thought you would save the world instead. Or maybe just save yourself—from the frustration of powerlessness." Emmerson smiled, a cold smile, and looked her in the eye. "I'm no monster. I'm a savior. Just like you wanted to be."

A security guard stuck his head inside. "Sir, there's a situation."

"Handle it!" Emmerson commanded.

Now Tanna could clearly hear the commotion from somewhere outside. She hid her relief and forced herself to stillness.

"Sir, they need you in the control room right now," the guard pressed. "You too," he said to Roman.

Emmerson took a long last lingering gaze at Tanna before he stormed out the door. Roman poked Jason in the chest with a stiff finger and said, "Don't go anywhere."

He began to leave as well, then stopped in the doorway and turned to Tanna. "Too bad you weren't strong enough to finish what you started here. Because I won't make it quick for you like I did for your roommate. No, you're in for a world of hurt. God, how I envy you."

CHAPTER 59

As Craig marched down the corridor, Roman on his heels, the shouting grew louder. He made out the words "money, liars," and "police." He entered the control room and found his lead security officer barking orders into his radio. On the wall of monitors, several red lights flashed in the corners, indicating active motion sensors.

"What the hell is going on?" Craig demanded. The screens showed at least twenty or thirty people walking around outside the lab. "Who are these people?"

"Don't know, but more are coming." The guard pointed to a monitor overlooking the parking lot. Cars and motor-cycles were streaming in one after another.

"Has Lauren's squad shown up yet? I understand you called her instead of me."

"No, sir. That was not intentional. Someone changed the protocol list in the system without my knowledge. All outgoing calls got routed to her. When the alarm tripped, she got notified automatically."

"Traitors everywhere."

Craig watched the screens as people began to crowd around the front door. "Get them out of here."

"We're trying. But I'll need to call for reinforcement guards."

"I don't care. Beat them bloody if you have to."

"Best not to bring the police here if you can help it," Roman interjected.

By now about fifty people had stepped through the broken front door and crammed themselves into the lobby. Many were holding up cell phones to take video as three security guards argued with them. The crowd surged forward, and the guards backed toward the security entrance that led to the lab, making sure no one got past them.

Roman pointed to a figure on the screen. "That one there. Perry. He's a friend of the other two. They're behind this."

The crowd pitched, and people got pushed into the guards. At the rear of the mob, someone had torn apart a chair, and people were now using pieces of the wood frame as weapons. One guard reached for his pistol, ready to pull it free.

"This is about to get out of hand," Roman said with a smile.

"You're damn right it is." Craig charged out of the control room and ran down the hall. When he reached the lobby, he burst through the door and came in behind the three guards. The room was packed with lowlife junkies and vagrants. He could feel their filth invading his building, his lab, his space.

"Quiet," he yelled. "Everyone quiet!" No one paid attention. "Shut the hell up!" he screamed at the top of his lungs.

That seemed to silence people for a moment, but they soon replied with their own shouts.

"I want everyone out right now! Do you hear me? This is my property!"

The crowd made another push as the people outside tried to force their way in, but there was no more room.

Craig grabbed one of the security guards. "What do these people want?"

"They keep saying they want money," the guard told him. "Apparently someone went online and posted that we're conducting a study on hybrid pain medicine. They think the first four hundred people to show up will receive two thousand in cash and free meds."

"Ridiculous." Craig turned back to the crowd. "There's nothing here for you! We don't have any medication, and we're not giving you any money! Do you hear me? No medicine, no money. Now get the hell out!"

The crowd heaved forward. It now moved as one interconnected entity, concentrated, solid, and too massive to stop. The guards tightened ranks and held.

"Leave now or I call the police. Everyone goes to jail!" Craig yelled.

"Fuck you!" someone shouted back.

The one named Perry shoved his way to the front. "Go ahead. Call the police," he hollered. "You promised us medicine and money. We're getting it one way or another." He turned to the crowd. "Isn't that right?"

The rioters screamed back their approval.

"So call the police," Perry said. "Unless you've got something to hide back there you don't want them to see."

Perry turned back to the crowd and whipped up a chant. "Money! Meds! Money! Meds! Money! Meds!"

Soon the building practically shook with the raucous chant.

"Shoot them! All of them!" Craig shouted.

The guards looked at each other and hesitated.

"Damn it." Craig reached down, unholstered a guard's pistol, and leveled it at the crowd.

CHAPTER 60

"I could have ripped his head off and he never would have seen it coming," Jason whispered. "First chance I get, I end him."

Tanna half wished he had done it. She was still reeling from Roman's glib confession about killing her roommate. In that moment, she had wanted nothing more than to beat him to a bloody pulp herself. Watch his broken body convulse on the floor as he drew a last breath through shattered ribs and a punctured lung. It was one thing to suspect that he had murdered Krystal, and quite another to have him throw the admission in her face.

"Next time," she said. "We need patience now."

"I know. But if they so much as lay a finger on you, that's it."

"Deal," Tanna told him, and she meant it. She wanted to hurt these people. But once she opened that door, touched that part within her, things would never be the same. Because the thought of vengeance excited her, and that excitement scared the hell out of her.

She pretended to walk the floor but moved closer to the door and waited. In the distance she heard a muted chorus of booing and shouting. "Something's happening."

"It's about time," Jason said. "I thought they'd never get here."

"We need to hurry."

They slid their hands out of the restraints. She gave hers to Jason, took a deep breath, slipped the black messenger bag over her shoulder, and placed her fingers around the door handle. Then she said a prayer for the third time in less than a week.

Jason pressed himself against the wall next to the door. He wiped his slick hands on his jeans, then readied the plastic straps. He looked at her and nodded.

Tanna pulled the door open and took a quick step into the hallway.

One guard stood outside. He spun, holding his pistol out in front of him with both hands. "Get back."

She stepped back into the office.

"Hands where I can see them," the guard said, still standing in the hall.

She put her hands up.

"Where's the other one? The guy?"

Tanna didn't let her eyes give anything away as she pointed to the spot behind the desk. "He's on the floor. He tried to get into the ceiling and fell. He's hurt and needs help."

The guard took a slight step forward and then stopped, the barrel of the weapon about to cross the door's threshold. He shifted his weight, tendons tightening and contracting.

And at that moment, Tanna knew he wasn't going to come in. He was about to call for backup.

Tanna's eyes darted to Jason, signaling him.

Jason leaped forward, gripping one of the plastic ties in his hand like a small lasso. He passed the loop over the end of the pistol and around the guard's hands. He yanked hard and the loop pulled tight, binding the guard's wrists together. The weapon fell free, and Jason tackled the man to the floor.

The guard screamed for backup, his legs kicking wildly.

"Grab his feet!" Jason yelled.

Tanna tried to, but when she came close, the man sent the heel of his boot into her face. Her head whiplashed backward and she bit her tongue. The sour taste of blood filled her mouth. She put all her strength and anger into a retaliatory kick intended to hit him in the stomach. It hit him square in the balls instead.

As the guard screamed in agony, Jason looped the remaining tie over his feet to bind his ankles.

But Tanna wasn't done. She raised her foot high and brought it down hard on the guard's abdomen. "How does that feel?" she shouted. She stomped down on him again. "Huh?" Again. "You like that?"

"Tanna!" Jason shouted.

She paused, then stomped down one more time on his rib cage for good measure.

The guard yelled for help, but Jason covered his mouth. He kicked off his shoe, peeled off a sock, and shoved it deep into the guard's mouth.

"Where's his gun?" he asked Tanna.

"I don't know. It fell somewhere."

Jason started to search under the desk, but Tanna peered out the door. "Just forget it. We need to go. Backup will be here any second."

Jason cursed and put on his shoe, and then ran out into the hallway. Tanna went right. Jason went left.

"This way," she called to him.

"You said the server room."

"We have to get to the lobby. We need their help."

"Dammit." Jason reversed his course to follow her. "This is a bad idea."

They ran down the hallway and turned the corner. But after they passed a row of offices and an open lab, Tanna felt lost. "Wait. It's not this way. Let me think."

But she didn't need to think. As soon as their own pounding footsteps stopped, she could easily hear the chant. "*Money, meds, money, meds.*" She took off toward the sound.

It led them to an armored steel door. She slammed her body against the emergency handle, and the door sprang open. Tanna fell forward into the lobby—only to find Dr. Emmerson in front of her, gun in hand. Three guards were with him, and they were surrounded by a raucous crowd.

Emmerson's eyes went wide and his face flushed with anger. "You."

"The money's in here!" Tanna screamed to the crowd. "All the meds you want! Come get it!"

Emmerson started to aim the pistol at her, but the crowd surged forward toward the open door and pushed him aside. Tanna was knocked to the ground by the bullrush and curled herself into a tight ball. Feet and knees slammed into her as people bolted past. She feared that she would be crushed under the assault.

Stand up!

She managed to stagger to her feet and immediately got swept up by the crowd and carried back into the lab's hallway.

People jumped, screamed, and ran into random rooms while breaking windows as they passed.

"Tanna!" Jason called from elsewhere in the flowing crowd.

Bracing herself against the rush, Tanna fought her way to him. Behind her, Dr. Emmerson and his guards were battling their way into the corridor. Shots rang out, followed by screams. One of the security guards was firing into the ceiling, threatening to kill anyone else who came down this hallway.

Tanna ran to the nearest door, but it was locked. Jason tried the next one, and it opened. "Here," he yelled and steered her inside. It was an overcrowded storage room. They wedged themselves between a deep freezer and shelving unit packed with glassware. Outside, they heard yelling over stampeding feet.

More shots, then silence.

"We need to get to Emmerson's private elevator," Tanna said. "It was in the information Eric gave me. That's the only way we're going to get down to the server room now."

Tanna cracked open the door and checked the corridor. She could hear shouts and breaking glass from other areas of the building, but this hallway was now quiet and still.

"You know where you're going?" Jason asked.

"No. But I memorized Eric's maps of the building the best I could."

She raced down the hall, took a left, then a right. Then she counted offices until she found it—the elevator.

She pressed the call button and the door opened. They stepped in, and Tanna hit the button for the fourth sub-basement floor. As the door closed, the distant noises of the crowd were silenced, and the car began its smooth descent.

Tanna had to put a hand on the wall to steady herself. Her nerves were raw and inflamed, and she felt as though she teetered on a knife's edge.

And then the lights cut out and the elevator came to a stop so suddenly that both Tanna and Jason crashed to the floor.

"What happened?" Tanna said.

"I think someone cut the power," Jason said. "They know where we are."

CHAPTER 61

The chaos played out across the monitors of the control room. Major sections of the first two levels had already been overrun, and although the guards had sealed off a few of the most crucial areas, others were being smashed and looted. More cars poured into the parking lot and more people forced their way in past the outnumbered guards.

Roman watched it all with a sick joy.

He clicked through several of the security cameras until he found them. Tanna and Jason, racing down a corridor.

"Got you," he said.

They slipped through an unlocked door into a storage closet. Roman didn't take his eyes off the screen. He waited. Before long they reemerged and ran down the hall, passing out of the camera's view.

"Come on, come on." Roman searched through several video feeds until he spotted them again. They were standing in front of Craig's private elevator.

Roman laughed. Tanna had shocked him at every turn. She had torn open this impenetrable fortress like a tin fucking can and let the ants pour in. A small bite here, a small bite there, until there'd be nothing left but a rotten carcass. He hadn't believed the woman was capable, and though he hated admitting he was wrong, he was. She had fucked things up good and rough.

Craig stormed into the control room. "What are you doing *here*?" he shouted.

Roman placed his body in front of the monitor to block Craig's view. "I'm not hired for crowd control."

"Those two are out there. They escaped. And that *is* your job."

"Are you sure? I would have seen them," Roman responded.

"I'm damn positive." Craig turned to the wall of videos and scowled. "Look at those disgusting, infested creatures. Polluting everything. Destroying everything. They'll pay for what they're doing. Everyone will pay. Lock them in." He reached over and pounded on the controls. "Then drag them out one by one if you have to."

Behind Craig's back, Roman grinned. Let the man be distracted by the crowd. Roman's quarry was right where he wanted them. They had taken the private elevator in the only direction it could go. Down.

CHAPTER 62

"You're getting heavy," Tanna said, adjusting her weight from one foot to the other. Jason stood on her shoulders with the upper half of his body extending through the ceiling of the elevator. She braced her back and did her best to keep him stable. "Anything yet?"

The elevator shaft was pitch black except for a handful of blinking LED lights at the top of the housing where Jason worked.

"There's still electricity," he told her. "But it runs through some sort of control switch. I have to figure out how to reset it or bypass it somehow."

"We're running out of time," Tanna said, shifting her weight again.

"Maybe if I had a socket set, screwdriver, wire cutters—"

"Quiet," she told him.

Voices seeped into the elevator from close by. Tanna couldn't make out the words, but she could tell they were security guards by the directness of their tone.

Jason jerked hard, and the quick motion nearly threw Tanna off balance.

"What are you doing?" she whispered.

"I need to get these wires out."

Tanna felt him yank again, and with a frightening crack of electricity even the LED lights went out, plunging them into complete darkness.

"What happened?"

"It's okay. If I splice the wires together, it might give us back control."

"Then hurry up. I can't hold you much longer."

"I just need to—"

Jason screamed, and a shower of sparks rained down on Tanna. But the motor up above chugged into action, revving and clunking into gear. The lights flickered on.

And the elevator car plunged into immediate free fall.

Tanna fell, and Jason tumbled down with her.

Some kind of emergency brakes must have kicked in, because the elevator stopped suddenly and the door opened. But it didn't lead to a way out. Through the opening Tanna could make out the bottom of an outer door and the top of another, with thick concrete in the middle.

"We're between floors," she said.

She tried to guess how far they had come before the elevator stopped, but she really had no idea. Still, when Jason started prying open the lower door, she stopped him.

"No. The upper one," she said.

"Are you sure?"

"Not really."

They both reached up and pulled at the door.

"There's got to be a trip latch or something," Jason said.

Tanna found a catch pin near the base, and she drew it back. "Got it."

Jason pushed the door open. He grabbed Tanna under the arms and lifted her up through the opening, then pulled himself out after. They found themselves in the eerie vacuum of a silent corridor cast in hard shadows from emergency lights.

"Is this the floor?" Jason asked.

"I think so." She led him forward. "Come on."

"Mary had three little lambs," she said as she passed three doors. "But right when she thought she had them all," she continued as she took a right down another corridor, "she realized she had two more left." They passed two more doors, and she turned to her left.

Before her was a reinforced steel door. "This has to be it," she said.

"You remember what to do?"

"Sort of."

Tanna had worked through Eric's rambling notes and had committed all his instructions to memory. Or at least, she hoped she had.

Here we go.

She waved her fingers over the security touch-screen panel on the wall, and it sprang to life. She entered the alpha-numeric password, then held her breath as she pressed ENTER.

The screen flashed red and went dark.

Her heart pumped red-hot panic through her body as she stared at the lifeless panel.

"What happened?" Jason asked.

"I don't know."

Tanna waved her fingers over the screen and it lit up again, her previous entry cleared.

"Maybe you mistyped the password. Try it again."

Tanna wrung her hands. "Another wrong entry locks us out."

"Tanna. You've got this." He put his hand over hers, guiding them back to the control pad. "Trust yourself."

She had just started to punch in the code again when Jason shoved her to the side and vaulted himself past her. A security guard had come around the corner, and Jason body-slammed him before the man could pull his gun from his holster.

"Go!" Jason screamed, struggling to keep the guard from reaching his weapon. "Open the door!"

"I'm not leaving you."

"Get in there."

But Tanna wouldn't abandon him. Not again.

Waiting for the right moment, she let loose a fierce kick at the guard's rib cage. She connected, but before she could pull back, the guard grabbed her foot, twisted his wrist, and jerked Tanna hard to the floor.

Jason grasped the man's hand and pulled back two fingers until they snapped. The guard screamed in pain and released his grip on Tanna's leg.

"Go!" Jason shouted.

Tanna jumped back to the control screen. She forced herself to concentrate, blocking out everything else. As the sound of fists hitting flesh faded in her ears, she entered the password. It was the words "Second Nature," but with characters and numbers replacing some of the letters. She had come to the last character when she stopped. She was doing something wrong. She knew it.

The "t" in Nature, her mind screamed.

That was it. The "t" had been replaced with the number seven.

She canceled out and raced to reenter the password. *5ec0ndN@7ur3!*

The screen flashed green, and she pulled the door open. "I got it!" she yelled as she stepped through. "Jason, come on!"

Jason held the guard's hands down and looked up at her. He smiled knowingly, then used his foot to slam the door shut with only her inside.

"Jason!" she cried. "Jason, what are you doing?"

She could still hear the struggle outside. And then she understood. If she didn't get this done, neither one of them would be safe. Ever again.

Tanna looked around. She was in a tiny security vestibule, like an airlock with another door directly opposite the first. On the wall next to it was a touch screen the size of a hand.

She pulled off her shoe and sock. There, tucked away between her big toe and second toe, were the USB flash drive from Eric and the microchip from Sol's hand, still wrapped in a piece of gauze.

One time only, Eric had told her. If this didn't work, there'd be no second chance.

She waved the microchip in front of the sensor. Nothing happened. Or at least nothing she could see.

"Please," Tanna whispered. She pressed a hand to the entrance. And when she felt the metal door sliding open under the tips of her fingers, she let herself exhale.

A cold blast of air hit her as she rushed through. Behind her, the door closed in silence.

"Oh God . . ."

She was in a room full of servers. That was expected. But it was nothing like the room Eric had diagrammed in his notes. Either he had it wrong or something had changed.

She stepped between the rows of server racks that shot down the center of the room, looking for something by which she could orient herself. She forced her eyes shut, recalling Eric's sketch from her memory, stretching her hands out to feel the servers.

Then she opened her eyes. Yes, the room was different from the sketch, but there were some similarities. There seemed to have been some additions since Eric was there last.

She followed her mental diagram to the proper server rack, then plugged the USB flash drive into an open port. The mini-LED light on the device blinked rapidly.

Eric had told her to wait until it stopped blinking before she could remove any of the drives. If she didn't, all the data would be destroyed. But it was taking too long. Her thoughts went to Jason in the hallway.

Still blinking.

Fighting the urge to go back and help him, she pounded a fist against her thigh.

Still blinking.

"Come on!" she shouted at the small device.

The sound of a gunshot pushed through the wall like a

punch to her chest. Tanna listened for Jason's voice—or for the guard's.

There was nothing but silence from the hallway.

She turned to leave the room but stopped herself. Envisioning Jason shot and dying in a pool of blood, she knew she would never get back inside this room. They would lose everything they had worked for.

"Jason," she said in a voice she hoped would reach the corridor. "Can you hear me?"

No response.

You promised him you wouldn't do this. That you'd be strong.

Her feet moved her closer to the exit.

So be fucking strong!

She turned to look at the racks of servers and the blinking light from the small USB device. Then she ran back and placed her hands on the specific hard drives Eric had told her to remove. She was ready. If only that damn light would finish blinking.

"The hell with it."

She unclasped the hard drives, each smaller than a paperback book, and ripped them out of the rack. Her mind raced as she worked to remember the ones she needed.

Unclip, pull. Unclip, pull. Unclip, pull.

It was a blur of slim black boxes. Her hands did the work while her thoughts focused on Jason. By the time she'd gotten everything Eric had told her to get—or so she hoped—the messenger bag was heavy and nearly overflowing.

She hurried back to the security vestibule. Once the interior door closed, she pushed open the outer door and peered into the hallway.

Jason was standing over the motionless guard.

"You're okay." She ran out and hugged him. "I heard a gunshot."

"I think he's still breathing," Jason said. "The shot went wild. I must have just knocked him out."

Tanna bent down and placed her fingers along the guard's neck. She felt a pulse and nodded.

"Did you get everything?" Jason motioned to the messenger bag.

She smiled. "I got it."

"So let's get the hell out of here. Which way?"

"We can't go back the way we came. Have to take the main elevator."

"Might be guarded."

"No choice." Tanna adjusted the messenger bag over her shoulder, and they took off down the corridor.

CHAPTER 63

Jason pushed the call button for the main elevator. "What's the plan?" he asked.

Tanna raised her hands. "You're asking me?"

"You don't have a plan?"

"I figured you did."

"I don't."

"Then why did you hit the button?" she asked.

"Because I thought you had a plan."

The elevator dinged to announce its arrival. Jason and Tanna looked at each other and pressed themselves tightly against the wall on either side of the doors.

The elevator opened, and three men charged out into the hallway.

Jason released a fierce shout and rushed them.

But then everyone stopped in their tracks.

It was Perry, flanked by two friends.

"Holy shit. I found you." Perry grabbed Jason around the shoulders and hugged Tanna with his other arm.

"Perry. Thank God," she said.

"We did good, didn't we?" Perry said with a grin.

"Amazing. But we have to go now."

"Screw that. We're storming the castle here."

"And now we have to leave," Jason said firmly and corralled them back onto the elevator. He hit the button for the ground floor, and as the doors began closing, a figure came charging at them.

Roman.

Perry lunged forward to stop the doors from shutting, but Tanna and Jason both shouted and grabbed his arms.

"What are you doing?" Jason said.

"I'm going to kill that dude. That's the fucker from the bar who gave me the cheap shot." Then Perry shouted through the crack between the closing doors, "Hear that, asshole? I'm coming back for you. This ain't over."

The elevator started to ascend, and Tanna fell against the elevator wall, fighting for oxygen.

"You got what you needed?" Perry asked.

"Right here." Tanna patted the messenger bag loaded with drives.

"What's going on up there?" Jason asked.

"Absolute mayhem. It's beautiful. I sent that info out to some real tweekers. They'd run over their mother for money and free meds. They'll get it one way or another."

"Can we find a way out?"

"Oh yeah, no problem. The place is a shitstorm. I can walk you right out the front and no one will notice."

When the elevator doors opened, Perry led the way. The hallway was littered with broken glass, but the place was silent.

"Where's the mayhem?" Tanna whispered.

Perry frowned. "Looks like they got bounced. What do you think, J-Bird? You want to go full frontal on this one?"

"Perry. They're playing for keeps here," Jason told him.

"Yeah, so are we."

Perry charged down the hall, giving the others no choice but to follow his lead. When they reached an intersecting hallway, Tanna shouted for them to go right.

They rounded the corner, and two guards came running straight at them. Perry knocked the first one over with a forearm to the face while Perry's two friends drove the other against the wall. They hit him with a flurry of knees and boots to the midsection that left him struggling to breathe.

"Take that, assholes," Perry said as he ran ahead.

They were getting close to the security door leading to the lobby when they ran into trouble. Six guards. They smiled when they saw Perry and his group.

"Well, what do we have here?" one said.

At almost the same moment, screaming and yelling came from somewhere behind Tanna. She grabbed Perry by the arm. "Hear that?"

He stopped and listened. Then grinned. "It's the god-damn cavalry," he said.

He shouted. "Money, meds! Money, meds!"

The chant was returned, and a crowd of people came around the corner, tearing toward them. Tanna, Jason, Perry, and Perry's two friends were now stuck in the middle, with both groups closing in at full speed.

The guards reached them first. Perry threw a body block but got thrown down. His friends joined the melee, and

Jason pulled Tanna behind him. The guards ripped at her messenger bag, but she clutched it in her arms and wouldn't let go.

The other group arrived and attacked, and it was all-out war. Rioters punching guards, guards beating rioters. The frenzy gave Tanna and Jason the opening she needed.

"Let's go," she whispered in Jason's ear. She grabbed his arm and slipped around the edge of the fight. As soon as they were free, they ran.

The corridor ahead was filled with smoke. Tanna heard footsteps pursuing them as they plunged into the thick gray vapor. She saw the security door through the haze and rushed through, bursting into the lobby. Small fires were burning here and there, and rioters were tearing the furniture to pieces to feed the flames. At the sight of Jason and Tanna, the place erupted in excited shouts, and when some of the guards burst through the door after them, the mob converged on the pursuers.

Tanna and Jason sprinted across the lobby and through the broken front door into the parking lot.

Only to stop short.

Black SUVs surrounded them.

They were trapped.

CHAPTER 64

Craig pulled pill bottle after pill bottle from his office credenza. Empty. Empty. All of them fucking empty.

He howled and marched across the hall to his private elevator.

It was dead.

"Of course."

Making his way to the front of the building, he trudged over scattered debris. Within the rubble he spotted part of a broken micropipette used for delivering an exact amount of liquids. He picked it up, remembering the first time he'd handled one just like it. After completing his first year of Harvard Medical School, he'd received an internship at SMDI Bio. They only picked one student a year, and everyone else thought it was such a great honor to get it. Not Craig. He expected it. And it didn't take long to establish himself at SMDI. The research in biomolecular engineering offered endless opportunities to make a name for himself. And it all started from working with a pipette similar to the one he now clutched in his hand.

"Sonofabitch!" The realization ripped through him, and he took off running.

Skidding to a halt inside the control room, he pushed the pipette under the nose of the officer on duty. "Do you know what this is?" he shouted. "Do you have any clue? It's used to dispense a precise amount of fluid. But do you know why it's significant? This comes from a lab on the third floor. How the hell did they get down there?"

The officer nodded sheepishly. "They've infiltrated several floors, sir."

"How many?"

"I'm not sure. Controls are still out in some areas."

Rage blackened Craig's vision. "I want them gone. Get everybody out!"

"I've already sent crews down for a manual sweep, sir."

On one of the monitors, Craig saw two figures run down a hallway. Almost immediately they disappeared into a haze of smoke, but it was them. He knew it.

"There!" he screamed. "Right there."

The security officer dialed up an exterior shot of the front door. "Here." He pointed to Tanna and Jason running out of the building. "Don't worry, sir. Reinforcements just arrived." He shouted a command into his microphone. "Nobody leaves the outside perimeter. Lock it down now."

"Go get them!" Craig yelled.

As the officer raced out, Craig took over in the control center. The scene in the parking lot spiraled into pandemonium as guards clashed with rioters. Some asshole rammed his car into an SUV while trying to escape.

He reversed the video feed to the point at which Tanna

and Jason first fled the building. There was a black messenger bag slung over Tanna's shoulder, and he zoomed in on it.

"God damn it!"

He ran out of the room, down the hall, and into the lobby. The reinforcements had finally cleared the space of all rioters, and outside, the mob had been herded to a spot in the center of the parking lot. Presumably Tanna and Jason were in the mix.

Except not everyone had been captured. Some were running off on foot. Shots were fired, and an SUV pulled out in pursuit.

Craig stormed out through the front door just as the guard from the control room came to meet him. "No sign of them yet," he said.

"They're here, and they took something from the lab. I need to know what it is."

"Yes, sir. Also, police are on their way."

"Then you'd better find those two before they arrive."

Roman came out of the building behind them.

"And where have you been?" Craig spat. "This is your fault. If you had done what I asked, we wouldn't be in this mess."

"They stole hard drives," Roman said.

"That's impossible. There's no way they could have gotten in there."

Roman opened his hand. Cupped in his palm was a microchip sitting on a bloodstained piece of gauze.

Craig stared at the chip. It could have only come from one place. His mentor. His partner. The one person who knew best how to damage him. And that meant they must have known exactly what drives to take in order to prove their innocence—and his guilt.

Now everything he had ever achieved, his life's work, his glorious future . . . all of it was in the hands of those two.

"That—that can't happen," Craig said. "It can't."

His voice sounded like it spoke from somewhere outside himself. He felt as though he was hovering above his body, looking down, able to pick out details in wonderfully sharp focus.

The smell of ash and burnt fabric wafting across from the lobby.

Guards rushing in and out of the building.

Roman standing there holding the microchip.

At that moment, something snapped deep inside him. Never to be fixed again. His world disintegrated, burying him under a crushing realization that drove out every ounce of anger, filling him with a treacherous black void instead.

"I have to get those hard drives back," he said, the words devoid of emotion. "That's all that matters now."

Craig took an aimless step into the parking lot when the air bubbled with the distinctive rumble of a motorcycle. He looked up, and there, on the dark horizon, he could just make two riders leaving the industrial park.

"Get drivers on the road," he instructed. "As many as you can."

He ran to the closest SUV and climbed inside. The keys were in the ignition. He started the engine and roared off after them.

CHAPTER 65

Jason pegged the motorcycle's throttle as far open as it would go, and Tanna shifted her weight behind him. The muscles of his inner thighs quivered as he clamped them tight against the body of the hurtling cycle. With the road racing past his wheels, he felt a calmness wash over him, a oneness with the machine beneath him. A feeling he had thought he'd never experience again after his accident.

The escape from the lab had been both easier and harder than he'd expected. Once they made it outside, they'd blended in with the people in the parking lot, and for a while there it looked like none of them would make it past the SUVs that had formed a barricade around the lot. But working with a handful of others, they edged their way around the perimeter, reached the rear of the building, then split off into the night. Tanna and Jason ran through the adjacent property and back to the open lot to where they had stashed the motorcycle. Jason didn't think he was going to make it—his legs revolted halfway through—but Tanna pushed him, and he wasn't going to let her down.

He was more than happy for the Modern Genetics building to be fading into the distance behind them. So much could have gone wrong—*should* have gone wrong—and yet somehow, they'd made it.

Now all they needed to do was get the information on the drives to the right people.

He looked over his shoulder to see an SUV on his tail. Possibly several of them. He worked the throttle but couldn't coax out any more speed.

The biting wind tore at his skin as they plunged through the darkness. They came up over a hill, passing a dark brown cargo van, and sailed through the air as they crested the rise. Tanna only half-stifled a scream, but Jason landed with smooth perfection.

He spotted a line of cars coming fast at him from a road on his left. The intersection wasn't far ahead, and he tried to calculate who would get there first, but it was too close to call. He considered finding another way, even slowing down and turning around, but that wasn't an option. He had to continue forward.

He leaned over the handlebars to cut down on the wind resistance, needing every advantage he could get.

The first of the cars would have reached the intersection before him, but instead it slowed. And that's when Jason understood: they weren't trying to cut him off. They wanted to run him over.

He pumped the brakes hard, and the motorcycle skidded sideways, whipping around with little control. The first car entered the intersection and swerved to hit him, but now overshot the collision.

Jason popped the clutch and gunned the throttle. The motorcycle leaped ahead, and he did what he could to guide it around the rear end of the vehicle. He didn't make it cleanly. The foot pedal tore into the car's bumper and the motorcycle jolted hard, but the bumper's pliable plastic couldn't hold up to the speed and steel of the bike. The bumper ripped away from the car's mounting brackets and fell to the ground, and Jason and Tanna blasted on ahead.

As Jason looked back, three cars turned in pursuit. Three more turned toward Modern Genetics. And the SUVs from the lab were still behind him, working to catch up. He wasn't quite sure how many were after him now, but he knew if he was going to slip the noose, he had to get out of the open.

CHAPTER 66

"Get up."

"Huh?" Duane responded, waking from a deep sleep.

"We need the room," said Deputy Chief Marcos, standing in the doorway and almost filling the frame.

"Oh. Yeah, no problem." Duane tried to rub some life into his eyes.

With nowhere else to go, he'd ended up in a back office at the San Francisco Police Department Headquarters.

"And clean up your mess before you leave."

Duane looked at the files he'd spread out over the desktop, many plastered with yellow sticky notes and his handwritten remarks. "Sure. Where do you want me to go?"

"Anywhere but here," Marcos said and walked out of the room.

Duane gathered up his things and followed the deputy chief into the main bullpen. The calm, reserved atmosphere of yesterday had now been replaced by a mad frenzy of activity.

"Whoa, what happened?"

"Problems at that lab you've been asking about. Modern

Genetics. Locals down there are responding to reports of a break-in. Shots have been fired."

"Someone broke into the lab?"

"More like a few hundred someones. We're trying to sort it out now."

"I want to help." Duane straightened up and ran a hand across the rough stubble on his face.

Marcos turned to him. "Help? Like when you went to interrogate Dr. Emmerson without my authorization? I said you could observe and assist, Detective, not run your own goddamn investigation."

"I'm sorry."

"You may not think it, but we have excellent detectives working right here."

"Emmerson is deep into this somehow. I just wanted to bring you something solid."

"And did you?"

Duane shook his head.

"Right. Go home, Detective. This isn't your case anymore." Marcos walked off.

Standing in the center of the swirling chaos, Duane deflated. He'd overstepped. And the truth was, the deputy chief had been right to cut him loose.

"He chew your ass?"

Duane turned to see who had spoken. He recognized the face. It was the detective who'd helped him at the convenience store.

"Didn't have to," Duane said. "I managed to screw things up all on my own."

"Well it's almost over now anyway. We got reports of

two people on a motorcycle hauling ass out of the lab with security on their tail. Every agency in four counties is on alert. Most of them ready to shoot on sight. Doesn't look like they'll make it."

"No," Duane said, his mind churning. "Doesn't seem so."

CHAPTER 67

Tanna's arms were the only things keeping her from falling off the motorcycle, but the razor-cold wind had numbed them to where she could barely feel them anymore. The world rushed by in a dizzying blur of raw speed. She tried to remember what Jason had told her about how to lean, how to be one with the bike, but the more she tried to help, the worse she did.

Jason yelled something to her, but she couldn't make out the words over the deafening roar of the engine.

They were on the freeway, flying along dangerously close to the left concrete divider with a car on their right. Jason blew through with what felt like less than an inch to spare on either side. Tanna turned her head to look back and saw the headlights of several vehicles still in pursuit, weaving around the slower traffic on the road.

Without warning, the motorcycle dipped and rolled hard to the right, pulling Tanna's breath from her body. At that moment she was sure they would fall over—just crash down into the road and get chewed up into bits of flesh and bone that would have to be picked out of the concrete for days.

Jason was pushing the bike hard across four lanes of traffic toward an off-ramp. Tanna couldn't figure out how he thought he could make it; the angle was too tight. Cars slammed on their brakes and blared their horns as the motorcycle cut in front of them.

"Now!" Jason yelled, throwing all his weight to the other side of the bike as he flipped the handlebars to the left. Tanna was slow to react, but she did her best to shift her weight with him. The left side of the motorcycle barely cleared the off-ramp divider, and Jason turned hard to keep it from overshooting.

Behind them, one of the cars didn't react fast enough and rear-ended another vehicle. But several SUVs made the exit and followed them down the off-ramp.

Jason blew through the red light at the bottom of the ramp. With quick turns, he weaved through the early-morning traffic of downtown San Francisco, maneuvering past a dump truck loaded with black dirt and splintered wood.

They passed along a tall chain-link fence encased in green fabric. A massive excavation was underway here, and signs proclaimed the site as the future home of a city center entertainment complex. The project extended for at least three blocks in both directions. Jason turned sharply and drove through a gate onto the construction site just as a truck was coming out.

A steep slope led down to a deep pit on one side, and heaping mounds of dirt were piled high on the other. Jason went around the mountains of dirt, past dormant bulldozers and backhoes, and stopped the motorcycle beneath an intertwined pile of rusted metal beams. He killed the engine, pulled off his helmet, and got off the bike. Tanna followed his lead.

"You okay?" he asked.

Tanna's hands were shaking, but she forced a smile. "I'm fine. See how easy that was?"

He wrapped her in his arms and whispered in her ear. "You're amazing. I don't know anyone else who could have done what you did."

As the adrenaline rush faded, her ravaging chills and exhaustion roared back with a vengeance. Her mind drifted to thoughts of a giant bed with velvety sheets and pillows so plush she could lose herself in them. She imagined a hot shower and room service. Coffee, croissants, fresh orange juice. And sleep. Endless sleep.

But the sound of a police helicopter circling high overhead put an end to such thoughts.

Jason frowned, then pointed to two black SUVs parked in front of the entrance gate. They were blocking all traffic in or out. "I was hoping they didn't see me turn. So much for that."

He climbed up into the tangle of bent metal beams for a better view. When he returned a moment later, she could read it on his face. "How bad?" she asked.

"Bad. Guards are crawling all over, and there are at least two SUVs still circling the perimeter. Probably more. Plus there's some of those paramilitary-looking assholes who attacked us at the restaurant. *And* the police."

"That's great," Tanna said.

"It is?"

"Yeah. We have the drives. We just need to get them to the police. Then everything will sort itself out."

"Maybe." Jason looked over the construction site. "Except those goons aren't about to let us just walk out and hand them over."

"Then we climb the fence. Get to the street."

Jason shook his head. "I'm in no condition. My legs are jelly and I'm working with one good arm. But I can distract them, and you can make it. You can save us both."

"I'm not leaving you again," Tanna said. She looked him directly in the eyes, letting him know she wasn't going to change her mind.

"Okay, then maybe we don't *climb* over the fence." He nodded toward the motorcycle. "Do you trust me?"

"I already told you—"

"No," he said, grabbing her by the shoulders. "The moment I start the engine, we become targets. So you need to trust me with everything you got. No matter what."

Tanna nodded. "I trust you. No matter what."

"Okay." Jason handed Tanna her helmet. "Remember, lean when I lean, move when I move. Stand when I stand and use your legs to absorb the shock. And never, ever let go. Remember that. Don't let go."

"I won't."

They got back on the motorcycle, and he pulled her hands tight around his waist.

"Don't let go," he repeated.

Tanna pressed her head down against his shoulder. Jason started the bike, popped the clutch, and threw open the throttle. The motorcycle rocketed forward with an explosion of sound, sending a giant rooster tail of loose dirt into the air.

CHAPTER 68

Craig scanned the construction site. Tanna and Jason were in there somewhere; he knew that. He just had to find them. After everything that had gone wrong, it could all still be fixed. Remove those two and get the hard drives back. The lab would continue to move on schedule. Any remaining loose ends would take care of themselves.

He grabbed a radio from his closest guard and spoke into it. "Where are you now?"

"Circling the perimeter," Roman responded through the handset.

"Get in and find them."

"Lauren's squad is out here too. And the police."

"I don't care. What we need is trapped in front of us. Do you hear me?"

"Understood."

Craig threw back the handset and ordered the guard to search the grounds.

"Wait," he shouted and stuck out his hand. The man unholstered his pistol and gave it to him. "Now go."

When the sound of the motorcycle ripped through the air, everyone scrambled toward the noise. Craig looked down at the weapon in his hand and slid the safety to the off position. In the end, it was always the same. He would have to take care of things himself.

CHAPTER 69

Jason barreled across the construction site, weaving around the mountains of dirt and piles of debris. The motorcycle was built for the streets, and driving on the loose ground felt like trying to push a Slinky over a sheet of ice.

He rode the bike hard along the outside edge of the open pit. Guards fired at him as he raced past, but they couldn't get a clean angle. When the motorcycle dipped down into a deep depression that threw Tanna backward, Jason did his best to reach around and pull her tight.

Ahead, a guard came over the top of a ridge and had a clear shot. Jason cranked the throttle. At the final possible moment, he wrenched the handlebars crosswise, threw himself and Tanna to the side, and drove the wheels into the top of the berm. The tires caught the last lip of dirt and destroyed the edge, sending the guard toppling over in a shower of rubble.

Jason eyed the gate but knew he couldn't get around the SUVs barricading the exit. Instead, he guided the motorcycle straight ahead and aimed it at a large pile of dense dirt near the fence. It wasn't ideal—the path leading up to it was short, and the bike was overloaded with two riders—but it would have to do.

As the ground beneath him became more compact, he picked up speed. The world outside his narrow path faded to a silent blur of motion. Jason rocked back and forth to feel the suspension of the motorcycle, the shimmy of the handlebars, the grip of the tires. He focused only on the ground in front of him, blocking out everything else.

When the front wheel hit the mound of dirt, it sank into the soil more than he'd wanted. The speed and force thrust it up the incline, but he hoped it hadn't lost too much momentum. Just past halfway up the slope, Jason stomped down and compressed the suspension. The motorcycle reached the crest, and he pulled hard on the front of the bike and released the tension. As he pushed himself off the seat, Tanna followed his lead, balancing on the foot pegs.

The wheels left the earth, and the bike rocketed into the air.

Peace. Tranquility. Harmony. Total connection with the world around him and the motorcycle beneath him. It had been so long since Jason had experienced it that he often wondered if he would feel it again. He wanted to let go of the handlebars and at least pull a no-hander, but a gust of wind pushed the bike sideways. He adjusted his body and straightened the angle.

As the fence passed beneath them, Jason heard gunshots, then felt impact vibrations in his hands. A bullet had hit the bike somewhere. He prayed Tanna wasn't hurt, but forced himself to concentrate on landing.

Several cars were parked on the street in front of him. Jason fought to correct the descent, but they couldn't be avoided. *Fuck 'em*, he thought as he aimed for a Mercedes. If he was going to crash, at least he wanted to do it with a little style.

The motorcycle barely missed the hood of the vehicle, and the wheels took the full weight of the bike as it hit pavement. Jason tried to use his legs to lessen the impact for Tanna, but they slammed down hard on the frame, sending shooting pain through Jason's hips and up his spine. The front of the bike absorbed tremendous force, and he did his best to fight the flex and wobble to keep it steady as it reeled.

"Tanna!" he shouted. "You okay?"

"I'm okay."

She squeezed his chest, and he let himself breathe again.

Two of the black SUVs pulled away from the barricade to pursue. As soon as the motorcycle settled down and straightened out, Jason opened the throttle, but the bike began to vibrate and shake. He couldn't control it. The front wheel slammed back and forth against the fork, and it took all the strength left in his arms to keep the motorcycle steady. He had to slow down.

With the bike damaged, he knew he couldn't outrun the SUVs. He turned off and tried to disappear onto the city streets, then pointed the bike north to find someplace safe, or at least public. He decided to aim for the wharf at the edge of the city.

He didn't make it far before a car filled with the paramilitary goons rolled into their path. Jason slammed on the brakes and started to turn the motorcycle around, but an SUV came up behind them, blocking any retreat.

"We're not going to make it," he said over the gurgling engine.

"There." Tanna pointed to a narrow walkway between apartment buildings.

Jason cranked the throttle and took the escape route. It emptied into the complex's parking lot and an open road.

Overhead, a police helicopter roared into view.

"Wave," Tanna yelled and threw an arm in the air.

Jason let go with one hand and did the same.

Then he looked back and saw the vehicles closing in on them once more.

When he spotted an on-ramp to the freeway, he took it. He wanted to keep everyone off his tail long enough for the helicopter to see them. But the bike was even more challenging on the freeway. The front shook and banged as he tried to cut between lanes.

They approached the entrance to the Golden Gate Bridge. Jason rushed through the electronic toll lanes and onto the bridge deck. The early sun had burned off the gray sky, and under normal circumstances, it would have been a spectacular morning, but Jason's focus was on the front of the motorcycle. He watched as one side of the fork twisted violently and spit fluid from an open gash in the metal tubing. It wouldn't hold.

"Jump off," he yelled.

"What?"

"Let go!"

"You said *never* let go!"

Jason hit the brakes and tried to rip Tanna's arms free.

But it was too late. The front fork gave way. The bike pitched forward.

Jason used the last of his strength to push her off, then himself, just as the motorcycle went tumbling through the air.

Tanna saw sky, ground, then sky again, floating there forever, suspended in some sort of timeless bubble where normal physics didn't apply. Wisps of smoke rose from car tires screeching to a halt. She saw Jason go airborne as the motorcycle flipped end over end, nearly landing on top of him.

And then she hit the ground. Her body bounced and pinwheeled, and her ears rang with the protective crack of her helmet. When she finally rolled to a stop, she was lying face-up on the asphalt deck of the Golden Gate Bridge.

It took a moment for her breathing to resume. When it did, she was relieved to find she could move her hands and feet. She pulled off her headgear and looked around for Jason.

The first thing she saw was the hard drives. The messenger bag had come off her shoulder, and it lay a few feet away, its contents spilled on the roadway. Just beyond that she spotted Jason, motionless, one leg bloody.

"Jason!" she shouted.

He didn't respond. Didn't move.

"Jason!"

He stirred. Tried to roll himself onto his side.

He's alive.

A shadow passed across her eyes, and she looked up to see Emmerson standing over her.

"It didn't have to be this way," he said, shaking his head. He picked up the bag and started stuffing the hard drives into it.

Pain stung the small of Tanna's back. She slid her hand down, afraid of the injury she might find. But instead of an open wound, her fingertips touched the edge of a solid plastic box.

A hard drive. I'm lying on a hard drive.

"You would have made one hell of a doctor," Emmerson said. "Too late now."

Tanna curled her hand around the end of the drive, digging her fingers in for a better grip.

Wait, she told herself. *Don't rush it.*

She saw Jason get to his knees, working to remove his helmet.

Emmerson gathered up the loose drives.

Tanna's mind raged as she looked at him. She thought of all the people he had harmed, all the people he'd killed. Each retreating memory seared with a name. Forever scarred with fear, and sadness, and loss. Then the braver part of her—the part that didn't care anymore, the part that wanted vengeance—took over, and the gray area between yes and no disappeared.

She harnessed every bit of fury within herself. Readied her muscles to move in perfect unison. Visualized her actions in precise detail.

For Krystal. For Solomon. For her mother and her sister. For herself.

Más vida. "More life."

She spoke in a voice so soft and calm that Emmerson paused, leaning over to hear her. Just enough. Just the way she wanted him to, stretching his neck and exposing his face.

Her body exploded in controlled movement as she pulled her arm out from behind her back and swung it through the air. The clasp end of the hard drive struck him in the side of the head with a baritone thump, like a hollow log caving in.

Emmerson staggered back, his expression a mixture of shock and panic. His cheek was already flowing with blood.

Go!

Tanna scrambled to her feet and grabbed the messenger bag, now full of the hard drives. She ran toward the sound of police sirens. Behind her, the heavy thump of footsteps filled her ears. Looking over her shoulder, she saw Emmerson chasing her.

"Help!" she screamed at the lines of idle cars on the bridge. "Stop him!"

Through closed windows, she watched startled drivers clutch their steering wheels, frozen, unsure what to do.

But up ahead, someone was running to help her.

Thank God!

She ran toward him between the rows of vehicles, then skidded to a stop as he came into focus.

Roman. It's fucking Roman.

With Emmerson behind her and Roman in front, she turned to the nearest car and pounded on the hood. "You have to help me!" But a panicked mother looked back at her through the windshield, and a sleeping toddler was strapped in the rear seat. "Shit."

Tanna cut across the lines of stopped traffic and flung herself over the low fence onto the pedestrian walkway along the outer edge of the bridge. In front of her, Roman did the same, then rushed toward her. Behind her, Emmerson moved up fast.

On the roadway, she saw Jason lurching his way toward them. *Stay down!* she wanted to scream.

Her thoughts swirled, dashing and darting through different scenarios. She tried to focus on anything that might help. Help her save Jason.

Think ahead.

Save the hard drives.

See what's behind it.

Save herself.

I can't!

Her mind felt like it was on the verge of shutting down.

And then her time ran out. Emmerson pulled out a pistol and pointed it at her.

"You won't kill me in front of all these people," she told him.

Emmerson merely looked at her, and she saw the profound desperation in his face. Yes, he would kill her. And Jason too. She had driven him to those lengths.

Her feet moved her to the edge of the bridge, her eyes scouring the water below. Beyond the railing, the suicide net extended out from the bottom edge, but she could make it.

She motioned to the messenger bag. "I'll throw it into the water. Destroy everything. We're the ones wanted for murder. Without the evidence on these drives, no one will believe us. There's no other proof. You can still save yourself."

She saw Jason working his way closer.

"Kill us now, and you'll be wanted for murder too. You can't escape that," Tanna continued. "But it's up to you. What are you willing to do for the future of humanity? For your future?"

She paused, waiting for Emmerson's reply. Police sirens descended on them.

"Throw it," Emmerson said.

Tanna didn't move. Didn't breathe.

He lowered his pistol. "Throw it now." Through his blood-streaked face, Emmerson smiled.

Tanna tightened her grip around the strap of the bag. She looked at him one last time, searching behind his expression of lies and false innocence into the man, this virus on humankind, who would do everything he could to survive, to continue infesting and destroying lives until he got what he wanted.

What's one more?

She launched the bag skyward in a high, arcing motion.

As he followed it with his eyes, Emmerson's empty smirk dissolved into an incredulous look of disbelief.

Instead of throwing it over the edge into the water below, Tanna had hurled it far off toward the center of the bridge.

The bag crashed down on the asphalt deck, splitting open on impact. Hard drives, filled with all of Emmerson's hopes and plans, his one and only future, scattered across the lanes and disappeared beneath cars. He'd never collect them all before the police arrived. They were gone from his reach forever.

"That's what it feels like to lose everything," Tanna told him.

His eyes were pure hate, and she saw his finger squeeze the trigger. Her ears rang with the sound of gunfire. First one, then several more in rapid succession.

But it was Emmerson's chest that spewed blood. He looked down, as surprised as she was, his face filling with deep realization. Then resolve. He pointed the gun at Jason.

Before he could fire, he collapsed.

Tanna spun around to see Roman lowering a pistol, its trail of fine smoke vanishing into the wind. Without even giving her a glance, he walked off between the cars on the bridge.

It was all too much. Tanna's legs gave way beneath her, and she tumbled down onto the walkway.

"Tanna!" Jason yelled and arrived next to her.

"What happened?"

"Shh, be still."

"Are you okay?"

"I'm fine. Don't move."

"The hard drives." Tanna tried to sit up. She saw the police converging, securing the area.

"They're fine." Jason eased her back down. "You're bleeding."

"So are you."

"No, you've been shot."

It hadn't registered until he said the words. But when Tanna tried to move again, the pain screamed through her upper body, and she couldn't fill her lungs.

"Easy." Jason clamped his hands over the wound in her chest. "Just breathe."

"It hurts."

"I know."

"Nobody move!" an officer shouted. "On the ground, both of you! Hands behind your head."

"She needs an ambulance!" Jason shouted back.

"It's on the way," another voice shouted, and a man appeared beside Jason. Tanna recognized him from what felt like a lifetime ago. Detective Lewis.

"Everything's going to be fine," the detective said. "You made it."

Tanna looked back at Jason. All around her, the sounds of sirens and shouting officers were slowly fading away.

"Tanna. You still with me?" Jason said.

She placed her hands over his. It was hard to stay awake.

"Hang on," Jason told her.

She looked into his eyes.

"You have to breathe."

The last thing Tanna saw was Jason's face. Behind him the massive cables of the Golden Gate Bridge reached high into a cloudless blue sky.

CHAPTER 70

"You don't know his last name? Where he's from? Where he lives now?"

"We already told you."

"And you don't remember anything else about him?"

"All we know is that his first name is Roman. That's it."

Tanna adjusted the pillow behind her head. She was stiff and uncomfortable and couldn't get used to the hospital bed. It had now been days since the surgery, and she was still in pain. But the pain reminded her she was alive. Emmerson's bullet had caused a pulmonary laceration that almost collapsed her lung, but thankfully it had missed the major arteries. It would take time, but she would heal.

Jason would heal, too. He sat in a chair next to her, his fractured leg in a cast. They both responded to Deputy Chief Marcos's questions as Detective Lewis observed from the corner.

"What about this computer guy, Eric? Do you have any idea as to his whereabouts?"

"None," Tanna said. "We haven't seen or heard from him

since he gave us instructions on how to get the drives from the servers. Have you found anything on them yet?"

"Some of the drives are too damaged to read, others are still being decrypted. We won't know if there's anything of value for a while. And the servers back at the lab are wiped clean. Even the backups. Everything's been overwritten with the words 'Second Nature' over and over again. Thousands of terabytes of just that." He paused. "So I'm curious why he told you to take those specific drives. What was on those and not the others?"

"Information to help us," Tanna said. "To prove our innocence and take down Modern Genetics. Proof of their live human trials, their use of synthetic XNA, and evidence of who's paying for the lab they're building out in the middle of the ocean somewhere." Tanna was losing patience with the questions, which kept coming around to the same points. "Listen, do you realize what we had to go through to get you those drives? You need to do your job and figure it out from here. We've done enough. We're out of it."

"You're right," Lewis said from the corner, and received a disapproving look from Marcos. "I believe you. And it's up to us to prove your claims."

Marcos huffed. "Detective, we don't know what these two are responsible for. They don't get to just walk away."

"We haven't walked away from anything. You did," Tanna fired back. "You made up lies and told them to the world. You accused us of murder. This is your mess." She adjusted the pillow again. "I'm tired now. My chest hurts, and I have to rest."

"Very well," Marcos said. "But this is an ongoing

investigation. We're going to need you to answer more questions."

"The moment we're discharged, we're out of here. I'm going back to my life. That's all I want. That's all I've ever wanted."

Jason chimed in. "We'll answer your questions." He tilted his head toward Lewis. "As long as they come from him. He's the only one we talk to from now on."

Marcos grumbled before turning and walking out of the room. Lewis followed, stopping to look back at Tanna. She held his stare for a long time before responding with a forgiving nod.

As the two officers left, Jason struggled to get out of his chair.

"Use your crutches," Tanna told him.

He bent down and kissed her.

"What was that for?" she said.

"I don't need a reason."

Grabbing him with both hands, Tanna pulled him down and kissed him back. "Neither do I."

CHAPTER 71

Deep inside Tanna's body, her T-cells had unleashed their final assault. Never stopping. Never resting. Slashing and drilling their way through any remaining viruses they could find. All the while, her B-cells and macrophages continued their brutal defense of her systems. They overwhelmed the retreating invaders, annihilating and engulfing everything in their path, destroying many of Tanna's own cells in the process. But that was the price that needed to be paid. The self-sacrifice required for her own survival.

With a final push, her immune system snuffed out the very last virus particle they could find. And then, with no more enemy left to fight, Tanna's immune system sent out signals to stand down. The war was over. The foe destroyed. The victory had come at a high cost—wastelands of devastation. But it was a victory nonetheless.

Except it wasn't. Not entirely.

The viruses' retreat had led them to the outer edges of Tanna's body, searching for a place to hide, a place where her immune system couldn't locate them. A place where they could remain undetected.

And they found one.

Her eyes.

They pushed deep into the cells of this sanctuary site. One of the few locations the immune system would rarely search—and would never attack for fear of causing irreversible damage. And once in place, the viruses settled in. Shut down. Turned off their reproductive machinery and went dormant. Without the chemicals created when they reproduced, they became invisible to Tanna's immune system. Unseen by her body. But they were there, hiding inside of her, looking out onto her world through her own eyes.

Days. Months. Years. It didn't matter. They would wait as long as it took. Then they would pick a moment of compromised immunity or debilitating stress. A moment when Tanna was least prepared to fight back. That would be their trigger to wake up. Emerge and attack once again. Stronger. Faster.

They even had the chance to mutate, to transform into something new. Something that her body never experienced before. Never fought. They were a ticking time bomb waiting to go off. That was their advantage and their everlasting future.

Because like all the viruses that went before them, they would adapt. They would adapt and evolve, or they would die.

It took several days for Tanna's symptoms to diminish. The doctors ran a battery of tests but didn't detect anything out of the ordinary. Eventually they concluded that she was suffering from a rhinovirus, the same type of virus that produces the common cold. They assured her it was nothing to worry about.

Tanna wanted that to be true. She wanted a simple explanation. Something unrelated to what she'd been through and what she now knew. Because she didn't want to imagine what a stronger, more destructive virus could do. A virus so lethal that her body wouldn't know how to fight it.

She thought about the unknowing victims of Dr. Emmerson's experiments. Their agony and suffering. And for what? It wasn't worth it.

She was just glad no one would ever have to experience that devastation again.

CHAPTER 72

Dr. Solomon Cabral was filled with renewed energy as he looked out over the waters of the Pacific Ocean from the lab's uppermost level, watching the rough waves break against the massive main spar of the converted rig.

"Feeling better?" he asked.

Lauren grasped the metal railing and drew a labored breath. "I think so."

"It can be a turbulent crossing on the helicopter."

"I'm not sure I'll ever get used to it."

"Don't worry, you won't be coming here often."

He guided her away with a wave of his hand, the wound on the back of it completely healed. As they walked into the first level, he led her past a lab with observation windows where a group of technicians worked on sequencing proteins.

"Not how I would have set it up, but under the circumstances, I think we've done an exemplary job," he said.

"The investors would like a report," she said. "I have to give them something."

"Tell them whatever you want. But I'll conduct business

on my terms and in my time, without their interference. They'll keep sending me money, and I'll provide results in due course."

"You didn't leave them much choice, did you?"

"The power of information, my dear. Those who have it, get to do what they want. And I made unimaginable sacrifices to acquire it."

"And you're sure you have it?"

Sol stopped in the middle of the hallway, reversed his course, and led her through a set of security doors. They were blasted with chilled air as they entered the computer server room.

"Eric," Sol hollered. "It appears we need an update."

Eric emerged from around a corner and greeted them both. Behind him were server racks loaded with the hard drives from his van. The ones still marked with red, yellow, and green labels.

"We got everything we wanted from the mainland servers and their backups. Except . . . it looks like Tanna and Jason pulled a few more hard drives than expected."

"And what's on those?" Lauren asked.

He looked at Sol as he answered. "Most of it is garbage, just like the other drives I directed them to take. Agro yields, counter-projections, inventory masters. But it's possible—just possible—that they got some information about a couple of the investors."

"What?" said Lauren, taken aback. "You can't be serious?"

"Oh, Lauren," Sol said to her. "You're looking at this all wrong. If some information about the investors' involvement were to leak, that may well work to our advantage. You can assure those investors who *aren't* exposed that their interests will remain safe here with me—as long as they keep funding the project. They ensure my security, and I ensure theirs."

Lauren shook her head and turned back to Eric. "But you have everything else? The work history?"

Eric grinned. "Down to the last calculation. Thanks to my brilliant program that turned the building's own electrical lines into one giant wireless network that I could access."

"You see?" said Sol. "It won't be long before everything we've ever wanted will be ours."

Lauren crossed her arms. "You still expect to get away with all of this?"

"You don't seem to understand," Sol replied. "It's already done. As far as the world is concerned, I'm dead. I've even got a death certificate to prove it. Modern Genetics is in shambles, and we've corrupted all their on-site data. There's nothing left. It's gone."

"You'd better hope you're right."

Sol guided Lauren out of the room and allowed her to tour the rest of the complex before escorting her back to the helicopter. He stood on the rig's upper deck and watched it disappear into the distance.

"Is it finished?" Roman asked, appearing at his side.

"For now," said Sol. "A few feathers have yet to be ruffled."

"Anything I can do?"

"Thank you, my friend, but you've done more than enough. Now I assume you want to go back and finish those two kids? I can only guess how difficult it was for you to show so much restraint and not eliminate them many times over."

"I'm not going back," Roman said. "Time for me to go home for a while. Enjoy my life, such as it is now."

"I don't want any loose ends."

"That's up to you. I did my job. I drove them hard, pushed them where they had to go, made them do what you needed. They earned my respect." Roman looked at Sol with a cautioning stare. "And now that they've played their part, do you really want to fuck that up?"

Roman was right. Sol still needed Tanna and Jason, just like he had needed them all along. If he had tried to do this on his own, there would have been too many strings attached to him. And if something went wrong, Craig would have never stopped hunting him. This way, his only crime was helping two kids prove their innocence. Something he'd reportedly given his life for, thanks to confirmation from the hospital nurse and a physician friend she was forced to recruit. The trail stopped with Tanna and Jason. End of story.

But if they disappeared now . . . well, that would only raise questions. Best to leave them be. Sol had what he wanted: he had the investors by the balls and was free to proceed as he chose, without interference.

"Understood, Roman. And thank you. For all your service."

"Don't thank me," Roman told him. "Just give me what you promised."

"Your nerve treatment is my number-one priority. I guaranteed you your life back, and you'll get it. Pleasure, pain, every feeling, every sensation you could ever want. I'll find a cure that will restore it all. I promise."

"You better." The two men shook hands. "Otherwise you'll end up like your predecessor."

As Roman departed, an assistant walked up and tapped Sol on the shoulder. "Sir, they're ready for you."

The assistant led Sol to the courtyard, where the entire staff waited. As Sol looked over the group, his heart swelled. They were the best of the best, the world's finest scientists and technicians. Men and women that he had handpicked from across the globe. And now they were his and his alone.

He was awash with hope, awake with the promise of unimaginable possibilities. He had already accomplished the impossible, and yet he sensed it was only the beginning.

Because he would never slow down.

Never second-guess his abilities.

Never become useless again.

"I want to thank you for being here," Sol said to the sea of eager faces. "I recognize the noble sacrifices you've made, and I pledge to do everything in my power to accomplish what we've set out to do. Know this: you are a part of something truly amazing here. We have taken the first step in achieving what no one else in the history of mankind has ever achieved, or ever even attempted. The road ahead remains difficult, and there will be setbacks, but we won't give up. Ever. We're united under a single desire, a single purpose, and a single goal."

Sol paused and took a deep breath. "From this day forward, the world will never be the same."

CHAPTER 73

Tanna sat in the front row of her Principles of Human Physiology class, listening to the professor discuss the process of cellular respiration as she sketched sausage-shaped cell mitochondria in her notebook.

She'd had to petition the university for readmittance, but ultimately she'd started the new semester as if she'd never left. She was overloaded with credits, trying to make up for what she missed, but she would handle it. It felt great to keep herself occupied, and she welcomed getting back into a routine.

All winter long, news reports had come out about Modern Genetics and Dr. Craig Emmerson. The whole thing unfolded like a conspiracy theory right out of a movie. If Tanna hadn't lived it herself, she probably wouldn't have believed it. The police and FBI had now proven that Modern Genetics conducted live human trials with unknowing subjects, and that Dr. Emmerson had orchestrated the murders of Krystal, Dean Atwell, and countless others. For a time,

Tanna had become a bit of a local celebrity around campus because of it, and she was relieved when her notoriety faded.

Authorities were still sifting through the data regarding XNA and the Second Nature program, but with Dr. Emmerson and Dr. Cabral both dead and much of the information missing, it would take some time to come to any real conclusions. Detective Lewis had told her that the drives had no information on any remote lab in the Pacific, and though she trusted him, she wondered if that was true. Perhaps someone in the FBI knew more than they were saying. Perhaps not. But it didn't matter. It was no longer her problem either way.

"Can anyone tell me what happens next?" the professor asked. "After glycolysis."

"Yes," a voice called out from the middle of the classroom.

It was Nick. Of course. Always Nick.

"The acetyl-CoA interacts with oxaloacetate to produce citrate," Nick said. "From there it undergoes a series of reactions to produce isocitrate, ketoglutarate, succinate, fum—"

"That's wrong," Tanna interrupted. The entire class looked at her as the mnemonic scrolled through her head. *Oh, can I keep speaking sternly for myself?* "You missed succinyl Co-A. It's citrate, isocitrate, ketoglutarate, succinyl Co-A, then succinate, fumarate, malate, and back to oxaloacetate, where the cycle starts all over. Here, let me show you, Nick."

Tanna got up and walked to the front of the room. She sensed the other students' eagerness to see her fail, but she knew she wouldn't give them the pleasure. Not this time. Not anymore. She stood at the whiteboard and drew a large circle. From there she outlined each point along the Krebs cycle where a carbon atom either gained or lost and when each reaction took place.

"Exactly right," the professor said. "Excellent explanation."

As Tanna walked back to her seat, she looked at Nick, making sure he could see the fuck-you in her grin.

When the class ended, Tanna strolled across campus, passing students lounging in the sunken garden, their voices and laughter floating along on the tender ocean breeze. She made her way to the parking garage where she found her little blue Mazda. It had sat at the impound yard for weeks while she recovered from the gunshot wound to her chest, and then for weeks more while Jason rebuilt it from one end to the other.

As she was driving east, a news alert popped up on her phone, and she played it aloud. It seemed that Beacon Global Investments had been exposed as a major investor in Modern Genetics. The executives at Beacon Global vehemently denied any knowledge of wrongdoing, but the publicity alone had sent the stock price into a nosedive, and the company appeared likely to fold overnight.

Tanna shut it off. She didn't want to hear about Modern Genetics anymore. She never wanted to hear about it again. She loaded her music, turned up the volume, and before long found herself singing out loud with the windows down.

When she reached the motocross track, she went directly to the pits. Jason was there, instructing a group of preteen riders. Among them was his niece, Samantha.

"Always look ahead," Jason was telling them. "And remember, hard through the turns—"

"Fast down the straightaways," the students shouted back in unison.

Tanna chuckled.

"Right. Races are won or lost in the corners, so go do it."

The kids jumped on their motorbikes and made their way to the track.

"You're early," Jason said to Tanna. "How was class?"

"It had its moments. How's yours?"

"They're having fun. Maybe they'll even learn something."

"You have a lot to teach them."

"We'll see about that."

Jason leaned on his cane. The cast on his leg had come off, but he still had months of rehab ahead of him.

Tanna ran her hand over the Steel Dukes tattoo on his arm. The knotted flesh of the scar rippled under her fingertips. He'd had the colors retouched, so the damage was almost invisible, but she knew it was there. It always would be.

"Looks good," she said.

"Yours too," he told her.

Tanna stuck out her foot, admiring the tattoo on her ankle. It was a wineglass with a splash of liquid rising out the top like a flame, wild and uncontainable. Just beneath it were two words: MÁS VIDA.

Always more life, her heart added.

Without realizing it, she released a light laugh, focusing beyond the sadness and loss to the best parts of her memories. The ones she would never let go of. The ones forever inked on her flesh and engraved in her mind.

As she stood in the refuge of the racetrack pit, surrounded by dusty mounds of dirt and belching motorbikes, Tanna realized there was nowhere else she wanted to be.

Jason reached over and pulled her close. She wrapped her arms around him and held on tight.

"Whatever you do," Tanna whispered through her deepening smile, "don't let go."

A NOTE FROM THE AUTHOR

Thank you for reading *The First Harm*. I hope you enjoyed the ride. For me, it's been a dream come true. I would be grateful if you'd take a moment to leave a review. Reviews help other readers find the book and tell them when an author is worth reading. And I'd love to hear your honest feedback.

For even more information on upcoming books, giveaways, and bonus material, visit: www.stevenpiskula.com.

Or send me a message at steven@stevenpiskula.com. I can't wait to hear from you.

ACKNOWLEDGMENTS

First, I would like to thank all the readers. You give these words life and meaning beyond anything I may have imagined when I wrote them. Without you, this book would be languishing on the proverbial bookshelf somewhere. And for those of you who have made the additional effort to write a review, I can't thank you enough.

I would also like to thank my incredible family. To my wife, who has inspired me throughout this journey. To my son, who still doesn't quite get why I stare at my computer so much. I could never have done this without their unwavering support and understanding. This book means so much more because I get to share the dream with them.

I want to thank my mom for her endless well of encouragement that never seems to run dry. And my dad for his guidance that continues to push me to be the best version of myself. Thank you to my brother, sisters, and the rest of my family for always being there. Sometimes you never realize how important you are to someone else.

A special thank you to Andrew Fracchia and J. Jason Hicks, talented writers, and friends who made time for passionate discussions about the craft of writing while keeping me focused on moving forward.

Finally, thank you to my amazing editors, Jim Thomsen and David Gatewood, for helping me shape the book into its final form. They forced me to examine what I couldn't see and didn't want to acknowledge, no matter how frustrating that was. Working with them has been transformative. To Stephanie Parent and Michael Garrett for their expert eyes. And to my early readers and everyone who has given me so much assistance along the way: Mary, Sarah, Mike, Miguel, Todd, Diego, Ed, Andrea, Bill, and so many more. You are an essential part of the process. Thank you!

I'm excited to do this again soon. Meanwhile,
please visit: www.stevenpiskula.com,
or contact me at steven@stevenpiskula.com.

ABOUT THE AUTHOR

STEVEN PISKULA is an award-winning screenwriter, former journalist, and passionate thriller author. His love of words led him to study English and journalism before earning a Master of Fine Arts in screenwriting. A native of Wisconsin, Steven now enjoys living in Southern California with his wife and child. They frequently travel to Spain, where he has found his second home while visiting his wife's family. When he's not writing or reading, Steven is busy attempting to learn Spanish, perfecting his paella recipe, and trying to keep up with his young son.

The First Harm is his debut novel.

Learn more at www.stevenpiskula.com.

Printed in Great Britain
by Amazon